Clearly well-researched, McHaf
told from several different vi
psychological issues, but with
turning the pages to find out w..._
characters. (It) raises challenging questions without simpifying
the issues or offering any easy answers. This is grown up fiction
in all senses, but the book might also be enjoyed by thoughtful
older teenagers.
LINDA GILLARD, AUTHOR OF *UNTYING THE KNOT* AND
EMOTIONAL GEOLOGY

...well researched, full of empathy and shows how wonderfully
Hazel McHaffie is able to get inside the skin of people who are
torn apart and tormented by deep and personal internal
struggles about their own image, identity and relationships. She
worms her way into the mind and heart of young people,
understanding their culture and appreciating the complex web
of their relationships with peers, parents and adults generally,
and is able to weave it all into a gripping story, full of
unexpected and emotional twists and turns. The tempo steadily
increases towards a climax which left me with a fresh
appreciation of how many unknown battles lie beneath the
surface of so many people's lives – including, of course, our
own – and of how we human beings need to be less
judgemental of each other.
JOHN SALTER, CANON IN THE CHURCH OF ENGLAND, GUILDFORD

...makes a gripping and compelling read. It is laced with
accurate insightful accounts of the physical and emotional
effects of eating disorders on young people and the dilemmas
faced by the parents and caregivers living with and planning
care for teenagers who themselves have reached the age of
consent. As a General Practitioner, I recommend it as a must-
read for anyone who might benefit from gems of accurate
information about the workings of the young troubled mind of
an anorectic as she desperately tries to take some control over
her life which was 'ruined' by adults. GPs, medical and nursing
students, and all parents of teenagers would do well to add
INSIDE OF ME to their wishlist.
MARIA GALEA, GENERAL PRACTITIONER, EDINBURGH

It flows very well, the characters are well drawn, and the moral issues are handled sensitively.

RICHARD ASHCROFT, PROFESSOR OF BIOETHICS, UNIVERSITY OF LONDON

Hazel McHaffie has once again managed to combine a sensitive and informed exploration of ethical issues with a strong human story that engages the reader from beginning to end. She provides an insightful commentary on both the individual and social context of anorexia and identity. By telling the story through the voices of the key characters she allows the reader to identify with, and thus understand, their different perspectives; a prerequisite for anyone wishing to really engage with any ethical debate. As such it will provide a useful educational resource for teachers of medical ethics as well as a thoroughly enjoyable read.

ANNE SLOWTHER, ASSOCIATE PROFESSOR, CLINICAL ETHICS, WARWICK MEDICAL SCHOOL

This novel gives a touching, sensitive insight into the effects of 21st century expectations and parental influence on the young impressionable mind. I enjoyed it very much and believe it should be in every school library.

PAT BOYD, FORMERLY PRINCIPAL EXAMINER FOR RELIGIOUS, MORAL AND PHILOSOPHICAL STUDIES IN THE SCOTTISH QUALIFICATIONS AUTHORITY

By the same author

Fiction

Over my Dead Body
Saving Sebastian
Remember Remember
Right to Die
Double Trouble
Paternity
Vacant Possession

Non-fiction

Crucial Decisions at the Beginning of Life
Life, Death and Decisions

HAZEL McHAFFIE trained as a nurse and midwife, gained a PhD in Social Sciences and was Deputy Director of Research in the Institute of Medical Ethics. She is the author of about one hundred published articles and books. *Crucial Decisions at the Beginning of Life* won the British Medical Association Book of the Year Award in 2002. *Right to Die* was shortlisted for the BMA Popular Medicine prize in 2008. *Inside of Me* is her ninth published novel set in the world of medical ethics.

INSIDE OF ME

HAZEL McHAFFIE

First published 2016

ISBN: 978-0-9926231-2-8

British Library Cataloguing in Publication Data. A catalogue record for this book is available from the British Library.

Published by VelvetEthics Press
12 Mayburn Terrace, Loanhead, Scotland EH20 9EJ

CHAPTER 1

Tonya

THE HEADLINE jumps out and hits me.
TEENAGER MISSING.
Maria Davenport. She's pretty, no question about that. Oval face, a tad too much make-up maybe, but this is no ordinary everyday snapshot; it's a special occasion photo-shoot judging by the pose and the quality of the picture. Long dark curls, wide eyes, finely drawn eyebrows, a single tiny mole high on her left cheek, notable in an otherwise flawless skin.

The picture blurs ... dark circles hollow out those luminous eyes, the cheeks and nose are etched into sharper angles, the expression becomes pinched. The shrinkage tells its own tale; a tale that haunts me daily.

I give myself a mental shake. Start again, Tonya. Concentrate on *this* girl. *This* girl is no one you know, d'you hear me? She's just some random kid who's missing. Probably had a row at home. Probably already regretting storming out. Probably crawling back home with her tail between her legs as we speak, surprised at all the fuss she's created.

'Maria Davenport, sixteen years old' ... still a schoolgirl ... mere months older than my India.

'Last seen walking alone along a canal path' after an uneventful Thursday at school. Six days ago. Has she done this sort of thing before? Did the parents assume she was with friends over the weekend? Have they only just reported her missing? Why?

The *'Regent Canal'* in London? Never heard of it. Did she slip? Fall in? Drown? Get tangled up in some weeds, under a barge, maybe?

'Missing since Thursday'...

Thursday ...

Thursday!

My heart gives a sickening kick in my throat.

Thursday ... London ...

The day before my daughter India thought she heard her father's voice for the first time in almost eight years ... *down in London.*

But ... no! It surely can't be connected. It *can't*. Not after all this time. Please God. Please God. Please God.

My hands clench involuntarily on the newspaper, a wave of nausea washing over me. I sink onto the nearest chair. Not again ... God, no, *please*, not again.

'Five foot five, long curly dark hair, slight build'. The curls were up in a practical ponytail that day. She was *'wearing a maroon blazer, navy skirt, black tights, carrying a dark grey bag, listening to her iPod'*.

Her mother, Tessa Davenport, says they're a normal happy family: mum, dad, two children, a dog and three cats. Dad, Douglas, 44, is an engineer; mum, Tessa, 44, a history teacher. Older sister, Amy, 20, is at Birmingham University, studying geography. I never understand why they have to put ages in. Who cares? What possible relevance is Tessa's age to Maria's disappearance? Unless of course, she was eleven when she gave birth to her, or seventy. Even then, it's nobody's business but theirs. It's of no consequence now.

There had been no big arguments, no history of bullying, or anything untoward ... not that her parents know about at any rate.

Maria's laptop and passport were still in her room. That's something.

Maria's headmaster says she's an *'able student, popular, confident, fun-lovin*g', with her sights set on St Andrews to study History of Art. St Andrews. Of course. How many young girls have followed in Kate Middleton's shoes, vaguely hoping to snare their own prince, I wonder?

Unnamed friends say she's special – of course she is. There's no known boyfriend, no ex, to put under the spotlight.

Family members are *'helping police with their enquiries'*. There are no leads at present. They've taken away Maria's laptop and the family computer. Imagine, strangers poring over all *India's* emails, Facebook, Instagram, Google searches. A shiver runs down my spine.

A small inset photo shows the Davenport home: an average-looking semi in a quiet street. Barnsbury – never heard of it. Islington area – have heard of that. Nothing pretentious or expensive. Not by London standards anyway.

So, an ordinary girl from an ordinary family, living in an ordinary street, going to an ordinary school, going about her ordinary everyday life. Most likely something quite ordinary has kept her from going home. She'll be holed up somewhere, hoping to escape the consequences of some minor misdemeanor, or the pain of a broken relationship, or the threat of a failed exam, or the cruel jibes of her peers. Some distorted teenage tragedy.

The police are appealing for anyone who may have seen the teenager after 5.30pm that evening to contact them urgently. They're *'keeping an open mind'*, not yet considering the circumstances as suspicious. Thank God for that.

My heart goes out to her poor mother even so. Beside herself. Imagining every conceivable horror. Hoping against hope. Dreading that ring at the door. How could you even go to bed, or go shopping, or walk the dog, knowing your precious girl's out there somewhere, maybe alone, or frightened, or ... worse? How could you simply stay in the house – 'in case' – not *doing* anything?

Last Thursday.

What was *I* doing last Thursday? Working at the nursery till 4.15pm, shopping at Morrisons, then home, cooking a meal for one. Marinated salmon with salad and fries; sticky toffee pudding. India was in London; I could eat what I liked, when I liked, without guilt.

She was away that whole week ... in the very place where Maria went missing ... and she's convinced that she heard her father's voice on that Friday afternoon. If that's true then Victor was in the London area at the same time as Maria and India. And now Maria is missing.

Surely, surely, surely, he couldn't be responsible. Not *Victor*!

But ... that's what I told myself the other times too.

CHAPTER 2

Tonya

EVEN AFTER NEARLY TEN YEARS the details are seared into my memory.

The first girl was Eva Daniella Demarco. An only child, like my India, fourteen years old, five foot seven. Bright, athletic, well-integrated, lively sense of humour, according to a spokesman from her school.

It was way back. In 2006. One grey, drizzly afternoon in July this teenager set off for an evening with friends at the cinema. Her mother, Jennifer, was out at work in the local hotel, earning money to 'provide the little extras' she wanted to give her daughter. Her stepfather, Bill, saw Eva leave the house at 5.25pm wearing only a skimpy jacket and cropped trousers, no umbrella, no raincoat. He shouted after her but she ignored his instruction. Nine people saw her board a bus at 5.47pm, laughing into her mobile phone; no one remembered seeing her get off. CCTV footage showed her sitting on the top deck for sixteen minutes but at that point the camera malfunctioned. The driver swore that he reported the fault as soon as he arrived at the depot although there was nothing recorded in writing.

Eva's three friends waited in vain for her to join them at the café a stone's throw from the Odeon cinema. Eventually they went ahead and ordered their hot-chocolates-with-everything. They giggled as they wiped the smears of cream and molten marshmallows from their glossed lips and crunched Maltesers. Between them they left twenty-one text messages for Eva.

They hung around waiting till the last minute before creeping into the cinema just as the adverts and trailers finished. The film was *Harry Potter and the Prisoner of Azkaban*. I remember it clearly on account of one of my neighbour's friends knowing JK Rowling's daughter's friend's aunt, and wondering aloud if the author herself attended local showings. Anyway, the film instantly absorbed their full attention and the girls assumed Eva had fallen asleep and forgotten their appointment, or changed her mind and gone off somewhere else. Afterwards they left more text messages telling her what she'd missed, which also went unanswered, but they remained unconcerned.

Odd really, when you think about it, modern communication. You leave a message; you assume it's arrived. It's now over to the recipient to reply in due course. Your duty's done, your conscience is clear. When the friends didn't hear from Eva before going their several ways, they even wondered aloud if they were being used as cover for some clandestine meeting she'd planned. They giggled about that too.

Not until Eva's mother rang each of their parents after 10.45pm that night to check whose house she was staying at, did alarm bells start to ring.

She was missing for eleven weeks during which time her stepfather, her paternal uncle, the bus driver, and six other local men, as well as four known sexual predators who might or might not have been in the area on the evening in question, had been grilled relentlessly by the increasingly desperate police. Eleven weeks plus two days.

For the whole seventy-nine agonizing days I followed that story, identifying with the parents of this only daughter who lived a mere twenty-eight miles from our house. I marked the days on my kitchen calendar. What if this had been *my* girl ... no, I daren't go there. For the whole of that time – minute by terrifying minute – I kept India glued to my side. And then they found Eva's decomposing body in a wood, buried under leaves. Or at least a gundog did. Odd really, I even remember the dog's name: Cerberus II. Like the hellhound of Greek mythology that guards the entrance to the underworld, to prevent the dead from escaping and the living from entering. Seemed somehow symbolic.

It was a particularly lovely autumn, I remember, and thinking about those crisp golden leaves covering something so macabre made me paranoid. India was only six years old that year and I stopped letting her scamper out of sight playing hide and seek. I saw shadowy figures lurking behind every tree and bush; I suspected every stranger who passed us in the street of sinister intentions; I waited until my precious daughter was actually in her classroom before I left school in the morning, and arrived at least ten minutes too early to collect her. I refused to let her go to play-dates, insisting the other children come to our house instead. I couldn't explain to her, of course, but I could see her mounting frustration at the limits I set, and she often rebelled, increasing my fear and obsession with her safety. She turned to her father more and more for fun and freedom.

No one was ever apprehended for Eva's death. The post mortem was inconclusive. Decomposition was advanced due to exposure and the warm weather. No cause of death could be found. No incriminating evidence. Nevertheless suspicion lurked and people muttered and theories abounded. Presumably the case is still open somewhere for someone. And there can be no closure for the Demarco family. Or those three surviving friends.

Every so often I revisit the collection of newspaper clippings I kept on Eva, and wonder and shiver.

Because I have absolutely no idea where my husband, Victor, was that day. He went out without explanation; he didn't return for two days, still no explanation; he was uncharacteristically withdrawn when he did.

Thirteen months and three weeks and four days after Eva's disappearance – in August 2007 – Rebekah Quindlan also vanished without trace.

She was fifteen, the same age as my own daughter is now. Her parents were – *are* – hard working, down-to-earth folk who belong to some small religious sect – I can't now remember exactly what, but I have this picture in my head of the mother looking like someone from the Amish people, or some such closed community where the girls all wear triangular scarves on their heads and long full baggy dresses and have a rigid code of behaviour. I remember thinking that, when I was a kid, I might have laughed with my friends about such a figure of fun, but not any more. Not when mockery could have this kind of result. Besides, the mum, Kezia Quindlan, was incredibly dignified. No wailing, no tears for the camera, simply a heart-wrenching appeal for anyone knowing anything about Rebekah's disappearance to come forward. Which I ignored.

She painted a picture of a dutiful daughter who was a model child at home, but an acknowledged misfit in the bigger society. Rebekah was the third of four girls, all dumpy, all frumpily dressed like the mother, none of whom had ever had their hair cut. The Quindlans lived fifty-four miles from us, and Rebekah was completely unlike Eva Demarco. Different school; blonde where Eva was dark; short where Eva was tall; of only average academic ability, hated sports. She was a loner and didn't join any clubs or social groups. The family had no TV or car, they never went to the cinema or the theatre, and they didn't celebrate Christmas.

Zachariah Quindlan, her father, was seen on TV only once when the police arranged a press appeal. He looked totally forbidding and inscrutable with his rough farming clothes, Abrahamic beard, and taciturn demeanour, and he spent the whole appearance before the press staring at the floor without expression. If he hadn't been a man of God he'd have been top of my suspect list.

Kezia Quindlan apparently thought Rebekah was safely in her room that evening doing her school homework.

This time though, the ensuing hunt unearthed bullying and cruelty that made me weep. They printed some of the messages in the paper. The wretched child was taunted for her size, her quaint ways, her dress, her old-fashioned plaits, her belief in God, her respect for authority, her refusal to try tobacco or drugs or sex. Forced to comment on the truth the police had revealed, her mother told of Rebekah sobbing herself to sleep, having nightmares, comfort bingeing. But, she insisted, their principles denied them the opportunity to do anything to right this great wrong: they would always 'esteem others better than themselves' and 'leave judgement to God' – the quaver in her voice made me think that her heart was at odds with her tongue here. How could *any* mother turn a blind eye to her child's suffering? Kezia's God forgive me, what wouldn't I do to any kid who tormented my India?

Counsellors spent hours every week with the Quindlan sisters who all maintained a stoical silence in public, refusing to name and shame anyone at all. Not one of them would admit to being bullied themselves, though to the outward eye they all closely resembled Rebekah in every respect. However, in time, two girls were suspended from their school, accused of being the ringleaders for Rebekah's ongoing torture. Countless others were reprimanded for forwarding taunts and unflattering pictures electronically. The school instituted rigorous checks and punishments for any form of bullying, and new sessions were introduced to teach acceptable moral behaviour within the community.

The police worked tirelessly to find the missing girl, and local groups joined in the physical search. Posters appeared in shop windows, on lampposts, in doctors' surgeries, on buses. Mainstream local churches as well as their own tiny sect, rallied to the support of the Quindlan family, plying them with casseroles and caraway seed cakes, listening ears and any-hour any-day phone numbers. They held prayer sessions, and offered confidential chats for anyone traumatised by Rebekah's disappearance.

And there were plenty of us. I didn't personally go to talk directly to anyone – I couldn't – but I prayed like I'd never prayed before that wherever she was, dead or alive, God would take care of this tortured girl who'd been a faithful servant even in the face of all that opposition and ridicule. Praying that she hadn't fallen into the clutches of the first kind man who tempted her with comfort and love. One specific man.

To this day she hasn't been found, and on good days I cling to the vain hope that she simply ran away from her tormentors and found peace in a different place where she could reinvent herself. And watching her mother, so composed, being interviewed on various programmes, I talked myself into believing that she secretly knew that her daughter was safe somewhere, so she was spared the doubt the rest of us continued to bear.

I picture Rebekah today, unrecognizable: a modern woman, with contact lenses instead of the hefty frames she wore in the photos, her blonde pigtails now a fashionable auburn bob, her mature face healthily clear of teenage oil and eruptions, her curves released from those shapeless pinafores, wearing ubiquitous skinny jeans, four-inch heels and expensive perfume. She'd be twenty-five now. Maybe married with kids of her own.

I forced myself to cling to that theory for years, in spite of the things I knew, in spite of what I found hidden in our house. But in truth I know that my husband was absent from home that night too. He remained away for two days, came home with no explanation, was unnaturally withdrawn, and took a bag of things to work with him next day that I'd never seen before.

And now *this*, blowing the whole question wide open again.

Where was he on all three occasions?

He was certainly in the area when Eva and Rebekah vanished. India believes he was in London the day after Maria went missing.

After eight years of silence, just when we might finally have evidence of his location, police are hunting for a missing schoolgirl.

Is he still alive?

Is he responsible?

CHAPTER 3

Chris

EIGHT O'CLOCK PRECISELY. Her time.

I place the white candle in the window.

I smooth the crumpled photo and lay it gently on the sill, transferring a kiss on my fingers to her cheek.

I lower the single white rose into the crystal bowl of water, watch the light sparkling on the tiny ripples I've created.

I light the candle, my hand trembling exactly like it does every year I go through this ceremony on this day.

I touch my taper to the incense cone, inhaling the evocative aroma. Sandalwood.

I open the window, send my silent prayer upwards on the scented air to where the clouds are trailing chiffon scarves against the sky. A light breeze is tugging the thin strands, carrying my whisper: 'Wherever you are, my darling girl, wherever you are ... I'm thinking of you.'

I leave the candle burning, the window open, for the rest of the evening until I go to bed. I won't sleep but I can rest my body. And in the darkness I'll add another plea for all parents everywhere who ache to hold their children one more time.

Nothing softens the pain but the annual ritual helps me to survive the anniversary. Every day is a struggle but this date in particular is laden with guilt and sorrow and if-onlys: the last time I saw my precious daughter alive and well and bubbling with life.

And that old saying: Time heals? Forget it; it's rubbish. You don't ever ever ever get over mourning for a loss this great. It's like a vital organ has been wrenched out of you and every day some malign presence pulls off the scab to make you bleed all over again, ratcheting up the pain, delaying the healing process. Some days even yet I want to *kill* somebody! Some days I want to kill myself.

The photo's fading now; they say you should preserve precious snaps in black and white if you want them to last, but I wanted to hold on to her warm skin tones, her grandmother's thick hair streaked through with sunshine. Oh, if only ...!

The girls wanted me to go out with them tonight, but I couldn't. Not today. This day, this night, belongs to her.

Some things can't be shared, not even with good friends, and I owe all three of these special people big time. Without them I wouldn't be here, not just here in London, in my job, in my flat; here in this world. That's quite a debt.

But they never knew my daughter. They are unaware of the significance of this day.

We agree to make it the following Tuesday.

It's an unwritten rule: no bringing problems to these night's out. They're about having a laugh, drowning our sorrows in alcohol and merriment: a tonic we all need.

Val's already at our favourite pub when I arrive, her face hardly visible in the gloomy atmosphere, but I'd know that defiant brassy crop anywhere.

'Darling! How are you?' she cries, leaping to her feet, planting extravagant kisses on both cheeks, one on my nose for good measure.

'*You*'re in a good humour,' I say instead. 'Good day pandering to the rich and famous?'

'Better day keeping secrets for the naughty and reprobate!' she whispers from behind her hand, rubbing her other fingers together to mime lucrative.

She's a bottomless pit of salacious stories about the guests who stay in the hotel where she works as a supervisor of guest services, and within minutes she launches into another apocryphal tale of secret assignations and innuendoes. As always I grit my teeth and humour her; after all I owe this woman my sanity. It was Val who rescued me when I first arrived in London, getting me a no-questions-asked job in 'her' hotel when I needed occupation, spinning one of her special brand of extravaganzas to cover my lack of papers, my inexperience in the catering industry.

We're already 'sneaking down the back stairs to avoid an irate husband' when Jane arrives. In spite of her elegant all-black outfit, she's looking grey and drawn, but I know better than to comment. I give her a brief hug, slip a gin and tonic into her hand, and return to the antics of the posh-lady-who-can't-be-named who isn't playing by the matrimonial rules. All three of us know we have to be ready to give Jane time to shed the burdens of her job before she can join the rest of the world. She's a part-time social worker, part-time counsellor for the Samaritans, full-time mum to a lad with attention deficit disorder who makes Usain Bolt look like a slowcoach. She's also the patient listener who stopped me swallowing a bottle full of aspirin when I hit rock bottom and found I couldn't go on with the burden of my loss. One day the powers that be have to give Jane an OBE; till then we have to double as her cheerleaders.

Georgie's always late; the rest of us always forgive her. Today she arrives breathless and flushed, her dull mousy curls a mess, her clothes dishevelled, her mind chaotic.

'Wow! Where have *you* been?' I say.

'More like, what you been up to?' Val says with a suggestive wink.

'Shut up, dumbhead,' Georgie fires back. 'The boss found me a whole stash of filing to do right before knocking-off time. Only just caught my bus. No time to be titivating in front of mirrors like *some* idle so-and-sos.'

'Well done for making it,' I say quietly. 'Take your time.' I push her red wine closer. Sometimes Val can be a moron.

Georgie's a rough diamond in many ways but she's had

it tough. A rebel at school, a misfit in every job she tried, slung out by the man who persuaded her into a ridiculously early marriage, begging on the streets by the time she was twenty-two. It was Jane who linked her up with Crisis, the charity that cares for single homeless people. It was Jane who somehow got her back into work – in the kitchen, which was where Val and I met her. She lasted less than a month before the chef screamed it was her or him. Her clumsiness was legendary. We stayed in contact and became outcasts together on the park benches of London. But Georgie gave me a reason to go on: she was more needy than I.

'So, how's life in the pretty world of flower arranging going?' Jane says, beginning to regain her natural colour after two drinks.

'Great,' I say. 'My boss is terrific, the work's fun, the pay better than in that hell-hole of a kitchen.'

'Still doing the evening classes?'

'Nope. All finished. Got the certificates. Thinking of advertising myself: Have secateurs, will travel!'

'Good on you, Chris. You're a fighter. I'm so glad it's worked out for you.'

'I love it. And I'm getting loads of experience.'

'Hey, you two, quit huddling and get yourselves outside these two beauties,' Val shouts, pushing brimming glasses in our direction.

I grimace. But she's right, distraction's the name of the game.

'Did I ever tell you about the porter we had in our place ...'

If it's a fiction it's acceptable.

And tonight all four of us are recasting ourselves in the carefree image of make-believe.

Relaxed by the acceptance of true friends and the kindly narcotic of alcohol, I sleep the sleep of the unconscious. In spite of all the lingering guilt, all the risks I'm taking, I now have a reason to get up in the morning.

CHAPTER 4

India

'WAY TO GO! *Yes and no!*' That voice on the platform. *Dad*'s voice! His Superman voice. I just can't get it out of my head.
Only, seven years ago, it was: '*Way to go! Yes and no! High and low! Thus and so! Top to toe! Go, kiddo!*' with a high five if he was near enough, and off he'd fly on some crazy mission or other. Awesome!
Mum rubbished it, of course, like she does. It's cos I've been thinking about him 'at some level' – I totally *hate* all that trashy psychobabble. They always said that kind of stuff when I was little.
It's 'like seeing somebody you love everywhere, after they're dead', she said, but it's not; that stopped ages ago.
'How could you possibly single out one voice in all the racket at King's Cross station?' she said. Well, I swear I *did* hear it, and that funny laugh he used to do at the same time. Cross my heart and hope to die, I definitely, definitely did.
See, we were coming back from a school trip – five days in London. I wasn't even *thinking* about him. So when I heard that voice, I grabbed hold of my friend Daisy's arm so's I kept moving with my class, but I swung round straight away to look behind me, back to where I'd heard him. At first everything went blurry – it does that these days when I turn suddenly or stand up too fast, but when it all settled down again, I couldn't see anybody remotely like my dad going away from me. Mostly guys were on their own, trundling cases and bags, glued to their mobile phones and newspapers, not talking to anybody ... ahhh, unless one of them was

saying 'Way to go! Yes and no!' *on the phone*. Could've been, I guess; I never thought of that. It felt like a totally *real* conversation.

But there were only two 'couply' kinds of people I could see who *might* have been talking to each other. Two women laughing together, one whitey-blonde and one reddish-brown; and a tall thin guy in a pin-stripe suit alongside a boy in baggy jeans carrying a super deluxe skateboard. They were both about Dad's height and build but the young one was too scruffy and too young, and the older one's face was long and thin – not remotely similar. They didn't look like they were having fun together either; nothing to make them say something cheerful like *Way to go!*

Now I wish I'd run back to check, stared at everybody really hard, but we were hurrying for the train, and Mrs Soutar goes totally mental about keeping everybody together when we're on these trips – especially in busy places like London. And I mean, I really don't blame her. *I'd* have freaked out if I'd got separated from my lot there with all those millions of people rushing everywhere.

Mum said it must have been 'a figment of your overactive imagination,' Well, she *would*. 'And starving yourself.' Not again!

But then she goes too far: 'You were only eight when he went away, India. I doubt you would really remember what his voice sounded like in real life. Things fade over time and get distorted. And besides, loads of men would sound the same saying *Way to go!*'

But now I *know* she's lying. She's only saying it cos she wants to stop me worrying inside. Dad made that stuff up. He *was* a one-off, and I miss him every single day of every single week of every single month of every single year. And that'll be eight years in a few weeks' time. Okay, I admit, I'm mad at him for going away – fizzing, hopping mad, if you must know – but I still want him back.

And whatever anybody says, I still don't believe that he's gone for good. Mum reckons he's dead but nobody's seen his body, have they? And now there's this new evidence:

the voice at the station. His voice.

I slam the door shut and fling myself on the bed, blasting the music, max decibels, and force my mind to concentrate on the beat, the lyrics: it's *My Immortal* by Evanescence.

I'm so tired of being here/Suppressed by all my childish fears. That's exactly how I feel: tired, tired, tired of being here ... of being me.

These wounds won't seem to heal/This pain is just too real/There's just too much that time cannot erase. Oh Dad. If you only knew! You'd be back like a shot. I know you would.

Your face it haunts my once pleasant dreams/Your voice it chased away all the sanity in me ...

It's the last straw. That voice ...

I bury my head under the pillow and howl for what should have been.

Bleugh doesn't begin to describe how I feel when I wake forty minutes later. I lie staring miserably at the ceiling hearing his voice, over and over again: '*Way to go! Yes and no! High and low! Thus and so! Top to toe! Go kiddo!*'

What if it really *was* him on the platform?

What if he really *is* alive? Somewhere in this country even. Wow!

Wicked!

But then, if he *is*, why did he ...?

Was it my fault?

Would I recognise him?

In the end I give up and pull out the memory box. I sit back on my heels and take several long slow breaths till my heart steadies and the room stands still again.

CHAPTER 5

India

I RUN MY HAND softly over the sides of the box, dented and scuffed from being lugged in and out of the wardrobe loads of times. I started collecting stuff when I found out my dad was probably not coming back – four years ago, give or take. 'Maybe dead.' 'Probably dead.' They said it would help me hold onto the memories of him, find 'acceptance and resolution'. They said to jot down anything: things he did, things he said, how you feel, what you'd say to him if he came back today. Put in photos. Anything that helps you.

Writing stuff to order was a right pain back then, but now I'm glad, cos it gets harder and harder to picture him clearly. Looking at the photos helps. Makes him come alive again.

The first thing, though, isn't about Dad at all; it's about my mum.

Funny that. Like somebody said, 'Tell me about your mother.' Like they understand she's the one who'll stop me now if she can. But I won't, I absolutely WON'T, let her; not this time.

'My Mum worries about everything' the childish writing says.

And it's true. Back then, after Dad went, she was always on my case, like everything, everywhere, was dangerous and she was dead scared she'd lose me too. *That slide's too steep ... No, India, it's too high ... Keep well back from the edge ... Hold my hand crossing this road ... Careful, that floor looks wet.*

Gran says I shouldn't take it personally, she was always like that, timid, afraid. When I was tiny, it was, *Stay where I can see you ... You need an afternoon nap ... You're not old enough to use scissors.* She was always, always, *always* checking up on me, even when I was in bed! I mean! Did she think I'd suffocate in my sleep, or climb out the window, or something, if she didn't hover? Crazy woman! Gran says it's only her way, it's cos she loves me to death. To death, pretty much sums it up. Death by suffocation.

See, Mum works in a nursery school, and I reckon being with tiny tots all day accounts for a lot. She has that sort of voice, you know? – the one people use when they talk to young kids. She even says things like, 'Shall we wash our hands?' when she means, *'Will you jolly well go and wash your hands, India'.* I hate it. HATE it! Makes me want to scream and throw things. I'd much rather she shouted at me than do that.

She's a wee bit better these days – not much, but a bit. Now she'll sigh and say, 'It was so much easier when you were small'. It's like she doesn't *want* me to grow up, which I think is true. Maybe she doesn't realise it, but it shows. I mean, I'm *fifteen,* nearly sixteen, and she still tries to choose my clothes, and tell me when to turn out the light at night, and what food I should eat. For goodness' sake!

But that's where my trump card comes in, my chance for freedom and independence. She *can't* rule my life totally.

I'm down another 86 grams today. Yaaaay! And that's real. No cheating with a litre of water on board or anything. I'm definitely getting there. At least 19 chews before every swallow. And I managed 22 lengths of the swimming pool on Tuesday – after missing lunch as well. That'll be up to 24 next week. Plus another 5 minutes of intense cardio, and an extra 10 of resistance training – that should really help. *Way to go, kiddo!*

Mental note to self: Be more careful where you stash food.

'India, there's a horrible smell in your room. Have you been leaving food lying around? Or brought something nasty in on your shoes? Check, will you?'

'Yep, will do.' Last thing I want is Mum poking around in my stuff.

Sure enough, I'd forgotten all about the prawn mayo sandwiches I stuffed at the back of the wardrobe. Minging they were. Watch out homeless people of Edinburgh, Christmas is coming! Fresh delicacies supplied daily! Wholesome, nourishing, guaranteed to build you up. She's really into 'building you up'.

But that's not what I want to think about right this minute. I want to get close as I can to my dad.

I pull out Scrapbook 1, jam packed with photographs and clippings. I've already had to Sellotape several of the pages to stop them falling out altogether.

Ahh, I love this picture. It's my fave. We're at the beach, and Dad's wearing these ridiculous long shorts that have ginormous flowers and parrots all over them. Way too OTT. Ridiculous things like Mr Bean might wear in Honolulu. And he's got my frilly sunhat perched on his head and my kiddie sunglasses on – two big white daisies with smiley faces. And there's a great big dollop of ice-cream on his nose. And there's me, in my red and black swimsuit with the sticky-out frill, (gross! all that fat inside hideous nylon), jumping up and down beside him, pointing and laughing, so not realising that the ice-cream's falling out of *my* cone, I'm that focused on my crazy parent. Mum must have been watching us all the time and managed to catch the exact moment when the vanilla swirl started to drop.

You can totally *see* how happy we were back then.

And here he is again, giving me a shoulder ride. We're at the zoo and I'm trying to reach my hands as high as the giraffes. Dad's grinning into the camera but I'm looking to the skies. And you can see the animals in the background chomping away on their food, ignoring us completely in that superior way giraffes have.

This whole page of photos in the scrapbook is about my dad as my number one buddy. He wasn't a bit like Mum.

No way, José! He trusted me. He'd let me play around water, and use real scissors, and start a fire, and run on steep slopes, and cross roads, and everything. And I wrote about that for the memory box:

> *My Daddy used to say, 'My filosofy is that kids should learn to accept responsibility for their own actions. So, I'll give you plenty of rope, Indie. Then its down to you.'*

He believed in me. He talked to me like I was sensible, capable, like I was totally plugged in. Awesome.

Of course, I was looking back from an older age by the time I started writing about it. Must have been about eleven. It was after Mum told me he was most likely dead. I was eight when he disappeared, and if I'm honest, I have to admit I can't remember much before I was four, but Mum let me have pictures from the family albums of him when I was a baby. He had this great big smile that showed his funny squint teeth, and a *lot* of hair in those days, long and brown and curly, and he even grew a mini-beard one summer. It was kind of reddish-gingery when the sun caught it, apparently. Mum said I used to run away squealing when he rubbed his rough chin against my bare skin. Can't say I remember that myself. He shaved it all off before it really got going seriously.

But I do remember him as one of those cuddly bear types; he sort of swallowed you up in his hugs. And when his big warm hand curled around mine, I felt totally safe. I've stuck in several pictures of us hand in hand and I still get a good feeling looking at those.

It was Dad who taught me to tie my shoelaces, and tell the time, and write with magic invisible ink, and identify the major stars in the night sky.

But best of all, he let me do a load of things Mum didn't approve of, and we swore together – underneath the table at midnight one birthday, I remember – that neither of us would 'clype' as he called it; it would remain our secret. Now, I know the books tell you that's bad, parents shouldn't play one against another with their kids, but I loved it.

He would pretend to lose at games so I could win. Let me play tennis indoors. Give me a real kitchen knife to cut up an apple. Sit me on his lap in the car and let me help change gear and steer in the driveway of our house. Pop a chocolate bar in my schoolbag for a surprise on special days. And the very best naughty thing? Smuggling me out of the house in the middle of the night and taking me up to the top of the garden to show me a shooting star. Boy, was it cold, but I didn't care. It was the best, standing there in my pyjamas, inside his big coat, looking up at that black velvety sky and listening to Dad's voice telling me stories of 'magic and mayhem' in heaven.

Cos that's what he did best: stories. I don't have any actual pictures of him reading to me but those are my best memories of all. I can still see him plain as day, and hear him like it was yesterday.

My dad absolutely adored books, all kinds, and whenever he could, he'd read to me. Not any old 'duty' father-child reading, oh no. He'd turn on all these magical voices that took me into different worlds. He could go from squeakily high to right down in his boots, and he never ever mixed the characters up. So, if Mr Badger was a growly Geordie, a growly Geordie he remained. No need to say, 'said Mr Badger'. I could *hear* it was Mr Badger. It *was* Mr Badger. You couldn't mistake him for anybody else.

See, that's how I know it was Dad at the station. It *was* Superman.

When I was very small, he'd bring the characters in Beatrix Potter or *The Mister Men* to life. Then it was Rudyard Kipling's *The Jungle Book* and the *Just So Stories*. He did some of the Greek and Roman and Norse myths and legends too, only I guess they were the abbreviated modern versions for kids. I wasn't as keen on those and I must admit I don't remember much about them now.

My teachers reckoned some of the material he chose was a bit questionable – 'too dark' – for a child, but I was completely enchanted by the music of the words. Longfellow's *Hiawatha* was my all-time favourite. I can still recite chunks of it purely because Dad made it sound so beautiful. It was his favourite too.

> 'Homeward hurried Hiawatha,
> Empty-handed, heavy-hearted,
> Heard Nokomis moaning, wailing:
> "Wahonowin! Wahonowin!
> Would that I had perished for you,
> Would that I were dead as you are!
> Wahonowin! Wahonowin!"
> And he rushed into the wigwam,
> Saw the old Nokomis slowly
> Rocking to and fro and moaning,
> Saw his lovely Minnehaha
> Lying dead and cold before him,
> And his bursting heart within him
> Uttered such a cry of anguish,
> That the forest moaned and shuddered,
> That the very stars in heaven
> Shook and trembled with his anguish.'

I didn't even know what 'anguish' meant back then, but old Nokomis had this ancient crackly voice, Minnehaha sounded exactly like a frail young girl with her words fading and dying away, and Hiawatha was strong and manly, and went into these rages and stormed about so brilliantly, I felt the pain of all of them and cried with them. But I guess the school had a point. I mean, what kind of father makes his little girl of six or seven cry with stories of young girls dying of famine and fever? *My* father, that's who. And it's thanks to him that I inherited his love of language and books. Mum isn't into that kind of thing really. She *does* read, sort of – romances and chick lit and stuff – but it's not the same when *she* reads out loud. I'd rather read it myself.

Our English teacher, Mrs Bakewell, she reckons it was probably Dad's influence that's given me a love of what she calls 'the melancholy writers': *Wuthering Heights*, *The Lovely Bones*, *We Need to Talk about Kevin*, Thomas Hardy,

Robert Goddard, the Brontës, Daphne du Maurier. I love love love them all.

Sometimes Dad would dress up too. Gran's apron over a cushion or two and an old fashioned mobcap, and 'Voilà! Mrs Tiggywinkle!' Trousers rolled up and a scarf round his head, a patch on his eye, and we'd be on Treasure Island. A dress of Mum's and one of my hair bands – hello, Alice in Wonderland. Anything that came to hand – Mum's hat, a flower in his lapel, a curtain – he'd use it and bring a story alive for me.

When he was around.

But that was the hard bit; he often wasn't. He worked at night, see. Chose to, what's more. He said humans were kinder at night and he had the chance to be a better nurse, he could really take care of the sick patients like he wanted to, make a difference, he wasn't bogged down in paperwork and endless ward rounds and official stuff. But of course, that meant sleeping in the daytime. And when he was asleep I had to be dead quiet, creep around, even in the school holidays. I used to get majorly fed up sometimes with Mum forever shushing me.

So I lived for his days off, when he'd be the one playing with me, taking me places, letting me do forbidden stuff, tucking me in at night, reading, reading, reading. It was way, way better than a going-abroad holiday.

Then one day everything changed.

I was eight years old. I have a picture of me at that age somewhere … yeah, there I am, fairish hair pulled back in two bunches, school uniform way too big so I wouldn't grow out of it too fast, one front tooth still missing, cheeks round and pink, grinning in that soppy way kids have for the camera. That's what I looked like last time Dad saw me. Thinking about that makes me feel really bad; my own dad wouldn't recognise me if he walked in the door now. Well, he'd know it was me cos it's the same house and he'd be coming expecting to see us, and all that, but I look totally different now. Thank goodness! I so do *not* want to be all pudgy and pink like I was then. No danger.

And Dad? Would he look much about the same? I put in the last picture Mum could find of him. He's in the kitchen and he's wearing this apron that says *IF YOU CAN'T STAND THE HEAT* in these huge capitals, and underneath there's this picture of an oven belching smoke, and Dad's holding a whisk and a wooden spoon crossed in front of him, and he's got his eyes turned in and his tongue rolled, and he looks totally hideous. But it's so him. He didn't care tuppence what he looked like. If it made us laugh, he was happy.

But see, that's what I absolutely don't get. If he loved us being happy, why, why, *why* would he ever *choose* to leave us? It doesn't make any sense. And that's why a great big bit of me never ever believed it. Something happened and he's out there somewhere, and if he can he'll come back to us. I'm certain he will if it's humanly possible.

CHAPTER 6

India

BACK THEN, when I was about eleven, they said, 'Write down your memory of how you found out about your daddy. What you thought, how you felt.' It was supposed to help me understand everything.

I tried, but when you're that young and it hurts really bad, it's majorly difficult to find words that are anywhere near how you feel. And somehow it makes it hurt even more writing it down. It makes it real.

Here's the first one I tried. You can see from the extra bits in funny places, somebody tried to help me remember the detail later on. Different pencil, different style of writing.

I was nearly 8 when my Daddy went away. At first they didn't tell me. I thought he'd just gone off on one of his trips. He would turn up again when he could.

Why did he start to go off on his own, sometimes for two, three days, on his nights off? Even now I don't know. Mum's always vague: something about him needing space.

I did all sorts of deals with God. If I don't eat a third roast potato ... if I don't have any cake at Carly's party ... if I give all my packed lunch to Jason, the fat boy in our class ... Boy, was he grosser than gross. His pockets bulged with his stash of crisps and snacks and sweets, and he gobbled up food like there was no tomorrow. Made you feel sick just watching. Everything shook and wobbled when he moved. His backside hung over the edge of his seat in class and we used to smirk and giggle behind our hands when you could see the crease in his bottom. Only of course you aren't ever allowed to say anything about kids being fat, definitely not anything remotely funny. Our teacher told us that. And Mum.

Where was I? Ah yeah, deals with the Almighty ... I thought if I gave up stuff I totally loved, God would send Dad home safely. They told me it was called 'bargaining' or 'magical thinking', but back then I'd have given up anything, *anything at all,* if it would have brought him back to me. Only God didn't listen. Or else he likes little girls to be sad all the way through to their hearts.

And I still remember the day Mum told me this time he might not be coming back. She was crouched down beside me, her eyes were all red and wet. Yeah, here it is. Here's what my younger self remembered about that conversation:

> *Mum: 'India, I'm so, so sorry but I'm afraid your Daddy has gone away.'*
> *Me: 'Where to? Where's he gone this time?'*
> *Mum: 'I'm not sure.'*
> *Me: 'When will he be back?'*
> *Mum: 'I'm not sure. He might not come back this time.'*
> *Me: 'What? Not ever?'*
> *Mum: 'Maybe not.'*
> *Me: 'Didn't he say?'*
> *Mum: 'No.'*
> *Me: 'Okay.'*
> *But I don't know why she didn't ask him. I would of.*

(Must've been an exercise they set me. They've put in the names and colons.)

But when he didn't return – not the next day, not the following week, not that month, not even on my *birthday* – then I started to get insanely scared. I was desperate enough by this time to miss whole meals, give away a big bar of my favourite Dairy Milk, on the off-chance God might be looking in my direction.

35

I knew – I just *knew* – the adults were hiding something, but I didn't know what questions to ask to find out what.

> Gran told me not to talk about him. That's Granny Knight, Mum's mum.
> She came into my room when I was in bed nearly asleep. I could smell her before I saw her. She smells of funny soap and something going off.
> 'India, sweetie,' she said, 'it's probably best you don't keep asking about your Daddy, honey. It only upsets Mummy.'
> So I asked her, 'Why does Mummy keep on crying, Granny?'
> She said, 'Because he's ... not here any more. She misses him.'
> Well, I missed him too. I told her that, even though she knows already. Like God. Or Santa. You say things to Santa but he knows already you want a puppy or maybe a pink bike for Christmas. And sometimes he's got it ready for you before you even say.
> Granny's the same. She got me a real china tea set for my Christmas and I never even told her I wanted one. I just put it in a secret letter to Santa cos Sonia at my school says, if you tell people Santa won't bring it. He likes secrets.
> Granny knows I ask God every night to send my Daddy home cos I told her that. Okay, God's not Santa but I mean he is God. Only he doesn't listen.
> I asked her then, 'Why doesn't Daddy come home?'
> And she said, 'You ask far too many questions. Time for sleep. Nighty night.'
> And I remember it, cos it wasn't fair. Nobody tells me things any more. Daddy used to tell me proper answers. He reckoned if I was old enough to ask the question I was old enough to hear the answer. Only Mum and Granny don't.

This was the longest stretch of prose I'd written at that time.

It must have made a big impression on my eight-year-old mind to be recalled so clearly three years later. If it was accurate, of course, but it sounds legit to me now.

The weeks stretched into months, a year, two years, and still he didn't reappear. Not for birthdays, not for Christmas, not for anything. And nobody ever said his name. You weren't allowed.

My imagination, inherited from my dad, went wild. I pictured him in terrible situations that meant he *couldn't* return to us. Kidnapped, blindfolded, hungry and cold. In prison, chained to the wall, listening to the screams and moans of fellow inmates, fearing he'll be stabbed if he goes to sleep. Marooned on a desert island, killing crunchy insects and slimy fish with his bare hands, eating them raw (yuck!) to survive. Dead, and lying undiscovered somewhere remote, his eyes picked out by vultures, his body crawling with worms and huge blowflies. I'd wake up whimpering, wet with sweat, but there was no one I could tell.

So how did I find out what the big secret was? From a bully, that's how.

It happened when I was two months off being eleven.

I rifle through the scrapbook till I find a school photo of me taken that term, before I heard the truth about my father. My hair's short this time, several shades darker than my eight-year-old self, curled over my ears, a tad too long in the fringe. (Miss Gidley, our maths teacher now, would have told me to get it out of my eyes cos it would ruin my eyesight 'in the long run'.) No blazer this time, only a pullover and the tie hardly showing. Must've been my last year at the primary school. Would my dad have known me, seeing me in the street then, I wonder? I flick the pages back and forth from me at eight to me at ten. Taller, thinner, less smiley. But I'd say, yeah, still the me he knew.

They told me to think about the time I was first told about my dad's 'probable death'. Write it as I might have described it at the time. Easy for them to say; a great big bit of me just didn't want to go back there. Ever.

*I'm standing in the playground at school, watching for my
chance to run in to skip in the rope. Daisy and Judith are
turning. Daisy's my best friend and Judith's okay. This
mean kid, Nancy Esterhausen, she's leaning against the
wall and she starts smirking at me.*

*'Go on then, what'cha waiting for?' she says in that nasty
kind of way.*

*She puts me off my stride and I start counting myself in all
over again.*

'Coward, huh? Must be in your blood,' she hisses.

I go all cold. 'What? What did you say?'

*'You heard,' she says. 'You get it from your dad. You're a
coward.'*

*Now, she's the first kid who ever said anything mean about
my dad. Everybody else is nice, and sorry he might be
dead and everything. So when she says that, I'm mad as
mad can be. If I was allowed to I'd hit her.*

*'You don't even know my dad,' I shout back, 'so shut your
ugly face and leave me alone!'*

*Granny Knight would tell me to wash my mouth out, but
she's not here and I <u>hate</u> Nancy Esterhausen. I really
really hate her. She's a mean bully. Everybody knows that.*

*'A coward and a nut case,' she says back, and she even
makes a rude gesture along with it. That's something nice
girls shouldn't ever ever do.*

*Daisy – she's really lovely, Daisy – she drops her end of
the skipping rope and comes over to stick her arm through
mine. She whispers in my ear, 'Ignore her, Indie, she's not
worth it. She's only making trouble. As usual.'*

*But I pull away from her. I walk right up to Nancy and stare
into her freckly mug.*

*'Shut your fat gob, Nancy Esterhausen. You don't know the
first thing about my dad and you have no right saying
things about him. So go boil your stupid face.'*

*'I do so know about him,' she jeers, stabbing her finger in
my direction. 'I know he was a nutter. So far gone he killed
himself. Only a coward does that. My dad says so and he*

knows. He's a policeman.'
I can feel Daisy pulling me away again and this time I don't stop her. It's like Nancy Esterhausen punched me in the belly and sent all the air out of my lungs. Only she never even touched me.

CHAPTER 7

India

READING THIS NOW, almost five years after it happened, I can still feel the sick dread in my stomach as I went home that afternoon. It couldn't be true. Surely not. My dad wouldn't have deliberately gone away and killed himself when he knew that meant he wouldn't ever see me, ever, ever, ever, again. He *wouldn't*. I was his 'special girl', 'his princess'. It had to be some terrible mistake.

I didn't go home, I went to Granny Knight's place. She lives in the next street but one to us, and I was allowed as long as she rang Mum to tell her I was safe. Only this day, as it happens, she didn't need to phone cos I was supposed to go to her anyway, on account of Mum having some in-service thingy or other. Which was just as well, cos Granny was the one who said not to talk about Dad at home, wasn't she?

I turn to the page from a lined notebook that records my memory of that conversation. How many times have I sat here reading and re-reading this bit?

Gran went a sort of greyish, whitish colour. She was totally quiet like she was searching around in her head for words. After ages she says in a peculiar voice like she was choking on some chopped nuts, 'We'll talk to your mother about this when she gets home.'
Well, blow me! After all she said! Sometimes I really don't get grown ups.
I couldn't help it, I said straight out, 'But you told me I mustn't.' And if Mum had of heard me, she'd of told me not

40

to cheek my elders and betters, but she wasn't there and I couldn't help it. I mean, that was so unfair.
Gran didn't tell me off either. She only said, 'I know. I know. But this has gone too far. You're old enough to understand now.' And she gave me two chocolate biscuits AND a hot chocolate with five marshmallows and chocolate sprinkles on top. In the middle of the afternoon! Unheard of. She always says, 'Not before your meal, it'll spoil your appetite.'
I kinda knew then I probably wasn't going to like whatever it was I was going to hear.
It seemed like ages and ages before Mum got home and before she could even get inside the door, Gran went outside to talk to her so I wouldn't hear. She made Mum a cup of tea and told her to drink it 'first'.

I can see from the different writing somebody else was writing down what I said. I guess it was too tough for a kid of eleven to write fast enough. Maybe they recorded it first, I don't remember. But the voice is me.

Mum didn't look at me while she talked. She was twisting a hanky round and round in her fingers, her voice all jaggy at the edges.
'We were only trying to protect you, darling,' she said. 'You were so young when ... it happened. I didn't want you to be upset. But the truth is, one day Daddy ... well, he ... just vanished. He walked out of the house and didn't come back. No explanation, he simply didn't come home.'
And then it was like she was talking through a puddle. 'A week later somebody found a pile of his clothes folded on the beach at Gullane with his wallet and money and reading glasses.'
'Gullane? You mean, our Gullane? Where Daddy used to take me to play in the sand dunes?'
'Yes.'
She sat there gulping for ages, and I desperately wanted her to get on with the story, but Gran was watching, and she

*put her finger in front of her lips to let me know I ought to
be quiet and wait till she was ready.*

Eventually Mum started up again.

*'A policeman came and told me. You were at school. He
said … it looked as if Daddy walked into the sea and kept
on walking, with no intention of coming out again. That's
what the police thought, anyway.'*

'But why? Why would he do that?' I wailed.

*I saw her jaw clench and it seemed like hours and hours
before she spoke.*

*'We don't know, India. He hadn't been happy for some
time. He was becoming increasingly moody, and … well …
wanting to be on his own. But we don't know what made
him decide to do … that.'*

Still it didn't make sense.

*'But, if he did walk into the sea, wouldn't they have found
him?' I said, 'You know, when the tide came in?'*

*Dad used to read me stories of terrible accidents at sea,
and the Cornish wreckers, and stuff like that. I knew things
washed up eventually.*

*She nodded and said, 'Everybody expected he would be
found, but so far there's been nothing. The most likely
thing is that he … his body … got trapped somewhere or
… but there's no point in you worrying about that kind of
detail. You and I, we've got to learn to accept that, for
whatever reason, he couldn't go on as he was, and that
he's not coming back.'*

*I know I banged my fists against my lap. No! No! No! I
won't accept any such thing. My dad wouldn't do that.*

*I had to make her see it. 'I don't believe you. He wouldn't.
He loved us.'*

*'He certainly loved you, sweetheart,' she said in that voice
– what did Dad call it? – patronising. Yes, that's the word –
patronising. 'He was devoted to you. You know he was.*

You had lovely times together, didn't you?'
*'So, if he did love us, he wouldn't up and leave us, would
he?' I said. I mean, it was plain as the nose on your face,
as Dad used to say.*
*'Not under normal circumstances, no,' she said in that
grown up-to-little kid voice again. 'But we don't know what
was going on in his head. We probably never will. Maybe
he had problems at work he couldn't talk about. Maybe
he'd done something, or something had happened, that
was more than he could live with. We don't know. We only
know he must have been terribly unhappy about
something.'*
I thought of something else right then, that minute.
*'If that's what you really believe, why didn't you tell me?' I
demanded. 'Why did you let me think he would come back
one day?'*
*'Because you were only eight years old,' she said, making
out I was a baby. 'You loved your daddy so much. I thought
it would hurt you too much if I told you he'd killed himself.
Besides which, there was no proof. No body. We didn't
know … not for sure. I thought it would be time enough
when they found him. When it was definite. And then
somehow the time never seemed right.'*
'But kids at my school, <u>they</u> knew.' How unfair was that!
*'One or two, maybe,' she said, making it out like it was
nothing. 'Some of the older ones, the ones with parents
that tell them everything. But it wouldn't upset them the
same. It wasn't their daddy.'*
'Did the teachers know?'
*She did go a bit pink this time and she was back to fiddling
with the hanky.*
*'Some of them saw it in the paper. Anyway they had to be
told so they could take extra care of you. But they knew I
didn't want you to be worried. As far as you were*

concerned your daddy had gone away. And to be fair, we still don't know for sure he is dead.'

I'm amazed that my young self could capture all that emotion. Of course, I know the counsellors and teachers were helping me work through my 'anger' and 'fear' and 'ambivalence', and 'express the emotions', and 'gain understanding' and 'acceptance' and blah-de-blah-de-blah in these different ways. But looking at that innocent wee scrap, not yet at secondary school, imagining her hearing the truth about her father for the first time, having to talk about this painful stuff, I want to reach back in time and protect her, keep her safe.

CHAPTER 8

Chris

I TAKE A LEAP and squeeze between the doors just as they start to close. Pretty good going, though I say it myself. Some days even yet I stand there watching the train slide out of the station, preferring late to injured. The London Underground, the sheer speed and relentless frenzy, the mad multitudes, is one of the biggest shocks for a country bumpkin like me. I live in constant dread of being sandwiched half in, half out.

To make absolutely doubly sure I twitch my full skirt. Yep, it's all inside. My reflection looks back at me momentarily as the train glides through a tunnel. I was right to match these two garments: the cropped jacket nicely complements the long line of the maxi.

Reassured I allow my gaze to scan the carriage. Right, a few of the usuals, plenty of new faces. Time for my game. I glance at my watch: I'm allowed one look to take in the whole picture, then I turn away and weave my story. Five minutes total for each person. I'm strict with myself even without an adjudicator.

Suzannah – that's my name for her – neat in her navy bank teller's uniform, hair glossy and more improbably red than usual. She's totally engrossed, applying eye-shadow, eyeliner, mascara. Must have pressed the snooze button once too often this morning. How she manages to keep a steady hand with all this lurching, I don't know, takes me all my time not to blot everything sitting still in front of the bedroom mirror with my elbow on a firm surface. Besides which, where's the mystery, the allure, if people *see* you making-up? She can't be wanting to impress anybody on this train, that's for sure. Ergo, she has someone special somewhere else. She's naturally pretty though as well as a smart dresser, doesn't need all that heavy stuff in my opinion. Nice legs too – I envy her those sculpted knees. Helped by the killer heels of course, easily four inches, but she must surely sit down most of the day; you couldn't totter in those for eight hours on the trot without doing harm. Probably kicks them off under the counter. Smallish flight bag with her this morning … hmm, I reckon she's going on a date after work with that significant other and has a snazzy black crush-resistant dress tucked in there, some sexy tights and underwear, and blood-red patent stilettos. She'll nibble at the edges of two courses at the restaurant, drink more Sauvignon Blanc than she intended, get home far too late, and be slapping on the face paint on the Tube again tomorrow morning. The day job's tedious enough to be automatic for her now; doesn't require the grey cells to be firing on all cylinders. She works in order to play.

Whoops, time up.

Pin-striped Anthony's sitting opposite her, studiously avoiding looking at those knees. Purple spotted tie – real silk – draped around his neck, ready to flick into a Windsor knot two minutes before he enters the office building; the only splash of colour on his monochrome person. He must be easily six foot five, probably has to get those luxury pure wool suits made to measure. As per every morning he's on his mobile pretending to be finalising major deals with venture capitalists around the world, but it's all social network stuff (I sat next to him once). He smirks when a mate sends him a salacious message; he smiles when the girlfriend tells him what she's doing right this minute; he adopts a serious frown and types madly with both thumbs when Suzannah happens to glance up and catch his eye. He'll be hard at work for the next ten hours ruling the corporate world, arrive home at 8, have to heat up his meal in the microwave because the indifferent wife's long ago fed the family and the dog and is ready to collapse in front of the telly for some mindless relaxation before bedtime. He'll drink two single malts and fall asleep in the chair that the cat keeps warm for him. Wifey will turf him out and send him to bed when his snores disturb her viewing. He'll be unconscious for six hours and wake to repeat the whole crazy process all over again tomorrow.

Time up.

Ah, Maggie's standing this morning; must have been cutting it as fine as me. Hmm, she's taller than I thought – five ten in her stockinged feet, I shouldn't wonder; over six feet in those canvas and cork wedges. Model height. Matronly figure but good posture. Probably, what ... early fifties? I always love her bohemian choices, every one of them courtesy of a secondhand shop or eBay by the look of them. Today she's a vision in olive green and gold. The full, almost floor-length skirt has embroidered flowers and little mirrors and beads and buttons scattered over two of the tiers, her waistcoat looks hand-crocheted, and the peasant's blouse reveals a tad too much of her crinkled bosom for an onlooker's comfort. Her mass of frizzy greying curls is restrained by a twist of green and gold scarf, below which brassy gipsy earrings dangle to her shoulders. She's strap-hanging and I can see both hands are covered in cheap and cheerful rings, nails chipped and unmanicured. Maggie's the other end of the spectrum from Suzannah; her plain asymmetrical face is bare as nature intended, no definition, no adornment whatever, wrinkled and freckled and bronzed as if she's gradually rusting into old age. I'd say she works for a charity and spends her days begging, beseeching and borrowing from the rich to feed the poor. She'll live in a sparse bedsit with next to no creature comforts and spend her annual leave (if she takes it) building schools in Burundi. Her tea tonight will be a basic salad from her Sainsbury's Local with olives, feta cheese and artisan bread, no pudding, Fairtrade decaf coffee with one square of Divine bitter 70% chocolate to supply her quota of flavanols. She'll sleep like a baby and wake every morning eager to take on the world. I'd like to get to know the real Maggie.

Time up.

In the far corner, a new-to-me commuter. Diminutive Qadira is squashed against the glass by the overhang of a huge hulk of punk, with enough metal in his ears, nose and lip to send a powerful magnet into a tailspin. She's swathed in black from head to toe but mercifully spared the veiled face. I doubt I'd recognise her with lustrous blue-black hair falling around her shoulders, a shape, a personality. She sits with head downcast: a crime to hide those beautiful dark eyes. I smile when she glances in my direction but she immediately averts her face, and gets off at the next station. Hmm, what kind of a job would keep her secure in her principles and boundaries? Maybe a legal secretary for a firm which specialises in cases involving ethnic minorities and suppressed women. She's meticulous to a fault and keeps impeccable records, never forgetting a face or a case. Some of her bosses are quick to judge, but Qadira is a calming influence who brings them down to earth and prevents them forming hasty verdicts. She goes home at night to an ailing and demanding mother whom she loves devotedly. Her five sisters and two brothers are still back in Iran, the country she called home until her father died and the widow decided to visit her last surviving sister-in-law in England while she still could. Qadira accompanied her and when her mother had a stroke in a supermarket in Battersea it was she who nursed her back to a semi-invalid existence. Her promised husband for twenty-one years is in the army, and she won't even see him until he has fulfilled his duty to his country. She's never met him; it was all arranged by their parents when they were two years old. What little free time she has is spent experimenting in the kitchen and exquisitely embroidering Egyptian cotton sheets and pure linen tablecloths ready for the marital home she may never have.

Time up.

Darren's a harder nut to crack. Ubiquitous dark chinos, crumpled blue shirt, trainers. Early twenties. Ears plugged, foot tapping. Nose down in the Metro … not the predictable sports pages though, so … I'm instantly intrigued. What does this tell me about our local mystery man? His nails are bitten to the quick already and one thumb's between his teeth being relentlessly chewed as he frowns in concentration at a photo of a young woman ... ahhh, might have guessed. He reads slowly. So would I with that din in my ears competing for my attention; I can hear the powerful beat even from this far down the carriage. He leaps up as the train slides to a standstill, throwing the free newspaper behind him. It hits the seat and falls to the floor shedding pages as it goes, a safety hazard if ever I saw one. I pick it up and try to reassemble it. There's the girl he was staring at. But ... this is no curvy page three type, this is a mere schoolgirl. A missing teenager. I close my eyes against the suffocating emotions.

Maria Davenport. She's from Barnsbury, only nine miles or so from where I work. I must have been busy making corsages for Friday's wedding when she was walking along that canal path to her fate. Twisting wires, piercing ivy leaves, anchoring cream roses and silver succulents ... like they mattered.

We're open late on a Thursday. Maybe someone who saw Maria, someone who knows what happened to her even, came into our shop that very evening. Gives you the heebie jeebies being that close to crime – if it was a crime. Especially *this* crime.

I look again at the girl's face. You can see why Darren was hypnotised. It's kind of haunting, seeing that teenager, knowing she's missing, any one of us might have seen her. *Have* I ever seen her? I'm into faces and people and weaving their stories; I think I'd have remembered this one. Except that last Thursday she'd have been in school uniform, simple ponytail, probably much less eye make-up than in this professional portrait.

I startle when the tannoy announces we're approaching my stop, and bundle the paper into my bag, tripping over the feet of a businessman snoozing quietly in the end seat beside the door. He drags his legs back with a grunt, nodding in recognition of my apology, 'Sorry, my big feet'. It's a relief to get back up into the openness of the streets after the cloying airlessness of the Tube. I don't think I'll ever get used to it, although it's been less of an ordeal since I started playing the game.

CHAPTER 9

Chris

PARMINDER IS UNLOCKING the security grill as I round the corner.

'Hi, Chris.'

'Morning, Parminder.'

'Gorgeous day.'

'Yep.'

I love entering the shop first thing after it's been closed up for the night; all that accumulated fragrance emerging and hovering like clandestine friends while we slept, leaving the whisper of their conversations behind. Somehow, for those first few minutes, you don't see the shabbiness of the building or the dropped leaves or the strategically placed bucket under the dodgy roof out in the working area. Today I inhale consciously ... and again ... willing myself into a different place mentally.

Parminder is the best kind of boss you could ask for, totally laid back but an absolute creative genius. She's taught me more than I ever picked up at college, and she's happy to give me plenty of free rein. Reckons I'm worth my weight in gold to her with my computer skills and financial acumen. Least she can do is give my career a hike. How she ever balanced the books before I came along, I'll never know. She absolutely hasn't a clue when it comes to figures.

Today she gets pitched straight into six orders for funeral wreaths while I top up the vases and rearrange the window. Balance ... colour co-ordination ... clean lines ... Parminder teases me for my peccadilloes but it's never

51

malicious, and customers often comment on the artistry.

'Got anything planned for today?' she says. She's so naturally skilled she can talk and work at the same time. Me, I need to concentrate the whole time when I'm arranging.

'Not sure. See how I feel after work. You?'

'Got a bride and her mum coming in after closing. I love those sessions. This one could be a biggie.'

'Great. All good for business.'

After a pause she says in a different tone, 'You all right, Chris? You seem a bit down.'

'A bit. Something and nothing.'

'Anything I can help with?'

'Nope. But thanks.'

She leaves it at that – another reason why I love her. She knows the bare bones: I was married, that I'm not in touch with my ex, that I lost a child, that this is my first proper (as in legal) job since moving to London, but she respects my wish not to talk about any of it. A rare creature, Parminder.

After a bit she says, 'Like to stay behind and meet the bride with me, see what it's like tailoring flowers to a specific person? I'm sure she wouldn't mind if you perched in the corner. No pressure though.'

'Sounds good to me.'

I know from the cards and messages she's brilliant at this, so I'd love to see her in action. Instantly I have something to look forward to, Maria Davenport's image is less pervasive, yearning for my own daughter not quite so unbearable.

'Great, then get yourself stuck into these two wreaths. This lady wants … let me see … 14 inch circle, white roses, pink gerberas, silver foliage. This one's a horseshoe, all red roses. I thought maybe some of this dark green ivy, ruscus maybe, and a few hypicum berries to set off that dark crimson. What d'you think? Okay with that?'

'Fine. Thanks, Parminder.' As if I'd dare counter her genius.

I'm in my absolute element.

I told her once, 'Flowers are my therapy' and she's never forgotten it. On a really bad day she puts me out the back working on bouquets and baskets and does the front of house herself. Like I say, a treasure. If I was going to confide in anyone it'd be Parminder, but I don't want to talk about it to anybody. My pain, my problem, my life.

At lunchtime I pop out to the park for my sandwich, calling in at the chemist for some nail polish; I'm all out of pearly pink, my favourite. I deliberately don't look at the newspaper, concentrating instead on the mums and toddlers feeding the ducks. Remembering good times. I wish I'd brought my camera. Before I leave I send a load of vibes to Maria Davenport's parents, and offer a swift prayer heavenwards, but then put the whole family resolutely out of my mind. I owe it to Parminder.

The bride, Ashley Crowe, isn't at all what I was expecting. She's minute, barely five feet, I'd say, and looking as if she's about eleven months pregnant. Apparently the wedding has been postponed to get the 'inconvenient' birth safely out of the way and allow the mother-of-the-bride to keep up appearances. This all rushes out of Mrs Crowe before they've even been ushered through into our back room. She's the one who rang our shop to make the appointment and at this moment she's clearly in the driving seat.

Parminder is her usual gracious self, a happy blend of hostess and supplier of wanted services.

'Let's all have a cup of tea first, then I want to hear all about you, Ashley, what kind of a girl you are, hobbies, what music you like, favourite colours, clothes, everything you can tell me about the real you.'

'Aren't you going to show us your designs first?' the mother says, rather tartly.

'Actually, no.' Parminder's smile remains wide and warm and friendly. 'The bouquet Ashley is going to carry doesn't exist yet. It will be uniquely hers. And the more I know about her and her dreams, the closer we'll get to something that's perfect for her.'

She's totally calm and unhurried and so in control. Under her gentle persuasion Ashley talks about her life and her dreams. Only after a good half an hour of chatting does Parminder move on to the wedding itself: the dress, hairstyle, bridesmaids, colours, venue, other choices already made for the big day.

She studies the samples of fabric and pictures they've brought along. Why *do* girls choose all that fuss and volume in unflattering white at colossal expense? And in Ashley's case presumably they'll be holding the baby amidst those acres of virginal tulle and lace and ribbon. I repress a shudder. Each to their own.

Parminder excuses herself for a few moments, returning with three blooms and a hefty reference book. 'I think, for you, Ashley, the main flower should be this phalaenopsis orchid, but in pinkish-lavender. I don't have the exact colour in at the moment but this will give you a sense of the shape it will create. Here's a picture of it. What d'you think?'

'It's *exactly* the colour I love. I wouldn't have thought of orchids but now you say ... Mmmm. I like it.'

'And then, around the orchids, these beautiful soft pink roses, Sweet Avalanche. Aren't they gorgeous? And maybe ranunculus in this slightly darker shade? D'you like ranunculus? If not we could have a different tighter rose ... like this ... or perhaps this one?'

'No, I like the original suggestion. They look lovely together and it's that little bit different.'

'And we could bring them all together with some lily of the valley which will give a lightness and delicacy to the whole effect and bring in the white.'

'That'll look fab,' Ashley breathes. 'I can't wait to see it. And the bridesmaids?'

'I'd suggest maybe pink roses and lily of the valley to echo and complement your bouquet, and as they're all young girls, a simple round posy is probably best.'

'Sounds pretty.'

'And Mum-of-the-bride? Happy with Ashley's choices?'

'If she's happy, I'm happy.' I've watched her mellowing

as Parminder wove her charm and she looks as if she believes what she says. 'As long as the bouquet is big enough to ... you know ...' She gestures across her own gently rounded middle-age swell. Ahhh, it's embarrassment not aggression.

Ashley flushes but says nothing.

A lesser woman might reply with some acidity, 'That's down to Ashley, exercise and a firm pantie-girdle. Not my problem.' Not Parminder though. She simply moves on swiftly, this time effectively involving both women in the choice of corsages and buttonholes, table decorations and church flowers. I can only hope I'll be as understanding and sensitive when ... *if* I ever get to this level.

It's 9.30 that night before I take out the newspaper and see Maria Davenport's face again. I must Google the story, see if there've been any developments.

I'm in no hurry to resurrect painful emotions. The vanilla latte I've brewed is silkily smooth on my tongue, Beethoven's Piano Concerto Number 5 is playing softly in the background, Sylvester warm and contented on my lap. How lucky am I? Most landlords aren't keen on pets but mine has a distinct weakness for cats, especially the long-haired ones like Sylvester, and as long as I pay for the house to be deep-cleaned when I leave, he's happy. It's a novelty for me. My ex wasn't keen on domestic pets of any kind so we never had one. Strange really, back then in my former life, we owned the house we shared; I can't possibly afford to buy in London, and yet I'm now more free to be myself than I've ever been.

Not that London would ever be my first choice for home, and I'm not sure I'll ever come to terms with city life. Everything seems to be grimy, smelly and noisy, even tea has a scum on it – not only in my modest flat, in the posh hotels too. But London is anonymous. Here there's no one to quiz and pry and criticise. Anything goes in the midst of the sheer vastness of anonymity.

CHAPTER 10

Chris

MARIA DAVENPORT: not much in the way of developments.

But still I'm shocked. Seems there are currently a hundred and twenty kids from the UK listed as missing, most of them teenagers, the majority from London. *A hundred and twenty*! One child reported missing *every three minutes*! I had no idea. Most are recent, but one of them's been missing since … *what? 1950*! Imagine waiting, wondering, worrying, for *decades*.

Information about Maria is sketchy. They are not *'at this stage'* looking for anyone else in relation to this enquiry. So they don't suspect foul play. That's a relief. But why then has she gone missing? What personal torture is she going through? She's only a kid.

The police are urging anyone who might have seen her since that sighting on Thursday on the tow path, or might have information as to her whereabouts, to contact them immediately. *'Maria may be in urgent need of medical assistance.'* Ahhh. Is she diabetic? Or asthmatic? Or epileptic, maybe? Recently given birth? Did she conceal her pregnancy? I check online again but no, no reports of a baby being found. What did she do with it?

They are combing the banks of the canal for clues. Blood? A baby? Discarded clothes? I guess it's something that they aren't sending in divers. Yet.

Poor Maria. How desperate was she? Was she suicidal? I hope, I devoutly hope, she didn't go through with it. It's not the answer. I want to tell her that. I know.

I hope she has someone somewhere she can confide in, someone who'll hold her close, listen, reassure, guide her into a safer place. Please God there's someone there for her.

Her mother makes a heartfelt appeal: '*Maria, we love you. Whatever has happened, whatever you've done, whatever you're struggling with, you aren't in any trouble as far as we're concerned. We just want you home. We miss you so much and we desperately need to know you're safe. Get in touch with us, please, please, please, darling. Ring home, leave a message. We only want to know you're okay.*'

Only it's not true. Simply knowing she's safe and sound *wouldn't* be enough. Then it'd be: *Where are you?* The police would be involved in a full-scale search – she's only sixteen. And when ... *if* they find her it's not like the mum would draw a veil over where she's been, what she's done. Nor the police. *Why? Who? Where? How? When?* They've got to account for all those man-hours, close the file with some kind of logical explanation that holds water with the powers that be. There'd be endless probing. The press would want the full story. No man – and certainly no pretty teenage girl – is an island.

Oh Maria, my heart goes out to you. And I too want to know you haven't come to any harm. Whatever you've done.

I didn't feel very safe myself tonight.

We're only officially open late on Thursdays, but Parminder and I often work on after closing time on other days to complete big orders for the next day. This time of year most nights it's getting dark by the time I start my walk from the Tube station, and tonight a low heavy mist was making it more murky than usual. Twenty minutes it takes me normally to get home, brisk pace, no holdups. I quite like the exercise before my meal. The usual crowd got off behind me and I didn't even notice the footsteps until I'd crossed the main road and started down the side street. But once I was aware of them, the old adrenaline surged. Every nerve was tuned to that sound. I speeded up a bit; so did they. I stopped to tip an imaginary stone out of my shoe; they stopped too. I turned down a different street; the footsteps followed. I took to my heels; so did they.

I wasn't about to risk going down my usual route out of sight of any houses or cars, so I swung round abruptly at the corner, and two lads in hoodies stopped dead in their tracks, a few metres away from me. I couldn't see their faces clearly but they were breathing heavily.

'What d'you want?' I said, calmly as I could muster.

'You,' they hissed. One of them gave a low wolf whistle to leave no doubt.

'Go away and leave me alone.'

'Yeuwww!' the taller one jeered. 'Got our knickers in a twist have we?' He advanced a step, keeping his face in shadow, laughing coarsely. 'Want me to untwist them for you?'

'Yeahh. We'll help you sort yourself out,' the other one said in a vile whisper, all the while inching out onto the road, and beginning to circle behind me.

What would have happened if a guy with a huge German Shepherd on a short chain hadn't come round the corner at that precise moment, I dread to think. One I could maybe have fought off; two much younger strapping youths? I doubt I'd have stood a chance, especially if they were fired up on something, which in all probability they were.

Anyway I simply fell into step a few yards in front of the dog walker and those would-be attackers melted into the shadows. Maybe I should get a large dog, the meaner the better.

I was still shaking when I tried to fit the key in my door and it took a stiff whisky to steady my nerves. Bastards! After I'd chased the alcohol down with a glass of ginger beer (it's a comfort thing) I gave up all attempts to read the paper, and instead cosseted myself – a long soak in a scented Radox bath. It helped to soothe my body if not rebuild my confidence.

I'm chopping vegetables in the kitchen for a kind of one-pot no-skill, minimum-effort stew, the news on in the background, when Maria Davenport's name impinges on my brain again. I stop what I'm doing and sit down to listen properly; the chopping can wait. There's no one coming home from work expecting a meal on the table any more.

'*Police have received four reports of sightings of the teenager. One in Cornwall, one in Yorkshire, one in Glasgow and one in London.*'

Sightings! They can't all be right of course, but still. She's more than likely still alive. How the Davenports will be clinging onto that possibility. Hoping against hope. Exactly like I would if there was the remotest chance that I'd ever see my own beloved daughter again. But I mustn't go down that road. I won't. I have to accept what's happened.

They give more details, most of which mean nothing to me ... except the London reference: '*in the area of Camden Market*'.

'*If anyone has any information of a teenager answering Maria's description in any of these locations or indeed anywhere else, would they please ring this number immediately.*'

The photograph of Maria from the paper fills the screen once more.

Camden Market, huh? Now that *is* close to home. I adore browsing in that place, with its craft stalls and quirky clothes shops. I rarely actually buy any garments there – they don't seem to cater for tall girls – but I get ideas I can then translate into my own wardrobe. And I'm stowed out with earrings, necklaces, bracelets from the women who're trying to make a living in a horribly competitive world.

Might I, in my wanderings, have inadvertently walked right by this girl, Maria?

What if I *had* seen her? Would I have reported the sighting? Or would I have contented myself with a whispered 'Want to talk? I'm a good listener. I understand trouble. Had plenty of my own.'

I don't know. But maybe I ought to think about it. In case. I'm planning to visit the markets tomorrow afternoon. Although, come to think of it if Maria's following reports she

won't hang around where she's been seen.
The news moves on. I resume chopping.

I push the empty plate away with a sigh. Not my finest hour,
but not my worst either. I'd rather have had a generous
helping of lasagne or shepherd's pie but I'm trying not to pile
on the weight now I've tripped over the milestone of forty.

Black coffee definitely tastes less bitter if I flick through
the pages of *Elle* while I drink. All those svelte bodies, the
fearless fashion, the effortless style these waifs can carry off
simply by virtue of their skinniness ... although I'm not so
convinced they'd be cuddly in bed! Heresy! Well, I'm not into
this triple zero rubbish, but I definitely don't like flab, so
maybe it's time to take up jogging or something.

I'm not vain – well, I don't *think* I am – but image
matters. I take a long hard look in the mirror, full length and
close up. Overdue: plucking eyebrows, shaving legs, painting
nails. Time to remedy all three. It's an abiding nightmare of
mine that one day I'll fall and break a limb. The plaster will
be on for six weeks and I'll have to endure the humiliation of
the nurse who cuts it off seeing my growth. I always
shuddered at my mother's reluctance to tidy up her arms and
legs, so I'm a bit obsessive about keeping my own limbs
smooth while I can. And I'm dying to try out this latest 'red
hot chilli pepper' nail polish.

Yep, I like it. Exactly right for my new gypsy skirt in
autumn colours.

Okay, I confess, that's another thing I'm a bit obsessive
about. I keep my wardrobe sorted according to the bands on
the old colour spectrum. Lipsticks and nail polishes lined up
in order of shade. Sad or what?! Eye make-up comes in
graded containers anyway so I cheat there and use the pre-
ordained hues.

My friends tease me about my fastidious tastes but I
laugh it off. It's enough for me that they don't make
demands, impose expectations, edge me out of my comfort
zone. And that's all I ask. Just to be myself.

When I'm done I settle down with a DVD I picked up in

Sainsbury's: *A Dangerous Method*. Says it's drawn from real life, a glimpse into the turbulent world of the early psychiatrists, Jung, Freud. Exactly what the doctor ordered tonight – a bit of insight.

CHAPTER 11

India

IT SUCKS. All this stuff with my dad. Not knowing.

What's more I've put on 22 grams this week. I feel fat
and disgusting and ugly and worthless, and I've no one to
blame but me. For not standing up for myself. I'm definitely
definitely going to skip lunch all this coming week, and up the
laxatives, but Mum's on my case and I *have* to eat something
at night or else she goes on and on and on and on till my
head aches and I feel like throwing things.

She's even started barging in when I'm doing my
exercises. 'You don't need all that at your age. Come on
downstairs.' And as soon as I'm downstairs she wants me to
have a drink. Not Diet Coke or lemon water, of course,
something 'nourishing'!

I wish I could talk to somebody about Dad ...
somebody who'd properly listen, not try to make out it's no
big deal. Hang on a minute ... maybe ...

Her name's Mercedes – how cool a name is that, huh?
And she's only been at our school for a term and a half.
Before that she was in this ultra, ultra posh place, all girls,
and she was a *boarder*. Imagine! Wicked! I've always
hankered to go to a boarding school. Only Mercedes reckons
it's nothing like as much fun as the storybooks make out. At
her place they didn't have dorm fights or midnight feasts or
even hover over the deathbeds of the sickly girls who were
always destined to die young. She reckons she felt homesick
for the first four weeks every term and was only starting to
'acclimatise' as she puts it, when it was time to start

preparing to go home for holidays. And then it all started up again.

She cried herself to sleep loads of times, and she's much, much happier in our ordinary everyday crummy school where she gets to go home every night. Hmm. She *says*! Me, I'd like to try it for myself. I think it'd be awesome. Dead romantic. But then, I'm a reader and whatever else she is, Mercedes is *not*. Never in a million years. No imagination at all, she reckons.

She had to move at any rate, cos her father – 'my Pa', as she calls him – ran out on them suddenly. Went off with a secretary half his age, Mercedes says. She doesn't seem to care that much, I have to say. Not like me and *my* dad. But then Mr Atkinson-Baker, QC, almost a judge, doesn't seem to have been the kind of father who did ace things with her like sneaking out in the night to watch shooting stars, or building her a tree house, or reading in all those voices. Anyway, her mother – 'my Ma' – reckons they can't afford the 'extortionate fees' now, so she has to slum it with us.

Mind you, she'll never *ever* be ordinary and everyday. Not Mercedes. For a kick-off, she has this really plummy lah-de-dah voice. I like it actually, but the other kids don't half mimic her. She doesn't *seem* to mind and she doesn't try to change either. I like that. She isn't going to be bullied into becoming something she's not. Besides which I reckon she'd get into a heck of a lot of trouble at home if she sounded all slovenly and dragged up in the gutter. You should hear her mother! If you think Mercedes sounds uppity, you wouldn't *believe* Mrs Atkinson-Baker's accent. Frightfully, frightfully superior and classy. Totally OTT.

But as well as that, she's stunning. I mean, pure drop-dead gorgeous. Mercedes, that is. (Well, her ma's pretty amazing too, come to think of it. That's definitely where it comes from.) Every single boy in the school fancies her and I shouldn't wonder if the men teachers don't too, although of course they couldn't let you see they're besotted. Not with all the scandals and everything – you know, Jimmy Savile, Cyril Smith, Rolf Harris, Stuart Hall and all that bunch of lowlife.

And those maths and music teachers that run off with under-age girls. Nah, our lot make sure they keep any feelings they might have under lock and key.

Anyway, she has this long, almost-black hair, cornflower blue eyes and skin that looks as if she lies on a tanning bed every day, only she doesn't, it's natural. Italian ancestors apparently. Some people have all the luck. She has this hundred-watt smile (I read that somewhere) and she makes you feel as if you're totally important to her when she talks to you. And I've never ever seen even a suggestion of a spot. It's so, so, *so* not fair. Usually if you have the kind of skin that browns, it's oily and you get acne at our age. Not her though. And what's more, she's as slim as slim can be. What wouldn't I give for a waist that size, and legs that long and skinny. Fab-u-lous.

I still have to pinch myself. I have no idea why she chose me as her best friend, but she did, and she's changed my life. And one of these days soon I think I might let her in on my secret; you know, about my dad and everything.

Better yet, Mercedes is really into fashion and celebrity. Big time. She knows the names of all the top designers and models and shows and fashion photographers. She has these pictures of famous models up in her room, too. You know, stick thin. The kind that look brilliant even in hideous dresses and clunky great shoes, with their faces plastered in outrageous make-up.

And her ma *encourages* her. Wow! My mum would do her absolute nut! But Penelope (that's Mrs Atkinson-Baker, only she says I must call her by her first name) defends Mercedes' obsession with thin.

'Nobody wants to see real life people in magazines and photo-shoots,' she says. 'We can all see them in the mirror, on the bus, on our streets, for free. Fashion magazines are about *fantasy*. Dreams. Ideals. People want to escape from reality and get a good vibration from what they see.'

Hmmm. Is that right? I'm not so sure. I mean, *I* don't always feel good seeing these *mega*-skinny girls. They make me feel even more gross than I am.

I told Mercedes that once.

'Rubbish,' she said. 'You're not gross. A tiny bit roundy in places maybe, if I'm brutally honest, but one of these days I'll let you into a secret. I know exactly how to get rid of those extra inches, have you looking as sensational as any top class model.'

Only she hasn't told me yet. She reckons we have to be totally committed friends first. I thought we were already but she says there's a threshold – whatever that is.

Her ma, Penelope, makes me wish I'd been born into a different family. Imagine inheriting those kind of genes! *Everything* must feel better. You don't have to even *try* and you have the world at your feet. Boys adore you, girls envy you, everybody admires you and loves to have you around. *My* mum's never going to be glamorous; there's pretty much nothing about her I wish I'd inherited. A crummy lot of genes if ever I saw them.

CHAPTER 12

India

WOW! Yesterday was secrets day. We didn't plan it, it sort of *happened*.

It all started when Mercedes came out of the school toilets at lunchtime looking a bit pink and watery-eyed and I thought she must be poorly or she'd been crying.

'You all right?' I asked.

'Yeaaah, thanks, I'm fine.'

But I knew she was lying, so after school I said, 'Want to do homework together?'

We have this stinker of an essay to do on the effect of global warming on the ecosystems of Antarctica. I mean, who *cares*? Shedloads of people are posting stuff about global warming all the time. All you have to do is look it up. We do our bit: cycling, recycling, switching off lights, and everything. I don't need to write a blinking *essay* on it!

So there I was, sprawled on the floor in her bedroom, when she told me. Talk about driving all ideas to do with science out of my head! She couldn't have done that better if she'd dropped a bomb in her room.

'Are you *really* okay?' I said. 'You have to tell me if you're sick or something. I mean, we're friends, right?'

'Honestly, India, I'm fine.'

The silence hung heavily.

She sighed. 'Well, if you *must* know, it was that disgusting macaroni cheese they served us. I mean, you could literally *see* the cholesterol oozing out of it, the millions of calories.'

'Why did you choose it, then?"
'Because it smelt so good.'
I stared at her. 'So? You didn't need to have two helpings.' It was a sore point; I adore mac cheese but I'd stuck to an apple and a laxative. I couldn't believe she could eat *two helpings* of all that fat and protein and carbs and stay skinny like she is. It's absolutely not fair. But then she's tall and small-boned exactly like her mother.

She laughed. 'You are such a kid sometimes, India. It's no big deal. There are ways of having your cake and eating it.'

'I have no idea what you're talking about,' I said, a bit huffily if I'm honest. Didn't help that my stomach was cramping big time.

'Look, I fancied that macaroni, right? I ate it. But it was only the taste I wanted, not its calories, certainly not the weight it'd put on me.'

I stared at her. No ... not *Mercedes* ...

She shrugged. 'I simply lost it again.'

But ... she wouldn't ... not *Mercedes* ...

She was looking a bit riled herself by now. 'Look, I vomit, yeaah? It's no big deal. That's how I stay the size I want to be.'

I'm pretty sure my mouth hung open here. 'You're kidding me.'

'No, it's true. When I need to. Like I say, it's no big deal.'

'But doesn't your mother ...? I thought ... you don't *need* to, you're so like her ...'

She gave a dismissive laugh. 'Oh, Ma's exactly the same. She knows how important it is to me to feel good about myself. Mind you, she was worse than me. When she was young she was hospitalised three times. They even sectioned her. She was a full-blown anorexic and bulimic. Vomiting, purging, excessive exercise; she did them all, to the nth degree. Then she moved on to not eating at all. She almost died twice. But she had loads of treatment and psychiatric help and everything and she came through it eventually. But she still has to be really careful. It's a huge priority for her to look good.

'While Pa was around she was going to all these important functions with him, having to be polite and eat and everything. But she couldn't bear to put on weight, so she just came home and got rid of it all again. It worked. She's been a size eight for donkey's years. I guess it's a kind of habit now.'

I'm totally speechless. *My* mother nags on at me all the time to eat more, not exercise so much, and Mercedes' mother *encourages* her to be sick! How unfair is *that*! I really really really wish I wasn't me.

I needed time to digest all this, (sorry! pun not intended) so we settled down to weightier matters (ditto): ways our planet's going off the rails, and what affects different parts of it, and then tried to relate it to Antarctica.

It was ages later we returned to the subject of her vomiting.

'You know, there's one thing I don't get,' I say.

'What's that?'

'Why you picked me as your friend. I mean, look at you. You're drop-dead gorgeous. You're popular. You have everything. And you seem so ... I don't know, content in your own skin, if you know what I mean. You aren't taking out your hang-ups on other people. You could've chosen anyone and they'd have jumped at the chance. I don't get it. Why me?'

'I knew you were a kindred spirit as soon as I saw you,' Mercedes says, flicking her hair in that casual way she has, and smiling that fab smile. 'You were someone who'd understand me like I understand you. Most people wouldn't. Not when they got to know the real me inside, the me who vomits, the me who's obsessed. But you do.'

'I've never tried vomiting,' I whisper.

'I'll teach you if you really want to. It's okay once you get the hang of it. And boy, does it feel good when it's all gone.'

'What *do* you weigh?' I ask her.

She knows to the gram. Like me. But in her case it's nine kilograms less than me. *Nine kilograms!* I feel majorly sick.

'Wow. That's awesome.'

'So, what's your target? How much d'you want to lose?' she asks, all matter of fact.

'I'm not sure,' I say vaguely. It's a lie. But if she's anything like me … 'I definitely want to drop a couple of sizes in jeans. I look totally obese in these ones.'

'No problem. That's good for now. You don't want to be a skeleton. You should see the pictures of Ma when she was really anorexic. Now that's what *I* call gross!'

Yep, I knew it; she definitely wants to be thinnest. They all do. I need to watch what I tell her.

'I can't *believe* your mother *lets* you vomit. I mean, my mum's always on my case, badgering me to eat, checking what I've had. She definitely wouldn't let me get away with what you're doing.'

'She doesn't need to know. Use plenty of mouthwash, disinfect the loo, all that kind of stuff. Piece of cake.'

I must look as dubious as I feel.

'No problem,' she grins, 'hang out here, then. We can gorge on rice cakes and celery to our hearts' content. I mean, *we* both know, nothing tastes as good as skinny feels. And I'll teach you how to handle things when you absolutely can't avoid eating.'

'Would you?' I breathe.

'Sure. Learn from a master. I mean, did you ever detect anything on me – before today?'

'No.'

'Well, there you are then.'

Could I *really* have a plateful of mac cheese and get away with it? A chocolate cupcake. Wow! What a bonus that'd be, eating stuff I like, whatever Mum cooks. I hate fighting all the time. I wish we could go back to being happy, like we were.

Like it was when Dad was still here.

My mind races.

Mercedes has given me so much food for thought. I mean she can do it, and look at her!

Once we've finished our stupid essays, she lies back on her bed and pats the edge. I perch awkwardly.

'So, your turn. One secret. In exchange for mine. A good one, mind. That's only fair. '

It's now or never.

Give her her due, she listens without interruption to my story.

'Wow! That's quite something. Like some romantic novel.'

'Doesn't feel very romantic from where I'm sitting,' I sniff.

'No, course it doesn't. I didn't mean it like that. But, Dad goes missing. Grieving daughter searches for him. Mum opposes her. Dad found. Now that's what old Doodlebug would call "a splendid narrative arc", wouldn't he?'

I can't help but snigger. She's a brilliant mimic. That's our supply teacher, Mr Doubleday, exactly.

CHAPTER 13

India

I HAVEN'T DONE IT YET. To be honest, I can't *stand* the smell of puke, but I daren't tell Mercedes that. She'd drop me for sure.

There's another thing too – I don't fancy needing false teeth. My Poppa had them and sometimes when he fell asleep they slipped and once they even fell onto the table. It was absolutely gross. But stomach acid rots your teeth, you know. I looked it up. I don't *think* Mercedes has falsies, but I suspect maybe her ma's had a lot of work done on hers. They look perfect anyway. But she could afford to get top-notch work done, way back when they had pots of money. Hers are probably porcelain or something.

Anyway, I'm not going to do it just yet. I'm keeping close tabs on everything – weight, cals, exercise, and I reckon if I'm extra extra strict and careful this week I'll get into the jeans Mercedes gave me on Friday. I've started having loads of green tea – black – to fill up; helps with the hunger pangs. My target in the swimming pool's up to 30 lengths now, 40 minutes skipping before school, 50 press-ups in my room whenever I can, morning and night. And if I do my contortion stuff on the floor, I don't have to worry about fainting and falling. I'm already somewhere safe.

Keep this up and I might not need to go down the vomiting route at all. That'd be dead cool. Trick is to keep Mum off my case. She's not exactly counting the cals but she's watching me and I'm pretty sure she's trying to check that I actually eat what she gives me. Oh, she thinks she's being subtle, but I'm not a fool.

It helps being at Mercedes' house so much of the time, of course.

In spite of the weight thing and food and my dad and everything, I'm feeling much better about things right now. Thanks to Mercedes again.

For a kick-off, she told me about a really cool pro ana website that has rules – 58 of them – that tell you how to keep yourself on target. I read them through every day before I go to sleep. And some thinspiration stuff, and blogs and chat sites. Awesome; all these people feeling the same way as me. Well, except for the dudes that don't get it, tell us we're on 'a pathway to suicide' and stuff. Don't bother reading it then, sister!

Plus, Mercedes has taken to giving me some of her clothes, the ones that'll fit me anyway. Her wardrobe's packed to the gunnels and she says she won't ever get around to wearing half this stuff, although, come to think of it, they're probably the things she's grown out of. She wouldn't *say* that, but I guess it gives *her* a kick being confident she won't need that size again; knowing she's smaller than me.

Whatever. I feel a million bucks in her cast-offs, things that fit beautifully. Believe me, this is no high street run-of-the-mill stuff; these are labels to die for! Not that I actually *like* it all, but you can tell it's expensive. It *feels* expensive, it *looks* expensive. It's the cut, she says. No, it's the *everything*.

And on top of that she reckons I've got flair for writing. Me? I mean, I adore making stuff up – poems, short stories and everything, but it's only for my own amusement. And sometimes I can hear my dad reading it out, using his voices. Of course, that makes me all sad again, but then I write poetry about being lonely. Like the 'melancholic' poets we did at school.

Mercedes found one of my poems lying beside my bed one day and before I knew what she'd picked up, she'd started reading it.

'Hey, that's mine, it's personal, private. Give it back.'

I try to snatch it back but she dodges and holds me off while she continues. She has this funny look on her face and I want to *die* of embarrassment.

'You actually *wrote* this?' she says. 'You made it all up? Out of your own head? '

'I know, it's pathetic,' I mumble. 'I only do it for myself, when I'm feeling lousy. But nobody else is supposed to see it. And that includes *you*!'

'You're kidding, right?'

'What d'you mean?'

'That it's pathetic.'

'No, I know it is.'

'It's nothing of the kind. It's *brilliant*,' she says with something like awe in her voice. 'You manage to get right inside the hurt and share it. I can totally relate to what you're saying.'

'You think?'

'I *know*!'

I can only blink at her. I don't know what to say.

'But how come you know about being that sad?' she says softly.

'Because ... because that's how I feel about my dad. He was my best friend.'

'Awwhh gee. I'm so, so sorry,' she says, and next minute she's giving me a king-size hug. 'I know how much that hurts.'

I pull back and she releases me.

'But ... well, I thought ... isn't your father ...?' I stutter.

'Oh, it wasn't my *Pa* I lost.' I wait, and after a bit she adds thickly, 'It was my brother.'

'I didn't know you even *had* a brother.'

'Why would you? I never told you.'

'But I haven't seen any photos or anything.'

'Ma and Pa took them all down. They don't like to talk about it.'

'It's dead weird that, isn't it?' I say slowly, thinking. 'My mum was the same. I remember my Granny told me I mustn't talk about Dad to her. Even when I was a wee kid, I wasn't supposed to mention him. But pretending, doesn't make it better. There's still the empty space, the hole in the family.'

'Exactly. And Archie was my only sibling, my best friend. I lost a hundred percent of my generation when he died. They don't seem to get that.'

'How did he die? Am I allowed to ask? Say, if it's too … you know.'

'He got in with a bad crowd when he was at boarding school. Started taking drugs, drinking, smoking, you know. Of course, we didn't know at the time, it only came out afterwards. And because he wasn't used to it, the stuff affected him more than the others. They reckoned he got hold of some really pure stuff on the street and gave himself a fatal overdose.'

'That is *so* terrible. D'you want to talk about him? To me, I mean? What was he like? If it's not too painful.'

She takes a big breath, shaking her head, but I can see the hurt written in her eyes.

'He was three years older than me. I was only twelve when he died. He was at this boys' school, the same one Pa went to when he was a boy. They're into cold showers and cross-country running when the snow's three metres deep, and short trousers till you're eighteen – you know the kind of stuff. Designed to toughen them up. "It'll make a man of you!"' She drops her voice to a growl, thrusts out her chest and flexes her biceps with a scowl on her face that makes me grin in spite of everything. 'But Archie took it all in his stride; he wasn't a namby-pamby Mummy's boy, Archie. Of course, Pa told him what was what before he went, warned him what to expect, so it didn't come as a shock or anything.

'What else to say? Well, he was really into sport. Rugby, rowing, cricket, swimming, cross-country. *Good* at everything too. Sickening really. I'm useless at anything sporty. Can't even vault over a horse in the gym, me. No hand-eye coordination. Two left feet. But Archie won trophies and stuff, he was that good. Come to think of it, I

have no idea what happened to them. Maybe Pa took them.'
She gives herself a shake.

'He was popular too; loads of friends. He used to invite
them to our house in the holidays, and I would listen to their
tales of what they got up to out of school hours. It sounded a
whole lot more fun than anything that happened at *my*
school. But I guess that was cos Archie was at the centre of it
all. He *was* fun. And he attracted other lads that liked a good
time too.

'He was bright as well, much cleverer than me, more
like Pa, I guess, so he would bring home these glowing
reports. The teachers always promised a brilliant future for
him. "Prime minister material",' – she says it in a
headmasterly voice – 'I suppose we all just expected
everything would fall into his lap, Archie included.

'Me, I was always the also-ran, but, hey, I didn't care,
cos it was Archie. He was my hero and I loved him to bits.
He never made me feel sub-standard or second-rate, you
know? I was his best pal too. He always made time for me
and I was hugely proud of him.

'So when we got the news ... well, there'd been no
warning, nothing. One minute he was Mr Golden Boy, the
next he was gone.' She breaks off and we sit in absolute
silence for ages.

'Nothing was ever the same after that. My Ma and Pa,
they were like broken things. The house was dead in the
holidays. I was away during term-time so some days I could
kind of pretend it hadn't happened, but it was like this
terrible black emptiness lurking inside me, that swallowed me
up when I didn't expect it. I couldn't concentrate; my grades
fell. They weren't up to much to start with, but now they
were totally abysmal. And that's when I started not eating. If
I couldn't be good at school-work, I'd at least *look* good, and
it kind of took over my life. As well as that, it was odd, but
the other girls, they started coming to talk to me about their
problems. I guess they sort of recognised that I knew what
pain was like.'

'Well, you *are* very good at listening. You really are,' I

interrupt for the first time.

'It sort of helps me to help them, if you can understand such warped logic. I can't help Archie, I can't stop it hurting for me, or for Ma, but sometimes I *can* help other people not feel so bad. I don't say the dumb things other people say, which makes me think I might have some kind of use in this world.'

'"Some kind of use"?' I repeat, staggered. 'That has to be the biggest understatement of the year. You're probably the most popular person I know. You're a one off. Everybody loves you. Everybody wants you as a friend.'

She shrugs. 'At home though, things got steadily worse. My parents drifted further and further apart. Pa spent all his time at work. To be fair, you could see why he did. When he was thinking about how to get the best deal for his clients, he wasn't thinking about Archie. And if I'm honest, Ma really wasn't much use to him. She couldn't get outside her own grief. So Pa took on these big cases and stayed in town more and more. He had this little city pad, you know? And in the end he simply moved his secretary in with him. I know – so clichéd, huh? Guess she didn't have all the baggage, she didn't remind him of the past. He could more or less put it behind him and start again.

'But for Ma it was different. She didn't have a job. She was a kind of trophy wife. Eye-candy. It was her husband, her son, who gave her her identity. And she idolised Archie. She couldn't move on. Having said that, she's been there for me through all of this. She never tried to make Archie's death less than the pits for me. You know, some folk are so lost in *their* grief, *their* loss, *their* pain, they can't find space for anybody else to feel bad about what's happened. Ma let me feel as bad as bad can be. She acknowledged that Archie was my world too. I didn't have to "snap out of it", or "look on the bright side", or "think of something else". You wouldn't believe the stuff people say – well, of course, *you* probably would.'

I give a half-hearted nod. It's not the same.

'So Ma and I were left, relying on each other to keep

going. She had all the money stuff to worry about and everything, too, of course. But I'll tell you something, I think we've been happier in some ways since we lost most of it. We're a proper mother and daughter now. I'm living at home, going to a day school, seeing her every night, and we've grown really close. I suppose we only have each other now. All she wants is for me to be happy again, and that's what I want for her. I don't think she'll ever be *really* happy again, but she makes the effort for me, and we keep each other going. If it comforts her to binge and vomit, who am I to say no? And I guess that's a bit where she's coming from. Mind you, I don't think she'd let me go *too* far, endanger my life or anything. No, in fact, I'm sure she definitely *wouldn't*. But there again, because she's listened to me and treated me like a responsible person, *I'd* listen if she said, "Wowwa. This is a step too far." D'you know what I mean?'

I nod. See, my mother still treats me like a kid, so I *don't* listen.

'So ...' I hesitate. 'Are you ... you know ... still in touch with your father sometimes?'

'Occasionally. He takes me out on my birthday, and I spend two weeks with him in the summer. We go on holiday somewhere hot, with a pool and exotic restaurants and everything. And then we have a few days round about New Year.'

'Is that good or what?'

'Well, he's still my Pa, and of course I don't want to lose contact, but to be honest, I worry about Ma all the time I'm away. I text her a dozen times a day, but it's not the same as being able to *see* for myself she's coping. I like it better if she goes to my uncle's, or goes away on holiday herself with other people while I'm away – people who'll make sure she's safe and not let her ... you know, do anything silly.'

I know exactly what she dreads.

'You know what?' I say, kind of wonderingly. 'You're a much better person than me. My mum's been left on *her* own too, but I don't spend all my time worrying about her. In fact, I get totally fed up when she keeps going on at me. I'd give *anything* to have a holiday with *my* dad. It wouldn't have to be anything expensive or exotic. It'd *be* special cos we were together. I wouldn't think twice about Mum.'

It makes me appreciate there isn't anything bad to say about him except maybe he chose to die rather than go on living with us. And I don't believe that.

'You should hang on to those great memories,' Mercedes says softly.

'Ahhh, well, see, Mum reckons I can't remember things like they really were. It's my imagination working overtime, she says. And it's true, I *do* have a vivid imagination. But she's not right about me not remembering his voice, not accurately, after all this time. I mean. As if!'

'Why would she say that?'

It's then I tell her about hearing Dad at the station.

CHAPTER 14

India

'NEVER!' MERCEDES SAYS. 'That is so cooool. In that case, we *have* to find him. If he's out there somewhere, we have to track him down. It'll be our very own detective story. So, what have you tried so far?'

'Tried?' I look at her blankly.

'What have you done so far to try to find him?'

'I haven't … I … Mum said it was all in my head.'

'And you *believe* her? *You* don't think it was real either?' Mercedes looks thunderstruck.

'No … I … yes … I don't know…'

'Look, India, this is your *dad* we're talking about! You loved him. You can't *not* follow this lead up. Imagine if he really *is* in London somewhere. Or *anywhere*. Imagine if you could talk to him again, hug him, do any of the things you loved doing with him. You know what? If this was Archie I'd have been hammering on the door of the Chief Constable's office by now.'

I close my eyes against the pictures. 'How would I even start?'

'Hey, *I* don't know. *You're* the one with the brains around here. But we could start with Googling *Finding missing persons* for a kick-off.'

The list of private investigators is impressive; names like *Reveal, Tracing, Look4them, Peopletracer*. But we home in on a site that gives seven tips for anyone trying to track down a specific person.

First sentence?

1. *It's important to act quickly.*

'Well, I guess we'll just have to forget that bit,' Mercedes says, running the cursor down the screen.

2. *Tell the police.*

'You'll have done that, though,' she says moving on.

'Well, actually … no,' I say, half below my breath.

She turns to stare at me. 'You didn't tell the police you heard your father's voice in London?' *I. Don't. Believe. What. I'm. Hearing* … is what she's really saying.

'Well, even *Mum* didn't believe me.'

'Never mind all that. We have to at least *tell* the police. It's their *job*! If they don't take it seriously, then that's a different issue. But look, that's what this site *tells* you to do. It's number two on the list.'

'I'll need to speak to Mum …'

Mercedes is already putting on her jacket muttering things about '… maybe he's lost his memory … maybe they have this guy somewhere and they have no idea who he is …'

'What if the police don't believe me?' I say weakly.

'Well, then we'll find a private investigator who will. Look, you know *loads* about him. Age, exact date of birth, height, build, colour of hair, eyes, birthmarks, rough weight maybe, habits, likes and dislikes. These people who search, they need all that kind of guff, anything, s'long as it's true. They feed in all the statistics and bits and bobs, and abracadabra, up he'll pop – if he's still alive. Says here, everybody leaves a paper trail.'

'Wouldn't that cost an arm and a leg?'

'No idea. But hey, money's the least of our concerns.'

She turns back to her computer and in minutes pulls up information.

'See? Look here. These guys specialise. We can trawl through the lists, find somebody who deals in finding lost adults – narrow it down, lost *fathers* maybe. Or … no, on second thoughts, maybe not. That might be for kids with single mums, or kids where the old man's scarpered rather than pay maintenance, or kids born by artificial insemination.

Anyway, we can refine our search. That's if the police won't listen.'

I grab a piece of paper from her bedside cabinet and scribble down:

1. Try police
2. Find specialist investigator (Google)

'Says here, the more details you can supply the better the chances of finding them ... ah, yeah, listen ... "*people don't tend to change their habits. If a person always read motoring magazines, he'll probably still be buying motoring magazines. If he used to love cats, chances are he has one now. If he had hay fever in the spring, he's probably buying anti-histamines today.*" See? You'll know heaps about your dad. Looking good! And you can always quiz your mum more about things you might not know.'

'Mum wouldn't let me waste anybody's time and effort. She'd say it's futile.'

'Don't tell her, then.'

'But you just said ...'

'No, dummy. Ask *casually*. "Mum, tell me what Dad was like when you first knew him." And "What kinds of things did he like doing before I came along?" Or "I'm afraid my memories are fading. Remind me again, what sorts of food did Dad like?" Idly. In passing.'

'Wouldn't an investigator need her consent? I mean, I'm still a minor.'

'Don't tell him. Say you're an orphan.'

'Hey, you said it had to be the truth.'

'Ah, that. Yep, you're right. Scrap that last comment. We'll think of a way round it. And we'll check if a minor can do it anyway without consent. I mean, if you've got the money, wouldn't they be desperate to take you on?'

'I have no idea. But ...'

She snorts. 'Look, d'you want to find him or not?'

'Course I do.'

'Well, stop being so negative and start thinking of ways

and means, then.'
    I write:

      3. List characteristics
      4. Find the money

CHAPTER 15

India

MUM GOES ABSOLUTELY totally mental.

'India! How *could* you? Wasting everybody's time like that. When you *know* he's dead.'

'But that's it – I *don't*.'

'And you didn't even talk to me about it.'

'I *did* talk to you! But you didn't believe me. *Mercedes* believed me, *and* she came to the police station with me. That's what the website *said* you should do.'

'*Website?* What website?'

'This one that gives you all the steps to track down somebody who's gone missing.'

'But the police *were* involved when Dad went missing. They were the ones who found his clothes. India, you know all this.'

'Yes, but they only *assumed* he'd gone into the sea. There was never any proof. And now there's evidence that he might still be alive. They *need* to know so they start looking again.'

'And what exactly did the police say?'

The police station was darker and more pokey than I'd expected. There were three middle-aged women with partially bleached hair and skanky clothes huddled in a row of four chairs under the high window, and that made it kind of crowded. And smelly. They kept whispering to each other, holding up their hands like kids so you couldn't watch their lips moving, like they were plotting something.

When the duty policeman looked up from his files he glared across at them before turning to us. His eyes stopped at Mercedes; I didn't even exist. You could see he was doing a full identity check: five foot eight, mid teens, long black hair, blue eyes ... but then he realises I'm watching.

'Can I help you?'

Mercedes did a grand sweeping gesture to indicate that I was the one waiting to report a crime. You can tell she's into drama and I felt a giggle welling up, but the policeman's cold stare stopped that dead in its tracks.

I waved towards the women on the chairs. 'They were before us.'

'They've already been seen. They're only waiting for somebody to be released,' he said dismissively.

Mercedes gave me a nudge towards the desk.

To be fair the constable heard me out. He even took some notes, and he wrote down my contact details. He asked for Mercedes' too but she said no, she was only here to support me. I reckon she's had too many guys trying to get her number to fall for that little trick.

'Leave it with me,' the officer said. 'We'll be in touch if we find anything, but ...'

'But?' I prompted.

'Well, I wouldn't hold my breath if I were you, lass. Not much to go on and finding the clothes and everything before ...' He shrugged.

Mercedes was great. I didn't need to tell her how I was feeling. She simply hauled me off to the shops and stuck me in a changing room and brought all these amazing clothes for me to try on. 'Choose anything. My treat.' Wow! She's always buying new stuff; reckons it lifts her spirits no end.

I was after a new pair of skinny jeans so I told her and ... guess what? ... a size four in this make was too big on me this time. What a boost! The ones I chose in the end were plain black and it felt like I was poured into them. That'll remind me not to eat. Imagine not being able to wear something as gorgeous as this!

Mercedes was so nice too.

'You look terrific in them, India. Perfect fit.'

Okay, I'm still way bigger than her but then, we didn't start in the same place – genes-wise, I mean.

'And it'll get better and better,' she promised. 'All you need do is believe in yourself, value yourself more. Set yourself a target, don't give up till you get there. I'll help you. We'll do it together.' Only I know she'd be sick to the back teeth if I went past *her* target.

I felt so good that night I even took a selfie of my legs in the new jeans. Not to share, only for me.

I can stare at that when I'm looking gross in two pairs of leggings under two pairs of fleece-lined tracksuit bottoms for bed, three pairs of thick socks. I can't seem to get warm these days. And it's a vicious circle. Lying there wide awake I keep thinking of things I absolutely must do. Bin my mango and raspberry lip glosses – extra calories? Check that gel I got for my mouth ulcers – does it contain sugar? Go back to that website – how much more weight has to go before I beat those girls who're the same height and age as me, Suzie and Anna?

Funny thing that, I can remember loads of stuff I read on these sites, exactly how many cals in a slice of cheese or a rice cracker, what's in sauces and drinks, loads of facts about diet and exercise and everything. But can I remember a single fact about stuff we've only just done in school? Nah! Weird. It's like I'm not really there.

CHAPTER 16

Tonya

I'D GIVE ANYTHING to ignore this whole thing, go back to the way we were. Get on with life as it is now. India and me, just the two of us.

But India has left me with no choice. Because *they* went over my head and reported India's fantasy, *I* have to go over the whole wretched business again, talk to the police – different officers, of course, but the police nonetheless.

We'll start off badly. They'll wonder why I didn't go to them straight away. They'll speculate about the kind of a relationship I have with my daughter, why I didn't believe her, what I've got to hide.

Now, *I* know, where the girls may not, that the police don't investigate adult disappearances the same way as kids. Course they don't. Alarm bells ring if it's a child or a young woman, but grown men, nope. The police are street-wise. They assume men've scarpered to make a new life for themselves, with or without a new woman. As far as they're concerned, if Victor is by any chance still alive, he'll have chosen to stay hidden. But if *I* say that, everybody thinks I'm callous, don't want him found.

What grieves me most is wasting their time. Thousands of people disappear. Every week of every month of every year. Literally thousands. Somebody new is reported missing about every two minutes! That's a heck of a lot of paperwork and time for these folk who're trying to keep our streets safe. I'd far, far rather they protected teenagers like Maria Davenport than be sent off on some wild goose chase looking for somebody who almost certainly drowned himself years ago.

The interviewer, Heather Rushton, is far too young, fresh, eager. Low down the pay grade? Even so I immediately wish I'd made more effort. My jeans and jumper, dash of lipstick, shout casual-approach-to-life against her seriously smart navy trousers and white shirt, immaculate hairstyle and perfect grooming. Too late now. I'd have preferred somebody a bit more battered by life, more resigned to reality, but you know what they say about policemen and doctors looking young ...

She leans forward and switches on the recording machine.

'You'll soon forget about it,' she says. 'I want you to relax and tell me all you can. I'll give you some lead questions but feel free to add anything or fill in things I might not know about, anything really that might give us some idea as to why your husband might have vanished, might still be alive. People don't change much, even in little things – tastes in reading, eating, sleeping, clothes, that kind of thing, so the more you can tell us about Victor, the easier it will be for us to get to know him and, if he's out there, find him. So don't think, oh that's too trivial to share. All the little details make up the bigger picture, help us understand the personality and behaviours. Maybe deduce what he actually did.'

I nod.

'Let's begin with how you met him.' She has her encouraging professional smile pinned on, but I know this is a warm up, to make me forget to be cautious. I wasn't born yesterday.

'We were add-ons in a foursome arranged by my best friend, Lisa.'

'So, what happened?'

'Well, she was mad keen on a boy called Nathan Samuels at the time. He didn't seem to notice her, though. Too busy preening himself, if you ask me. Then, one day, Lisa suddenly came out with, "Tonya and I are thinking of going to North Berwick on the train on Saturday. You interested in bringing a mate and joining up with us?" First I'd heard of it but hey, I wasn't going to be the one to rain on my best pal's parade.'

'So, did he agree?'

'Yep.'

'And what happened?'

'We waltzed up at the station early, but they were already there.' I smile involuntarily, remembering. 'The two of them: Nathan and his pal, Victor. Looking like aliens – well, you know how dark and dreary Waverley station looked before its makeover. There they were, in the middle of all that greyness, complete with gaudy Bermudas, mirrored Ray-bans, snazzy flip-flops, psychedelic beach towels, the works. They'd obviously been in cahoots, not only about dress, I mean, but about giving us a good time. Between them they'd packed stuff and organised things to fill the entire day.'

'And did it go well?'

'It was great, even though the wind was raw and the sand got in our Mr Whippys, and I cut my toe on a ring-pull half-buried on the beach, and we had to wait absolutely ages for the queue to go down at the chippie. We laughed ourselves silly playing crazy golf. We chucked a Frisbee around for a good hour or so. I'm useless at that kind of thing usually, but somehow it didn't matter. We were having fun, pure and simple, and the boys weren't too serious about any of it, not like blokes often are. Later, us girls sat on the low wall, you know, reading, watching people, chatting, while the guys tried to outdo each other swimming way out to sea. They were both strong swimmers, but ...'

'But?'

'They went way too far out, I thought. It wasn't like they were my responsibility or anything, they were grown men, but they were *with* us and if they got into trouble probably nobody else in the world knew where they were. I kept my eyes glued to those two little heads bobbing in the water, willing them to be safe.'

'And why is that still making you feel tense?'

'Well, it's like ... you know ... they found his clothes ...

on the beach …'

'Ahh. I see. We'll come back to that, but for now, could we stick with that time at North Berwick? They went too far out and you were worried.'

'Silly, I know. And when they *did* get back, I felt such a dawk for worrying, so I hid myself away in my book and pretended not to notice they'd returned.'

'And Lisa, where was she in all this?'

'She couldn't take her eyes off all that muscle and brawn and … you know.'

Heather gives a lop-sided half smile. 'So what happened next?'

'Turns out Victor was a qualified nurse and he did a neat little number on my damaged toe. I was going to let it bleed into a paper hankie, but he produced a packet of antiseptic wipes from his bag. I mean, talk about being prepared! And he insisted on cleaning it thoroughly and sticking plasters on.'

'And how did that make you feel?'

I pause. 'I guess, that's when I started to really notice him, if I'm honest. He had such a lovely gentle touch and he did it all like he really cared. It was nothing really, but he made me feel like it mattered to him that I was hurt. Most blokes would totally ignore something so trivial. *I* would have.'

'So, that was your introduction. Then what happened?'

'Well, this is going to sound kind of big headed, but you said I have to be honest and tell it like it really was.' She nods. 'Only when we were saying goodbye to the lads at the station afterwards, Nathan asked me out on a proper date.' I grimace.

'*Nathan?*'

'Yeah, Nathan. Lisa didn't know, thankfully. She'd have been sick … and probably mad at me. But I didn't do anything to encourage him, I honestly didn't. I wouldn't. In my mind, he was Lisa's guy.'

'And you said?'

'I turned him down flat, of course. But then,

afterwards, I felt pretty mean. The poor bloke probably had no idea Lisa had the hots for him, and it wasn't his fault if he didn't feel the same way. But in any case he wasn't my type. Too full of himself, good-looking but knows it, thinks he's God's gift to women. You know the type.'

'And Victor? Was he good-looking too?'

'Well, yeah! But not so flashy. And he didn't know it.'

'Can you describe him to me?'

'Tallish – five eleven. Slim, but solid muscles, toned. Brown curly hair, very blue eyes. Gorgeous smile. Front teeth slightly overlapping. Lovely hands, long fingers with the kind of nails I wish I had – you know, perfectly shaped.' I indicate an oval. 'Mine are always too squared off. Oh, and he had great legs – the sort that'd look brilliant in those old fashioned hose men used to wear. And such a warm ... generous kind of personality. You couldn't help but like him.'

'So, you fancied him?'

'Not at first. But enough to say, yes, when he rang to suggest we went to see the film, *The English Patient*. I hadn't seen it, so we went together, and the rest, as they say, is history.'

'And what was he like, would you say, during those early weeks and months when you were getting to know each other?'

'Great company. No, he really was. He was into music, art, gardens, books, theatre, films. We were never short of things to do, stuff to talk about. I suppose you'd say we were sort of kindred spirits. It was brilliant. He even came *clothes* shopping with me! I ask you.'

'And how did that go?'

'Brilliantly, surprise, surprise. He had a much better sense of what would suit me than I did. But then, he was much more clued up about colour and shape and texture and all that kind of stuff. I muddle along somehow but he had ... flair, I guess. He was naturally artistic. '

'And was there anything at that stage that bothered you, or gave you pause for thought. Anything that jarred, made you think, hmmm?'

'Not that I can think of. He was lovely. Thoughtful, kind. The nicest guy I'd ever been out with. Maybe it's only what you'd expect from somebody that chose to be a nurse, but I hadn't had that kind of experience before. Most blokes I knew were more into football and fast cars and looking macho and getting you into bed. Not interested in books beyond the old car manual.'

'So, how did things develop with Victor?'

'Fine. We got along great.'

'And whose idea was marriage?'

'Well, I must admit, that was mine. Not because I wanted the frothy dress and cute flower girls and soppy speeches stuff, though, don't get me wrong. I didn't. I really didn't. I'm not into that kind of ridiculous extravagance for one day. No, I wanted *marriage*, security, not the wedding itself. And I wanted it with this guy.'

'Can you pinpoint why "this guy"?'

'Because we had something special together. We were in love, yes, but it was more than that. He represented … stability, security, the kind of rock solid I was after for my kids.'

'So you proposed to him?'

'No, not exactly. But I was the one who first suggested making it permanent and legal. Not immediately, but at some point.'

'And how did Victor respond to that?'

'He was all for it. I think, anyway. And after a bit he did the romantic on-one-knee bit, with a second-hand ring ready in his pocket.' I hold out my hand to show her the diamond solitaire that flashes in the overhead light. 'He actually got it from the pawn brokers and he reckoned it was worth three times as much as he paid for it, and much better quality than anything he could afford new. That was Victor. A romantic at heart, but down-to-earth practical when it came to money. So he was the one who actually proposed, but he told me I'd given him the courage to do it because I'd virtually said yes already.'

'And how long would it have been you were engaged

91

before you got married?'

'Five months. Long enough to get everything arranged, let folk know. He reckoned there was no point hanging around for years like some of our friends did, endlessly arranging and rearranging things. But then, in our case, the wedding itself wasn't an elaborate affair. We did the whole shebang on a skimpy budget in the registrars office with a few friends and family, meal in the local hotel. We wanted to put what money we'd saved into property, like sensible mature adults.'

'And that was a joint decision? What you both wanted?'

'I think so. I certainly did. He *said* he did too.'

'Honeymoon?'

'A week in a self-catering cottage in Brittany.'

'And how was that?'

'Magic.' There's a long pause.

'Want to say any more?'

'Nope. It was exactly what we both wanted. I know you're thinking it wasn't much of a honeymoon. No fancy hotel, no month in the Seychelles, no trip of a lifetime to Thailand or any of that jazz. But just the two us, in our own little cottage in France, that was us. I only wanted to be with him. I'd have been happy anywhere ... just with him.' I hear the break in my voice and blow my nose hard. I know she's watching me, analysing, psychoanalysing.

'Take your time.'

'I'm okay.'

'When you're ready.'

'Because we were sensible about spending, it meant we had our three-bed semi, our affordable mortgage, our secondhand Volkswagen Passat, our washing machine and fridge-freezer all in place by the time India arrived.'

'Before we move on to India, can I ask, did you observe any changes in Victor once you started spending a lot more time together?'

'Not that I can remember.'

'Was money an issue for the two of you?'

'As in?'

'As in you found it hard to make ends meet, or you had different ideas of how to spend it, or ... well, anything really. Did it – or the lack of it – cause any problems for either or both of you?'

'No, I don't think so. We were never exactly flush, and neither of us were what you'd call well paid, but we both had jobs and we were buying our own house. We managed, and we more or less stayed within our means. We weren't all the time hankering for a higher standard of living, but we could afford the occasional treat. Holidays, meals out on special occasions, that kind of thing.'

'And marriage? Did it live up to your expectations? Were you happy?'

'At first we were. Really happy. It was only the last couple of years ...' I don't want to acknowledge any of that.

'Okay, we'll come to that later. Let's try to keep things in sequence, chronologically if we can, for the sake of clarity. It's still early days, you're both happy in your marriage, living within your means. Any issues other than money?'

'Nope.'

'So tell me about your little girl. When did she come along?'

'Eighteen months and eleven days after our wedding.'

'Planned?'

'Yep.' Strange really that she feels she can ask about such personal stuff. But I don't want to antagonise her. It'll only make her think I'm hiding something.

'And did you both want children?'

'We both wanted *her*.'

She darts me a penetrating look but doesn't challenge my statement yet.

'Let's take a short break. How d'you take your tea?'

'Black, thanks. No sugar.'

CHAPTER 17

Tonya

HER NOSE IS FRESHLY powdered when she returns from our comfort break. Why does she have to outdo me yet again?

'So, let's start with your pregnancy. How did you feel when you found out about the baby?'

'Over the moon. We'd not long started trying. I couldn't believe it had been that easy.'

'And the pregnancy? How was that?'

'Mixed. Loads of sickness early on. Good bit in the middle. Heartburn, swollen ankles, high blood pressure towards the end. Then pre-eclampsia, emergency caesarean section. *Not* what I'd planned.'

She waits, looking at me in that still kind of way she has.

'Then my wound fell apart. A hospital-acquired infection, it said in the discharge letter. Mastitis set in. They gave me several different antibiotics but some of them gave me the runs and a terrible itchy rash. I was a mess.'

'And the baby?'

'She cried all the time. It was relentless. She absolutely refused to latch onto the breast, but then went and vomited after every formula feed. She hated being cuddled. The health visitor came every day for ages. Victor said that was unusual, but she was somebody he knew, so I guess it was a bit of "looking after our own". But eventually the baby settled down and took the bottle and started putting on weight and sleeping for longer than two hours.'

'Sounds like a nightmarish time. How did you cope

with all that?'

'D'you have any kids?' I suddenly fire back at her.

'Uhhh … no.' I knew it. Hence the perfection.

'So you probably don't know what it's like to feel absolutely crushed by the sheer weight of responsibility for this helpless little creature you've brought into the world.'

'So tell me.' She doesn't appear to be at all rattled by my attack.

'You're her mother but you don't know the first thing about why she's crying, or what to do, but she's totally dependent on you knowing – and that's when everything goes smoothly. In our case, India screamed morning, noon and night. I was so exhausted I used to nod off eating my meals. And I felt desperate. Depressed doesn't begin to describe it. I remember, several times, I felt like walking out in front of a lorry, ending it all.'

'What stopped you?'

'I don't know.'

'And where was your husband in all of this?'

'He was amazing. He was brilliant with the baby; she'd settle with him. He was so calm. And … confident, yes, that's the word, confident with her. And she seemed to love the sound of his voice. She'd lie there with her head on his shoulder, eyes wide open, seeming to listen to him singing or talking. She was like a different child.'

'And with you?'

'What d'you mean?'

'How did he react to your low mood and everything that was going on for you at that difficult time?'

'Accepted it, really. Told me it often happened to new mums, it was only a matter of time, we'd get there. And sometimes he'd bring me flowers or wee gifts to cheer me up. It was always better when he was around. But of course, he worked long hours and we needed his income. Especially now we had another person to feed and clothe. It's an expensive business, having kids.'

'So how long would you say, before things started to improve for you?'

'Hard to say, really, but if I'm pushed, I'd have to say sixteen, eighteen months maybe.'

'That's a long time to feel low. Did you have treatment?'

'As in psychiatric help, or drugs, or that? No. But I did have help from my friend, Kaetlyn. She's from Ireland and she lives three doors down from me. She's one of eleven kids herself and by that stage she'd got five of her own already, and she's a natural. She'd breeze in and take over sometimes, whisking India away to play with her brood. They were all so used to babies that they knew exactly what to do to keep her happy. It's like instinct with all of them. And she reckoned one more nipper, as she called them, more or less, didn't make much difference once you were past four kids. And while she had the baby I could sleep and sleep and sleep. And gradually things got better. I watched Kaetlyn too and learned a lot from her, although ...' I break off.

She lifts one eyebrow.

'Well, I could never be as casual about things as she was. I still worried about India.'

'So, how long would you say before you felt you were coping on your own with India?'

'Probably I'd say it took what, twenty months maybe, till I was pretty much back to my old self, but I was managing okay *physically* for about six months before that, even though I still felt quite low mentally a lot of the time.'

'And at what point did you decide to go back to work?'

'When India was two. See, I worked in a kids' nursery, so she could come along with me, and because I was on the staff, it was all free. It worked out really well. My colleagues were there to help look after her, and I could do my job with the other toddlers. I got on fine with all of *them*.'

'Did it bother you that you had such problems with your own – well, as you perceived it anyway – when you were trained to care for children?'

Did it? I'm not sure.

'It's completely different when it's your own.'

'Fair enough. So, you're now back at work and India is

progressing well, and you're starting to feel more like your old self. How are things between you and your husband at this stage?'

'Fine.'

'Sorry to probe, but money-wise? In the bedroom? Deciding things? Any problems?'

'No. None that I knew of anyway.'

'So, what comes next?'

I think hard about this. Was it the baby or the overtime?

'We started arguing. Not big noisy fights or anything, but, well, not agreeing.'

'About anything in particular?'

'About another baby. I wanted one, he didn't.'

'Ahh, hence your earlier comment about wanting *India*.'

Blast it! I don't want somebody remembering every chance aside.

'Can you tell me more about that?' she says mildly, as if it's run of the mill, no big deal.

'I didn't want India to grow up an only child. I wanted her to learn to share, have somebody there for her whatever, when life's difficult, when other people give her a hard time, when I'm gone. Like Kaetlyn's lot have each other.'

'And Victor?'

'He didn't agree.'

'Did he say why not?'

'Oh yeah, he said, all right. There were two cast iron reasons that nobody could deny, he reckoned. First, the world's over populated as it is. He used to get quite worked up about Kaetlyn and her husband, Dermott, breeding so prolifically. Called it irresponsible, and he didn't know back then that they intended to have *nine* altogether. And his second reason was, having *one* baby had pretty nearly turned me stark staring bonkers. He wasn't prepared to risk a repeat of that. Or worse.'

'So how did this affect your relationship, would you say?'

97

'It did affect it, course it did. It was the first big thing we'd ever fallen out over. And he absolutely wasn't going to budge, easy-going as he was normally, this was something he felt passionately about. And he was totally convinced he was right, and I wasn't acknowledging how bad the time was with India as a baby. I *hadn't* forgotten, how could I? But I reckoned it had been worth it to have her, so, if I was prepared to go through it again, he ought to support me in that.'

'And you told him that?'

'Did I ever!'

'And?'

'Didn't make a blind bit of difference.'

'How did the tension between you manifest itself?'

'We'd argue, he'd walk away, I'd cry. He'd go all quiet, I'd sulk. He'd sleep in the spare room. If I'm honest, it was usually Victor who made the first move to heal things. But sometimes I'd cook his favourite food and he took that as a sign.'

'So how did you resolve this between you?'

'We didn't.'

'And how did that affect your relationship?'

'Most of the time it was fine on the surface, but there was always this shadow lurking just out of eyesight. Especially as I was seeing Kaetlyn's gang all the time and watching them with India like she was one of theirs. I guess we both tried to ignore it for the sake of our family life.'

'Did you ever threaten, or try to blackmail him?'

I'm taken aback by the question. Where's she coming from now?

Did I?

'I don't think so. I don't remember doing so anyway. I didn't have much to bargain with, did I?'

'You could have withheld sexual favours, threatened to get pregnant with someone else, said you'd leave if he didn't give you what you wanted. That sort of thing.'

'No, I couldn't. He wouldn't have believed any of those things. He knew me inside out.'

'As you thought you knew him.'

Touché, but below the belt. I see from her look she knows that was uncalled for.

'Sorry, Tonya.'

I shrug.

'Okay, so, you've reached an impasse in the matter of another baby, what else is going on at this stage in your lives?'

'He changed his job.'

'Right. Tell me about that.'

'Well, like I said, he went into nursing because he's … he was … he used to be, one of those really caring folk who want to make a difference in people's lives. And if you were ill or in trouble, he was exactly the kind of person you'd want to have alongside you. But in his job, like in lots of professions nowadays, the higher up the ladder you go, the further you get from what you wanted to do in the first place. He got to a stage where he reckoned he spent nearly all his time in the office or attending meetings or running round clearing up other people's mistakes, and he got pretty scunnered by it. All the bureaucratic nonsense and official stuff, it didn't need his training and skills. So he decided he wanted to get back to the bedside.

'He took himself off on a couple of courses and went into ITU – you know, Intensive Care nursing, where you look after fewer people, but they're critically ill. And he absolutely loved it. He used to come home really buzzing again. And things started to be more like they were in the beginning. We were happy together again. Okay, they had a lot more deaths and some really tragic cases, but he seemed to cope with that fine, he liked helping the families through these kinds of traumas. But most of all he loved being able to maintain a really high standard of care. What he did made a real difference.'

'Excuse me. One mo.'

The girl leans forward to check the recorder and I wait while she does something to it. The electronic equivalent of turning the tape, I figure.

'Sorry about that,' she says. 'But before you go on, you say about high standards and all that, would you say your husband was a perfectionist?'

I think for a moment. 'Yes, he was. He liked things to be done well.'

'Thank you. Sorry to interrupt your story. Carry on, please. You're doing brilliantly. So, Victor's in a new job and loving it. What happened next?'

'Well, then he begins to realise that the same thing could happen as he moves up through the ranks, so he decides he'll get even more patient contact and job satisfaction if he goes onto permanent night duty. Seven nights on, three off, eight on, four off, that kind of thing.'

'And how old was India by this time?'

'She would have been ... four coming up for five, something like that.'

'So, how did he find this new working pattern?'

'He loved it. He absolutely thrived on it. It suited him down to the ground. He was one of those people who can sleep on a clothes line any hour of the day or night, so he had no problem getting a good nine, ten hours, through the day.'

'What did *you* think about all this?'

'At first I was pleased for him. He was so much happier. But it also meant we saw far less of him. And gradually things changed. It was the upside-down life really – he was out of kilter with everyone else. And that made him more irritable than he used to be. It was tough for India too. I'd often have to take her out somewhere so she could let off steam.'

'What effect did *that* have?'

'Hard to put a finger on it,' I say slowly, 'But I guess, when I think about it, that was the second thing that came between us. I know inside I sometimes resented his freedom to do his own thing, concentrate on himself. *I* was the one getting up in the night when India was poorly, doing the shopping, meals, all that stuff. He slept and went to work, full stop. It's no worse than those couples where the guy's away for work during the week, I know, but I'm only talking about me and how I felt.'

'Which is exactly what this is all about: you and Victor and how things were. No need to be apologetic.' This time the smile seems more genuine. Maybe she too carries a disproportionate share of the family burden, simply by virtue of her gender.

'Were there any other significant changes in this period soon after India started school?'

'Not that I can ... Oh no, wait, I tell a lie. My mother went into hospital during the first term of India's second year at school. She needed quite major surgery for a growth on her ovary. It was benign actually, but we didn't know that initially.'

'And what did that mean in terms of your little family?'

'Actually, Victor was brilliant. He took annual leave and looked after India and the house and everything so I could go off to Fife to stay close by the hospital and visit every afternoon and evening. Mother was only in four days but, of course, still very weak and poorly when she got home, so it was great being able to devote my attention to her needs knowing everything was ticking over smoothly at home. And India *loved* having her Daddy to herself for two whole weeks. She had a ball. And the garden was absolutely immaculate when I got back!'

She smiles broadly. 'He was the gardener in the family, I take it.'

'Absolutely. Me, all I do are the basics – keep the paths swept, borders weeded, plants dead-headed. Nothing imaginative.'

I am already anticipating her next question. 'So, when did things change?'

When *did* marriage start to be so difficult? Where did it all go wrong?

But she switches off the machine and says, 'I think we'll call it a day there. This must be pretty exhausting for you. Take a break and we'll start fresh tomorrow.'

CHAPTER 18

Tonya

AS SOON AS I WAKEN next morning, I remember, and feel that horrible sick feeling you get when you know you're going to be put through the wringer – by India as well as that policewoman.

I very nearly called Kaetlyn last night after the interview when India refused to eat a thing at dinner. But I know exactly what she'd say. We've been here before.

'You need to lighten up, Tonya, so you do. She's a teenager.'

'Your kids don't talk back to you like she does.' More aggressive than I intended.

'It's different when you've got a tribe of them. You can't afford to be that intense. My lot have to get on with life, make the best of it for themselves, muck in at home. Not so much opportunity to get all tied up in knots.'

'Even so.'

'Your India's a great kid, so she is. Give her some space. She'll come round.'

I find myself wishing that India could still hobnob with Kaetlyn's kids. They're such a down-to-earth, practical, no-nonsense bunch, and they always said she was like one of them. Well, she practically lived with them in her early years.

I guess genes will out in the end, and not even my best friend would call *me* laid-back. Like Kaetlyn said, I have to let her choose her own friends. She's moved on since her days of playing tig in the garden, and besides, most of the O'Leary brood around her age are either working or reproducing themselves now, and that's *not* an example I want my only daughter to follow!

The second instalment of my interview starts at 9 and I arrive ten minutes early determined to keep the upper hand this time.

I feel nauseous. I so don't want to talk about this bit. All marriages have their ups and downs, and ours had taken a hammering over the two years from India's birth till I started to recover. Okay, I know it wasn't anybody's fault, merely the cards life dealt. But still.

On the other hand, rehearsing my story ready for somebody impartial, has made me appreciate what a good husband Victor was back then. In spite of all the months when my libido was at rock bottom, and I was too exhausted to make the effort, he'd been content to hold me, so gently, not demanding more than I was ready to offer. He never made me feel inadequate, he laid it all at the door of my hormones, and reassured me it would all come right in the end. As it did. Eventually, with patience and perseverance – mostly his, I would have to say – we got back to something better again.

It strengthens my resolve. Even now, knowing what I know, suspecting what I suspect, I don't want to paint him in a bad light.

Heather is as brisk and businesslike as yesterday, but this time I'm dressed to equal her. It's a start.

'So, last time we got to the point where you were struggling with the changes in Victor which you put down to his work patterns, sleep deprivation and being out of kilter with normal daytime living.'

'You're good at this,' I say, 'remembering all that.'

'Well, thanks. Actually this is what I want to go into: profiling. Eventually. And you're very good at telling the story.'

'That's because you're keeping me on track.'

'So, tell me more about that period in your lives.'

103

'Victor would be out of the loop for a week or so at a time working and sleeping, then we all had to adjust to him coming back into play on his nights off. But I guess it's much harder for couples in the armed forces, or where one of them is away abroad or on the rigs or whatever for months or years.'

She acknowledges this with a tiny lift of a shoulder but doesn't offer an opinion. Of course she doesn't, this isn't about what *she* thinks.

'But it felt like we were always playing catch-up, never quite getting back to where we were. And maybe that's why I didn't notice at first.' I break off, remembering ... the creeping realisation, the anxiety, the ...

'Notice?' she prompts.

'That something wasn't right. Something was troubling him. He wouldn't admit it, but I could sense it, see it in his face, when he didn't know I was watching.'

'So what did you do?'

'I tried to get him to share it. Was it work? No. Were all the deaths getting him down? No. Had something specific happened, something gone wrong, a mistake perhaps? No. Was it me? No. Was there someone else? No. Was it the baby thing? No. He kept reiterating there was nothing, he was fine, only tired.'

Listing it to her makes it sound like an inquisition. It wasn't like that. It was gentle, over time, often when he was in my arms. I could feel his tension, I could show him I cared. I couldn't force him to divulge his inner demons.

'How did that make you feel?'

'Lonely. Rejected.'

'What effect did that have?'

I ponder this before answering. 'We drifted further and further apart. The old closeness had gone. This is going to sound childish, but I stopped telling him about my day too. If he was going to clam up and have his secret world, so could I! Pathetic, I know, and probably the wrong response altogether if he was struggling with some deep-seated problem or other.'

'It's always easy to be wise after the event.'

'I suppose. Anyway, we can't change the past.'

'No indeed.'

'He started to spend more time away from the house, us. It was only for a few hours at first. I asked him, mildly, where he'd been. Out. Out where? Nowhere special, just out. Doing what? Nothing in particular, trying to sort his head out. He'd be back in time for our meal in the evening and he was still every bit as keen to do things with India. She was always his number one. But he said he needed breathing space, which in a way was acknowledging he had a problem.'

'How did you feel about that?'

'Even more sidelined. And more suspicious that he'd found somebody else, he was having an affair.'

'And was he, d'you think?'

'No, I really don't think so. He swore he wasn't and I believed him. He said he had mental stuff to sort out, and given how good he'd been when I was the one depressed and withdrawn and behaving like a lunatic, it was only fair that I should give him the benefit of the doubt now. It was his turn. Besides, he never once threw all that stuff up at me. *I* was very conscious of it though, and I did wonder if this was some kind of delayed reaction. You know, they tell you, don't they, that sometimes couples take it in turns to be the needy one?'

She pauses a beat as if registering this but doesn't respond verbally. 'And then?'

'The times away got longer. He wouldn't always be back before bedtime. Once it was even the following day before he returned. He left a wee message, I remember. "Back tomorrow. Stuff to sort out. Big hug for India." He'd even left the meal all ready for us to microwave.'

'Ahh, that reminds me. You said earlier that when he was on a run of nights you did all the domestic chores. What about on his nights off? How did you sort out who did what then?'

'On the first day he'd be sleeping. On the day before his first night back on duty he'd sleep in the afternoon. In between he'd do most of the cooking and collect India and play with her and help her with her homework.'

'And did he have hobbies of his own? How did he fill the days you and India were both out at school and work, when he wasn't off "sorting his head out"?' She repeats my phrase matter-of-factly, mimicking my air apostrophes, no scorn or criticism in her tone.

'He read mostly, and did the garden. He was a voracious reader. Always was. Oh, and he took up swimming. Said he was starting to put on weight. It'd keep him fit.'

'And was he?'

'Not that I could see. He was always slim.'

'And friends? Did he do things with friends?'

'Not a lot. A couple of work colleagues maybe, occasionally they'd meet for a pint or maybe a film. But mostly he was on his own, or so he said.'

'So, you'd got to the stage where he'd started spending longer out of the house, sorting himself out, and it was beginning to impinge on family life.'

'That's when it started to get really difficult. During the day, it didn't affect India. She was at school anyway, and often went to play with her pals afterwards. She would see him in the evening and have his undivided attention then. But when he didn't come home on his days off, that required some kind of explanation and any excuses I made always sounded kind of lame.'

'How did *she* take it? Did she challenge him?'

'No, actually. She didn't altogether understand his rotas anyway, so she was glad when he was around, and took his absences in her stride. It was her norm. And I suppose I encouraged that. I always downplayed his time away.'

'Why d'you think you did that?'

'Because he was her dad. Because she loved him to bits. Because we both knew he loved her totally. I didn't want to spoil what they had.'

'How did you feel about *their* closeness?'

I pause. I don't want to answer this question; I don't

like the answer.

Eventually she leans forward slightly, 'Tonya?'

'Jealous. Excluded.'

'And yet you didn't take advantage of this situation to undermine it?' Is she doubting my version of events?

I look straight at her, hold her gaze. 'No, it's true, I *didn't*. I'm telling you stuff that puts me in a bad enough light, so I don't have any reason to lie about this.'

'I'm not suggesting you're lying, I'm simply trying to understand. Sorry if it was too challenging. It wasn't meant to be.'

'In a funny sort of way, it made me feel good that he was such a brilliant dad. I'd chosen him, I'd recognised his potential as a family man, that's why I'd married him. And my prediction had turned out to be spot-on right. He was even better than I ever dreamed of. And I think all that time when I couldn't really bond with India and he took over, that helped to forge that special closeness they had. That and his natural affinity with kids.'

She nods as if to acknowledge the legitimacy of my response.

'You're doing really well, Tonya, but I can see this is emotionally draining stuff, so how about we take a wee break, get some fresh air? Shall we say fifteen minutes?'

CHAPTER 19

Tonya

EVEN HER VOICE sounds refreshed. Maybe she was the one needing the break.

'So, you're worried that there's something troubling Victor, he's not sharing it with you, but he and India are as close as ever. More than usually close. Could he have been sharing it with *her*, d'you think?'

'Not that I know of, and I must say, I seriously doubt it. She was still a little kid. And he wouldn't want to trouble her. Besides, over the years, she's never said anything. I'm pretty sure she'd have said if she knew.'

'He might have sworn her to secrecy.'

I shrug.

'Listen, Tonya, don't take this the wrong way, but I have to ask. Is it possible he had an unnatural interest in India, d'you think?' she says, watching me.

I close my eyes.

'Ahh. The thought did cross your mind then.' Her voice is gentle.

'Not at the time, no. Only afterwards, when I was trying to make sense of everything. Seeing them together, hearing him in her bedroom for ages, all the cuddling, their secrets, the changes in him, why he used to go off on his own, why he left so suddenly without explanation, India's reaction when he left. *Something* made him go away. It has to be a possibility. Maybe he couldn't live with the feelings he was developing towards his own daughter; what he might do.'

'And did you share that idea with anyone at the time?'

I shake my head fiercely. '*No!* I *couldn't*. Besides there was no evidence of anything untoward. *Ever*.'

'Did you ever ask India?'

'Not directly, no. But I gave her plenty of opportunities to talk about her daddy and the things they did together.'

'And was there any suggestion, any hint, of impropriety?'

'Not a shred of anything.'

'Does she confide in you now?'

'Not much, no.'

'Do you confide in her?'

I feel a wave of panic rise into my chest. She watches me with a strange stillness as if she's filming every twitch, every emotion, unravelling my unravelling.

'No.'

'Why not?'

'Because she's his daughter, and because she's still only fifteen, and because I don't want to spoil her memories. And she's got enough problems of her own growing up in this modern world with all its pressures and stresses.'

'D'you think she's having a hard time with her teens?'

'Yes.'

'More so than normal?'

'I don't know what normal is, but I worry about her.'

'Would you describe yourself as a worrier generally?'

'Probably. And *definitely* where India's concerned. But I don't see that's anything out of the ordinary. All parents are concerned about their children, aren't they?'

'Could you tell me what sorts of things you worry about with her?'

'That she might get in with a bad crowd and start taking drugs or alcohol or something. That somebody might hurt her.'

'Any somebody in particular?'

'Nobody I can name, no. But any guy who wants more than she's ready to give.'

'You say "might", have you any concrete reason to suspect she's under these kinds of pressures?'

'Well, no, not exactly, but young people are today, aren't they? And you can't watch them twenty-four seven.'

'So normal teen pressures, nothing specific. But you think she's having a hard time with her teens. What makes you say that?' There it is again, that intensive listening, picking up on things I say, things I don't say. She's good at her job, I grant her that.

'Because I know her so well. She's not the happy soul she was a few years ago. She's moody, shuts herself away in her room, secretive, snaps back at me, that kind of thing.'

'And this is more than becoming a teenager, you think?'

Oh, it's so easy for her, young, free, no kids, no worries. I want to shock her out of her too-trite interpretations.

'I think she's becoming anorexic.'

Yep, she's taken aback. Good. But she bounces back quickly like a true professional, her tone even and non-committal as always.

'And what makes you think that?'

'Food left on her plate, meals in the bin, losing weight.' I break off before my voice betrays me. Two can play at this game.

'And have you tackled her on this?'

'I've mentioned her weight loss and how it worries me, but I haven't let her know I've seen the wasted food. They tell you to go carefully so the child doesn't have to lie and isn't on the defensive.'

'"They"?'

'Experts. On the internet.'

'Ahh.'

'And Kaetlyn, my neighbour with all the kids, says it's best to encourage, reassure, not criticise. It's maybe only a passing phase. She'll grow out of it if nobody makes a big deal of it.'

'I see. And do you attribute any of this to her father's disappearance?'

'I have no idea what's down to him and what's normal

teenage angst.'

'You said earlier you haven't shared all you know with her, you don't want to spoil her memories of her dad. So what do you know that might risk that, Tonya?'

Now I've done it. My mind sifts through the facts and attaches the consequences at lightning speed. Go cautiously. Once it's said it can't be unsaid.

'Well, at first I didn't tell her they found his clothes on the beach. There was no body and there could have been an innocent explanation. I thought, best leave it till there's some evidence one way or another.'

'So what *did* you tell her? She was eight, presumably aware of time, and she would have expected him home?'

'I told her he'd gone away and I didn't know when he'd be back.'

'And does she know now?'

'Yes, of course.'

'So, how old was she when you judged her old enough to know the truth?'

'Eleven-ish. But ...'

'But?'

'Well, it wasn't a case of me judging her old enough. A kid at her school told her he'd committed suicide.'

'Ahhh. And how did she react?'

'She was terribly upset, naturally, but I don't know how much of that was because I'd kept it from her, and how much because she hated that her dad had left her deliberately. She felt betrayed by both of us, I think.'

'And since then, have you kept her in the picture?'

'There hasn't been much to tell. There's still been no body, no sightings. So *I* don't know anything more either.'

'So, what do you *think* happened, Tonya? You knew your husband better than anyone else. What do you make of his disappearance?'

'None of it makes sense. Okay, yes, he had something preying on his mind, but he was so besotted with India. I can't see him killing himself. He wasn't the type.'

'Is there a type?'

'You know what I mean.'

'Can you tell me why *Victor* wasn't the type?'

'Because ... he wasn't self-centred. He cared about us, India specially. He wasn't low enough to want to end it all.'

'So you don't think it was suicide?'

'No, I don't.'

'What do *you* think happened?'

'An accident, maybe. I don't know. But like I told you last time, he was a strong swimmer.'

'So, this latest development, India thinking she heard his voice in London. What d'you make of that?'

'Wishful thinking. And they do say that your senses are heightened when you're hungry. I think India's permanently hungry and that's making her sort of hallucinate.'

'I see. So you came to see us because?'

'India forced my hand actually. But she needs to know I'm listening to her, reporting her experience. Getting something done. '

'In your mind, then, this is about India's trust in you, not your belief that your husband is still alive, is that correct?'

'That makes it sound terribly devious and underhand. It's more making sure India knows no stone has been left unturned in the search for her father.'

'I see.'

She looks directly at me for what feels like ages.

'So, is there anything else at all that we ought to know?'

I hesitate. I'm in enough hot water already with this woman. Better not leave any more room for mistrust.

'Well, there is one other small thing ...'

'Go on.' She's poised like a cat waiting to pounce. I mentally rehearse the sentence that will change everything.

'I didn't ever tell India this, but Victor left a note.'

'Ahh. And did you tell the police?'

'No.'

'Why not?'

'Because I decided not to tell India, I wanted her to

have some closure. If I'd told the police, they might have told India.'

'And what did the note say?'

Even yet it's hard to say, though I know it by heart. '"*I'm sorry. I can't go on like this. Please forgive me. Let me go. Don't try to look for me.*"'

'But you went to the police anyway?'

'No. It was only when somebody found his clothes that the police became involved.'

'And the note didn't say whether he intended to commit suicide or not anyway.'

'Exactly.'

'Anything else you haven't told us?'

'Well ... after ... after they found his clothes on the beach, I went through his things – really to see if anything else was missing.'

'And was it?'

'Not that I could see.'

'So?'

'Well, I found something I didn't expect ... buried in the bottom of his underwear and sock drawer.'

She waits patiently. There's obviously no going back now. No need for a prompt.

'Lingerie.'

'Ahhh.'

'A pair of ladies' silk panties. Lacy ones.'

'Not yours?'

'Not mine.'

'Which makes you think, what?'

'I don't know. An affair, maybe?'

The alternative is unthinkable. Definitely unsayable.

'But earlier you said, you believed him when he swore he wasn't having an affair.'

'I did. I do.'

She quirks an eyebrow and I know she doesn't believe me, but I can't, I *can't* tell her what I really suspect. It's her job to make the deductions.

'Can I ask you something?' I blurt out before she has a

chance to put me on the spot. 'Talking about missing people
…'

'Of course.'

'This girl near London. Maria something.'

'Maria Davenport.'

'Yes. Are they looking for somebody in connection
with that disappearance?'

'Not that I'm aware of.'

'So they don't think there's anything sinister about it?'

'Not at the moment, no. Why?'

'It's … I've been thinking about all the people on the
police records that are still missing, and wondering how they
decide who to follow up.'

'It's a combination of lots of factors.'

'Right.'

'What are you really trying to say, Tonya?'

CHAPTER 20

Chris

I DO A DOUBLE TAKE. Can it be ....? Surely not ...? Inside that oversized parka, behind the hood and sunglasses ...?

She flits from car to car, fingering the occasional piece of jewellery, eyeing up the backpacks, brushing the back of her hand against the fabrics. She looks thinner than in the pictures, more androgynous. This local car boot sale isn't Camden Market but maybe she'll find a better bargain in the midst of this seething disorganization.

I follow at a distance, feigning interest in the merchandise when she glances over her shoulder.

Eventually she plonks herself down on a pile of cardboard behind a stall set up at the back of an ancient Range Rover. She takes off the glasses ... Yes, it *is* her ... She rummages in her canvas bag. From the way she sinks her teeth into the plain bread roll I guess that a) it was salvaged from an out-of-date bin; b) she hasn't had a proper meal in ages; and c) she's currently of no fixed abode.

I slip round the back and I'm crouching down beside her before she has time to move.

'Hi, Maria, fancy running into you here. Long time no see.'

She shrinks into herself, bundling up her possessions, preparing for flight.

'You don't remember?' I say, with what I hope is a teasing look. 'Chris?'

She shakes her head slowly. 'Don't think ...' It's no more than a mumble.

'Well, good thing my memory's better than yours then. Recognised you immediately. Even with the hood!'

I pass her my lunch box. 'Go ahead, tuck in.'

She stares at the food, each item neatly wrapped in film, looks back at me, and then tears into it. I watch with a mixture of horror and relief as she demolishes it in minutes. She can't have tasted anything properly. Waste of Gorgonzola and walnut bread and shortbread and fresh strawberries.

'Better?' I manage a smile.

She gives one sharp nod. 'Thanks.'

I wait until she's drained the carton of raspberry and banana smoothie before speaking again.

'Good. So, how're you doing?'

She shrugs, doesn't look at me.

'I know you're on the run, but don't be scared. I've no intention of turning you in.'

She continues to stare at the ground, grimy fingers scratching her shins. Fleas, maybe?

'Have you got anywhere to sleep, Maria? Anywhere to stay?'

Silence.

'I take it that's a no?'

She screws her eyes up tightly.

'How about you come back to my place for a nice hot shower and a good square meal? Looks to me like you're in need of an old friend.'

She darts a brief suspicious look at me.

'Please. I'd really like to help. I know what it feels like to be all alone in a big city. I ran away once myself when I was younger.'

'Honestly?' It comes out all croaky and crumpled as if she hasn't used her tongue for ages. Come to think of it, it's perfectly possible she hasn't.

'Really, truly, honestly. Cross my heart and hope to die.'

'To London?'

'To London.'

I can see she's swithering.

116

'You won't …?'

I shake my head.

'I only want to help, not get you into trouble. Home isn't a palace but it's dry and warm. Food in the fridge.'

Still she hesitates.

'Oh, and I've got a cat: Sylvester. You used to like cats. Still do, huh? Three wasn't it, you had? Three cats and a dog, if I remember correctly. Want to come and see Sylvester? He's a real character.'

The thaw has started.

'Come on, then.' I scramble up and extend a hand. Her small fingers are cold and she snatches them away as soon as she's upright. She keeps her distance as we head away from the market and I adapt my stride to her weaker pace, alert for a sudden dart away. Now I've found her I've no intention of losing her.

Huddled in my one armchair, dwarfed by my fluffy bathrobe, her hair still wet and clinging to her scrubbed face, stroking Sylvester, she looks, if anything, even more vulnerable. I hand her a mug of hot chocolate laced with extra cream and she wraps both hands around it, inhaling the smell with a familiar look that catches in my throat. My daughter was a chocoholic too.

But this is no time for nostalgia. I flick on the TV and leave her to relax while I make up a bed in the cupboard the agent called a compact spare bedroom. I fish out more towels, toiletries, tissues, books. I hunt for undies, a couple of ribbed tops, a skirt, a cluster of safety-pins – they'll serve until I can buy her the right size, wash her things.

Maria is my very first staying guest; I get caught up in the excitement. I want my welcome to be palpable.

I don't know if you've ever tried to entertain a complete stranger without asking a single question about their lives or telling them a single thing about your own, but take it from me, it's not easy. When that stranger is a monosyllabic troubled teenager the difficulty is compounded. By the time we get to dessert that evening, we're pretty much running on empty.

I can see the kid is exhausted, probably hasn't slept properly in ages, but there's something I have to do before I let her crash out here.

I kneel down beside her chair and lower my voice to a soothing tone.

'Maria, before you go to bed I want you to listen to me. Okay? Hear me out.'

Her face remains averted. Guarded. No promises.

'I'm your friend, right? I'm on your side. You're perfectly safe here. So what I'm going to say is as much for your benefit as anyone's. All right?'

Still no quarter given.

'I'm not going to bore on about my troubles but, like I told you before, I was very unhappy once, ran away myself, so I understand where you're coming from, how you want to stay hidden in this great big, dirty, impersonal city. I can also tell you I once had a daughter and something bad happened to her, so I can kind of see both sides of this stuff. I don't know what's gone on in your family, and I'm not going to force you to tell me anything. It's your life, your story. No Spanish inquisition, promise.' I can see this allusion is lost on her. 'I'm sure you have your reasons.

'But I want you to do one thing for me. I want you to seriously consider letting your parents know you're safe. Not where you are, or anything more, simply that you're safe. See, I know what it's like to worry like crazy about your kids, and right now they'll be going out of their minds, thinking you may be dead or injured or being held against your will or whatever. You can tell them you don't want to be found. Ask them to tell the police not to look for you, if you like. Could you do that, d'you think?'

She doesn't agree. But she doesn't say no either.

'Or how about letting your sister Amy know, if it's too hard to contact your mum and dad. She'll be worried sick about you too.'

There's a small glimmer.

'D'you have a mobile phone?'

She nods.

'Course you do. Daft question. Sorry.'

She glances sideways at me, a question in her eyes.

'Ahh. You haven't been able to use it, of course. No way of recharging.'

'The police could track me down.'

'You could use mine ... no, same risks, huh?'

Another nod.

'Riiight. So, let's see ... How about sending a postcard?'

She's not ruling it out.

'We could put it in an envelope. I could type the address for you if that would help. Post it miles away from here.'

Before she can change her mind, I fish out a postcard showing Big Ben. It was lying in the corridor of the hotel where I worked when I first moved to London. I offer a blank envelope and stamp tentatively.

She takes them both, scribbles something on the card, addresses the envelope to her sister in block capitals using her left hand, puts it in her pocket ready to mail herself next day. Okay, I wouldn't trust me yet either.

That night I hardly sleep a wink; my guest barely stirs. I know because I check on her fifteen times. Miraculously she's still here in the morning.

I have some urgent shopping to do.

CHAPTER 21

Chris

AS SOON AS the market stalls open, I slip out silently, locking the door behind me. A gnawing anxiety lends speed to my spending spree. Will my guest find some way to vanish by the time I get back? Would fear be enough to catapult an exhausted teenager out of bed before ten o'clock?

I choose two of everything. Jeans, t-shirts, jumpers, underwear. Guessing. I dared not rootle through her possessions for size labels.

Checking trainers was simpler. I nearly stuck them in the machine they were so foul; a guarantee she couldn't run away before I got back, but I reckoned she'd see that as an abuse of trust. The new trainers are cheaper, more gaudy than I'd have chosen, but they're all I can find in the time. In the chemist I slide vitamin supplements and fortifying compounds, toothbrush, sanitary products, hair rinse, towards the woman at the till. I don't look at her or speak. I can't afford to be memorable if the police come calling door-to-door, shop-to-shop.

Maria is still unconscious when I get back. A weight drops from my shoulders. I quickly change back into casual at-home garb, and inch quietly into her room. Memories flood back as I lay out the clothes ready for her, like I used to ... no, not now. This is no time to be wallowing in my own loss. This other girl is my priority now.

She doesn't surface for another ninety minutes, and the shower runs forever. When she appears in the kitchen her long hair is hanging in damp strands, staining the purple sweatshirt, but the clothes fit her remarkably well, showing off her slim figure. Her face, innocent of makeup, is touchingly young.

'Good sleep?' I ask.

'Thanks, yep.'

'Found everything you need?'

She nods.

'Can I?' She gesticulates towards the washing machine, her arms clutching the evidence of her former existence.

'Go ahead,' I say with a smile. 'Colour-catchers on the top shelf. Maybe stick your trainers in separately?' Typical kid. No idea of fabrics or machine cycles.

'Sorry. I know they stink.'

'No problem. They'll be good as new when they come out.'

She tucks into cereal and scrambled egg with the unselfconsciousness of the desperate. It's gone so quickly I'm satisfied she hasn't even noticed I've bolstered her calorific intake.

'Maria ... can you remind me? D'you have any special likes, dislikes, in food?'

She shakes her head, her mouth full of toast.

'Any health problems we need to see to?' I keep it bland and casual. *Maria may be in urgent need of medical assistance.*

She shrugs. I have no idea what that means but let it go for the time being.

I busy myself putting ingredients into the slow cooker, giving her space to finish her breakfast without scrutiny. When she's cleared everything on the table she leans back and says, 'Don't you have to get to work or something?'

'I told my boss I wouldn't be in today.'

She's suddenly tense. 'Did you tell him ... about me?'

'Her. No. Promise. I only said something unexpected had come up. She won't pry, she's lovely, very understanding.'

Sylvester slinks into the room and Maria swoops on him. For the first time I see the smiling girl in the photo. I watch her stroking his long fur, forgetting her troubles for a few precious moments.

'What d'you fancy doing today?' I clear the table so she doesn't feel under pressure.

'Dunno.'

'Want to go out? Stay in? Watch a film? Do some baking? Chill out on your own?'

After an age she says, 'Watch the telly?'

'Sure thing. Help yourself.'

I sneak a look every once in a while and within an hour both she and Sylvester are asleep again, lulled by the voice of some middle-aged presenter droning on about glorious views and fake ceiling beams and the size of a utility room. Maria's features are softer in repose. She's a schoolgirl again.

The world-weary runaway emerges in time to tuck into baked potatoes and stew and declare herself in need of some fresh air. We strike out away from my usual haunts and take a path through a lovely wooded park. Conversation is spasmodic, on my side because, fortified, she sets a brisk pace; on hers because, I suspect, she isn't yet sure she can trust me.

But I learn that biology and English are her favourite subjects, she's worried about one of their cats who's started lurching 'like my Uncle Jack when he's had a few too many', she despises all politicians, envies her sister her sporting ability. It's a start.

'She's at uni now isn't she – Amy?'

'Yeah.'

'Enjoying it?'

'Yeah.'

'D'you miss her? *I* did when *my* sister went away to college. Even though we argued pretty much all the time, I still missed her.'

'Kind of.'

'Feels empty. Too quiet, doesn't it?'

She shrugs. 'We text.'

After a few minutes she surprises me. 'Is it just you and her?' It's her first direct personal question.

'No, two brothers as well,' I say. 'All older than me. I was the misfit. The afterthought. A pest to my brothers and an irritation to my sister.'

'Were you lonely?'

'You bet I was! Lived in an imaginary world most of my childhood.'

'Did your mum know?'

'She was too busy keeping food on our table and a roof over our heads to bother with finer feelings.'

'Mine's too busy with her own career to notice.'

'She's a teacher, isn't she, your mum, if I remember correctly? Geography, history or something?'

'History. Head of department now. Loads more work. She's never done. Weekdays, evenings, weekends. Always work, work, work.'

'Ahh. The old rat race. Promotion's not all it's cracked up to be, is it? My dream job's doing something I love during the day, but that I can leave behind when the shift ends, so's I have a life outside it.'

'What *is* your job?'

'I'm a florist.'

'And is that 9 to 5?'

My snort is spontaneous. 'I wish! No. If we have a function coming up – conference, wedding, funeral, whatever – we have to do a lot of the preparation when the shop's closed. At the flower market, in the back of the shop, out at the venue, getting everything ready on time. Don't get me wrong, I absolutely love it, I really do, but it plays havoc with the old social life. I guess, ideally you'd make enough doing the big events not to need to do the more mundane stuff, but we aren't that big – yet – and we need to survive.'

'But floristry's what you chose to do, right?'

I nod. 'I adore it.' Enough for now.

'See, what you said, that's what I think too. I don't want to spend my whole life working at some boring old job.'

'Not History of Art at St Andrews Uni then? '

'Not if I can help it! Nah. That's Mum's idea. See, in my family that's what's expected. You go to uni, get a good degree, in a proper subject.' She snarls the last two words.

'Ahh, poor old you. The dreaded expectations. So, what would you rather do?'

'Acting.'

'Really? Wow. You any good?'

'School thinks so. Some reviewer chappie thought so when he wrote up a show I was in. Mum reckons it's a phase, a hobby thing, not a real career job, not secure, no guarantees. I don't *care* about guarantees.' She breaks off suddenly.

'So what've you been in?' I ask.

She rattles off five or six plays, only one of which I recognise: Oscar Wilde.

'Ever been to a show in London?'

'Naah.'

'Like to?'

'Would I ever!'

'Right. Let's see what's on when we get back, huh?' I'll be on bread and water for a month at this rate.

'Musical or stage play?' I ask.

'Not fussed.'

'*The Lion King*? *Phantom of the Opera*?' I know they're suitable for a teenager. 'Or if you prefer stage plays, there's *War Horse*? *Mamma Mia*?'

'Whatever.' A long pause. 'Have *you* seen them?'

'*Phantom* – years ago. Not in London, though. And *The Lion King* ... with my daughter, also years ago. How about you have a browse through the bumph about all of them and see what takes your fancy. Nothing to offend my delicate sensibilities, mind!'

I pray I can get 'cheap seats' – a relative term I know – for the one she likes the sound of.

War Horse is spectacular and worth every penny. It was her choice: 'Let's go for something *you* haven't seen before.' I'm touched.

The sight of her enraptured face makes it doubly special. And afterwards she enthuses about the effects, the puppets, the lighting, the music, the plot; becomes impassioned about the futility of war, animal abuse … this must be the original Maria before disillusion and despair tore her from her family. Michael Morpurgo would be chuffed to know he was responsible for her rescue and our bonding.

Back at the flat I surreptitiously watch her fingers caressing the glossy programme, turning the pages again and again as she relives the experience.

I dig out a stack of DVDs of films she hasn't seen and she pounces on *12 Years a Slave*.

'Ahhh, that one. It's pretty shocking in places,' I caution. 'Are you okay with that? Did your parents set limits?'

The cloud descends. 'I'm sixteen. I can decide for myself.'

'Fair enough. But say, you know, if you want company or to chat. It's disturbing – well, at least, *I* thought so. Don't want you having nightmares. Neighbours might complain!'

'Okay.'

I hover during the worst bits, but she takes the violence and gore in her stride, analytical in her comment – how they created such realistic scenes; how well the actors portrayed the pain, the terror, the sadistic delight. A serious observer of the craft of her chosen profession.

'So, to be an actor, tell me, how'd you go about it?' I ask companionably afterwards. 'I have absolutely no idea what these guys have gone through to get to this point.'

'You can do degrees in drama or performing arts. Or you can go to performing arts centres, acting schools, film academies, stuff like that. Or you can do classes and workshops and summer programmes, and learn on the job. Depends.'

'And what route would *you* choose?'

'Degree, probably … if I could.'

'Uhhm.'

'They reckon folk take you more seriously if you've studied the different aspects of the job.'

'What kind of qualifications do they ask for?'

'English lang. English lit. Theatre studies, or something like that.'

'Makes sense. So have you got all that?'

'Nah. Mum wouldn't let me do drama as a subject. Wasn't a *real* subject she said.' The voice of Mrs Davenport, schoolmarm, head of department, echoes in the scorn.

I click my tongue in sympathy.

'So, what d'you need if you go down a different route?'

'Reading and speaking skills. Ability to memorise. Confidence performing in front of an audience. Stuff like that. And they like it if you've done some amateur productions.'

'So you've got all that behind you. Anything else?'

She shrugs.

'Persistence?' I say with a wry smile.

She grins lopsidedly. 'Yeah, that too.'

I wait.

'Flexibility helps. You need to be able to adapt to the needs of each production, do different things.'

'Such as?'

'Sing. Dance. Ride a horse. Acrobatics. Stuff like that. Stamina's another quality they look for.'

'So? You're looking good so far. Where's the problem?'

'Parents. End of.'

'Because they're looking for security, and you want risk and adventure.'

'Yeah, but see, I *know* it'd be a struggle. I *know* very few people get big breaks that make them into household names. I don't *expect* to be a Scarlett Johanssen or a Cameron Diaz or a Maggie Smith overnight. *Ever*, even! But so? Mum's not a history professor on the telly, is she? She's only jogging along in an ordinary everyday kind of job too. Dad isn't a modern day Isambard Kingdom Brunel, but he's doing a decent job and getting paid for it. He's not minted, but he's doing what he *enjoys*.'

'Hey, I'm impressed! Isambard Kingdom Brunel, huh?'

'Did about him in class.'

'Phew! That's okay then.' I grin at her. 'Dad's an engineer, as I recall, yes?'

'Yeah.'

'What does *he* think of your ambition to be an actor?'

'Dunno. He's always made it a rule not to let Amy and me play him off against Mum, and cos Mum's in education he reckons she knows best about careers and stuff.'

'Fair enough.'

'No, it's *not* fair!' she explodes. 'None of it's fair. Amy always was a high flyer. She always *wanted* to go to uni and become a teacher, like forever. But I'm not Amy. Why should I do the same as her, when I want something different? I never ever for one single second wanted to be stuck in a classroom with a bunch of cheeky kids trying to teach them dreary stuff they couldn't care less about. I want to do something I totally totally love. And I don't care about secure. What's the point of secure if you're miserable?'

'There's another qualification you have in spades then. Passion.' I smile broadly.

She grins back. 'Sorry, only ...'

'Oh, don't apologise. You'll need loads of passion if you're going to succeed in a job like acting. And persistence. And like you said, flexibility, versatility. You might find yourself doing something pretty menial during the day to scrape a living while you're waiting for that next break, or when they pay you tuppence an hour for some miniscule walk-on part as a street urchin or something.'

'I know. I really *do* know that. But I reckon I could stomach pretty much anything if it meant I could do what I really want to do.'

'Except cheeky brats, huh?'

'Like me, you mean.'

'If the cap fits!'

'I guess I could be a convincing street urchin now, huh!'

We laugh together.

CHAPTER 22

Chris

LATER I SAY, 'How about writing out a five-point plan of the steps you need to take if you *do* get a chance to go down this route? See what it would take.'

She grunts.

'You can use my laptop to look stuff up.'

'Thanks,' she says flatly, without moving. Ten minutes later she goes to the side table and picks up the computer. I set her up with a password and leave her to it.

Only after she's scoffed two helpings of everything at dinner, do I casually enquire how she fared.

She fishes a folded paper from her pocket and pushes it across the table to me. Her writing is tiny but absurdly neat.

1. Work on a resumé
2. Gain experience acting/stage-hand/backstage
3. Join an acting group?
4. Check out auditions
5. Apply to unis
6. Make some money!!

'Brilliant. Like to use my laptop to start on your resumé tomorrow?'

'You sure?'

'Sure, I'm sure. Only one snag though. *I* need to go back to work.'

She nods.

I take a gamble. 'You're welcome to chill out here, but

I do have another suggestion. An idea for you to think about. No pressure, mind, but, you know what I said about maybe doing menial jobs to pay your way while you accumulate experience in the acting world?'

She nods, an alert expression on her face. Careful, Chris.

'Well, you could come to the shop with me. Parminder – she's the boss – she could use another pair of hands to do odd jobs. Tidying up, answering the phone, sorting the orders, that kind of thing. We're getting loads more work these days. Word of mouth recommendations, and everything. It would free us up to concentrate more on making up the orders. The pay wouldn't be much but it'd be something. Get you started. You don't need to say immediately, but think about it and I'll ring her back if you want to give it a whirl.'

'You told her about me?' There's something in her eyes that sends warning signals.

'The bare minimum. I had to explain my absence. I owed her that. Trust works both ways. And she's really lovely, she won't pry or gossip. She's a brilliant florist but she's also a terrific person.'

She shrugs.

I don't tell her I asked Parminder to dock a small wage for her out of my own salary.

Not till she's off to bed does she reply, 'Okay. I'll give it a go.'

It's the best I can hope for.

'Oh, by the way, I gave you a different name. Rea. Rea Portland.'

She grimaces but doesn't protest.

'Sorry. Corruption of your real name. Maria – Rea. Davenport – Portland. Best I could come up with.'

She shrugs again. 'Catch ya later.'

'Sleep well.'

We don't talk on the Tube on the way to her first day at work. She keeps her head in a Metro, her ears plugged with her iPod. I'm free to play the game but don't; I have other priorities now. Instead I find myself scanning the commuters willing them not to notice my young companion, moving in front of her if I see an eye straying anywhere near her. Dressed in a combination of her own clothes and the ones I got from the local market, hair shining with a new chestnut-rinse and neatly secured in a bridal plait, sparingly made-up, she looks unexceptional, nothing like the photo in the paper ... but I recognised her, didn't I?

Parminder's already in the shop when we arrive, even though we're fifteen minutes early. She's matter-of-fact with 'Rea'. And give her her due, the girl makes a real effort – smiles, replies civilly, even occasionally with warmth.

She looks almost happy sorting the new stock, filling the flower buckets, sweeping up the detritus Parminder leaves in her wake as she fulfils orders at breathtaking speed, alert for new opportunities to clean and tidy. Ahh, what bliss! Long may it continue. That's the one aspect of working with Parminder that screws me up – she doesn't care what mess surrounds her. Me, I need to tidy up as I go along.

'Can you drive?' Parminder asks her as they work side by side.

'Nah. Sorry.'

'Okay.'

I let out my breath slowly. Delivering orders would further expose her to possible identification. I didn't mention that Maria was a runaway when I told my boss about this 'young friend, Rea'. I will, but not yet. For now I need to concentrate on keeping her backstage.

That night we have our best conversation yet. She's eager to know more about the flower business. We have a shared common ground now, safe territory for both of us. It's agreed: she becomes 'Rea' at home as well as at work, help to prevent a slip-up in public. It's agreed: she'll give this job a proper trial. It's agreed: she'll send a card to her sister once a fortnight. It's agreed: she'll stay with me meantime. It's agreed: I'll help her seek acting opportunities. It's agreed: I'll tell Parminder who she is.

'You're brill at listening,' she says in the kindly twilight.

'Thanks. That's a nice thing to say. I guess I know how important it is to talk. That was my problem, clamming up, not sharing my problems.'

'Do you now? Talk to anybody?' she asks.

'Not much,' I admit.

'Did you talk to your parents … when you were a kid, I mean? Or your sister or anybody?'

'Not much. You?'

'My sister. Used to. Not recently.'

'Would it help, d'you think? Sharing your thoughts?'

She shrugs.

'Happy to listen.' I keep it casual. 'If you want to. No pressure though.'

'Thanks.'

'I once got to rock bottom. Thought about ending it … you know?'

Her eyes widen. 'Suicide?'

'Yep. Not a good place to be, take it from one who knows. Don't let yourself get that low. Talk to somebody – if not me, somebody else. Somebody who can take it. I went to a therapisty kind of person in the end. Made a world of difference. I worried hugely about confiding my deepest darkest secrets, but guess what? She wasn't in the least bit fazed. Reckoned she'd heard far worse. But she understood what a burden it was keeping it all bottled up.'

'So, you're okay now? I mean, you *seem* … well, normal-ish.'

I smile. 'Cheeky bandit! But yep, I'm okay now. She helped me to accept myself, be who I am.'

'Guess that means you understand other people better, huh?'

'I like to think so. I don't pretend to be a professional counsellor or anything, but I *am* willing to listen, share troubles.'

'You don't talk about yours, though, do you? I know pretty much zilch about you. Four kids in your family. You're the youngest. You ran away from home. You once had a daughter but something awful happened to her. You work in a florist's shop. You've been suicidal. You're kind and you're a not-bad cook, but you have lousy taste in clothes.' She grins.

'Thanks a bunch!' I laugh with her. 'At least mine are clean, you ungrateful beggar!'

She's so pretty when she forgets to be miserable.

The grin dissolves as fast as it appeared. 'Sounds like you've had it worse than me. I never felt like packing it all in – life and everything. I just felt ... suffocated. Needed to escape.' Past tense.

'Ahhh, I have to say, I don't feel over the moon about that. I've been a parent, and I guess I wouldn't be too keen on some stranger helping my kid do the very thing I've said she shouldn't. I'd totally respect your parents if they hunted me down, had me hung, drawn and quartered!'

'Well, they won't. I'd tell them. You haven't forced me to do anything I didn't want to do anyway.'

'You and I know that. They might not see things in the same light.'

'And you were right. Sketching out a plan, starting to take some responsibility for seeing it happen in real life. It's a whole heap better than slouching about feeling sorry for myself, and hard done by.'

'Good show.'

'So, thanks.'

'Hey, missy, you'd better shoot off to bed or you'll never be up for work in the morning, and believe you me, there ain't no way *I'm* rocking up late cos I've had to wait for you. Not after all Parminder's done for the both of us.'

'She's brill. I really like her.'

'Cool, hugely talented, and a gem of a woman to boot.'

Long after she's fallen into the deep sleep of youth, I lie awake worrying. Never mind *her* family, what did I do to mine?

CHAPTER 23

India

MY ROOM'S BEGINNING to look like Mercedes'. Her cast-offs hanging in the wardrobe; piles of her fashion magazines on the bedside table; pin-up posters of size zero models on my walls – Codie Young, Kendall Jenner, Sarah Jessica Parker, oh and Eliana and Luisel Ramos (my little tribute to them). Awesome.

I keep my clothes sorted in size order now. Lets me see the progress I'm making. I've decided, if I manage to stay on the right side of size four by this time next week, I'll get rid of the bigger stuff, take it to a charity shop. On second thoughts I'll maybe keep a couple of things for bloated days. There'll be room then to have different colour sections for jeans, skirts, dresses, in the wardrobe. Make it easier to choose what I'll wear.

Mercedes laughs at me for having everything precisely so, but see, I can't function if my shoes aren't in neat rows, and my pencils all sharpened and lined up end to end, and my books arranged exactly according to height. I feel all churned up inside, can't settle to anything. It's not only me though. The girls who blog on this new website I found, they're the exact same so it's no big deal. Besides, it's one less thing for Mum to go ballistic over!

Mind you, some of these girls are way, way further down the track than me. I mean, they look like corpses. But it's fine, cos Mercedes is going to tell me when enough's enough, like her Ma does for her, so no need to worry on that score. Weird though, sharing stuff like that. There's absolutely no way I'm going to let anyone see *my* body on the internet. For once I agree with Mum. She's banged on about that for years, and she's dead right. I mean, you hear about girls getting groomed by nutters and paedophiles and everything. Even if *they* don't see you, other folk – strangers – can, and heck, *I* don't like seeing my body *myself*, never mind anybody else gawping at me. These girls that take semi-naked selfies and plaster them all over their pages, they must be out of their tiny minds.

Mercedes agrees. She wouldn't either, even though she's pretty near perfect. She's such a pal, Mercedes, says the nicest things, and it's dead helpful to have her to measure myself against. Wearing her cast-offs is an incentive in itself. Reminds me she's ahead of me, in a size smaller. She's where I want to be. But even *she* doesn't get to see me without clothes on.

She reads the poems and stuff I write, though. I was mega-embarrassed at first, but I've kind of got used to it now. And I must admit, it's great to get feedback. Usually she's really positive, but every once in a while she'll home in on something that isn't clear or doesn't ring true and I like that. It's never threatening or bullying or putting you down. I'm dead chuffed that someone like her thinks it's worth reading. 'You understand emotion. You get right *inside* things.'

She's also urging me on with the profile of my dad. I'm getting occasional snippets from my mum and my gran, but I can't *keep* asking or they'll get suspicious.

But then I bump into Kaetlyn O'Leary from down the street. I used to play with her kids – there were millions of them – when I was little, and she's like this born mother, nothing seems to faze her. I used to envy her lot. They got away with murder cos she couldn't watch the whole bunch of them all the time, but d'you know what? they've had it much harder than me. Right from when they were little they've had to muck in and take responsibility for the babies and do chores and live in secondhand stuff and hand-me-downs. Mrs O'Leary's lovely, but she hasn't got time to do the house up or the garden, and Mr O'Leary moonlights as a cab driver to get a bit of extra cash to take care of the tribe, so he's next to never around. Not much time or money left for luxuries.

While she's blethering on, a thought strikes me: she was around at the time my dad went missing. Maybe she'd talk. So I hang around, listening to what her grandkids are up to these days and how Tommy's been in trouble at school and Gilly's turning into the spitting image of our Franny only much wilder.

After a bit she says, 'Here's me rabbitting on as usual. Fancy a cuppa, India?'

I can't stand the smell of tea so I say, could I maybe have a hot water with a slice of lemon. Well, she doesn't have a real lemon but she sploshes in a bit of stuff from a bottle and calls through, 'You'll be needing sugar with that, so you will. Or honey?'

'No, it's fine as it is, thanks.'

'Yuck. Don't know how you can bear it. Fair sets my teeth on edge *thinking* about it.' She grimaces as she puts it in front of me.

It tastes … of nothing in particular. Certainly not sour or bitter.

Maybe because there's a fantastic smell of fresh baking as soon as you walk into the kitchen. Everything's higgeldy piggeldy on all the surfaces and I clench my fists and try to block it out before I sit down at the table. But suddenly it all fades cos there … right in front of me … is this rack full of doughnuts, homemade from scratch, golden brown and totally lathered in sugar. They smell divine. She doesn't even ask if I want one, she plonks the plate down in front of me and there it is. A million calories staring me in the face. No choice. I can't offend the woman, not after all the kindness she's shown us. I *have* to taste it. I take the tinsiest nibble.

Delish.

She's pretty much finished hers already.

This is exactly the kind of occasion when Mercedes says you have to grit your teeth and remember that you can get rid of it straight away once you escape. It'll be my first time. I need to hang on to the threat of not being able to wear my new white jeggings.

Before I know it I've scoffed the lot. It tastes amazing.

'Enjoyed that, huh?' she says, grinning.

'Scrumptious,' I say. 'I'd forgotten what a brilliant cook you are.'

'Help yourself.' She pushes the temptation closer.

'Oh, I couldn't, but thanks. I'm absolutely stuffed.' I launch into a diversion. 'Can I ask you something, Mrs O'Leary?'

'Sure you can, honey. Ask away.'

'You remember when my dad went missing.'

'Uhhuh.'

'What did you think happened?'

'When we first heard? Me, I didn't believe it, so help me. He was such a nice man. We couldn't take it in.'

'Mum hates to talk about that time. It's too painful, but I was only eight and it's all a bit vague in my memory. Besides, I don't know how much I really remember, and how much is what other people have put into my head.'

'Ahh, you poor bairn. You were nothing but an innocent child.'

'So, what do *you* remember?'

'What do I remember? He was a real family man. Worshipped the ground you walked on, so he did. He couldn't ... he *wouldn't* ... not ... *that*!' She crosses herself automatically. '*Victor*? Your daddy? Of all people. Saints preserve us, *never!*'

'What did they tell you had happened?'

'He'd ended it all ... in the sea.'

'So what *did* you think?'

'Sure, we didn't know *what* to think. It didn't make one whit of sense.'

'Now, though, looking back, what d'you think?'

She places one worn hand over mine and gives it a squeeze. 'Listen, dearie, if he was still alive, there's no way in this world he'd be missing you growing up. So, likely he's dead or his memory's gone – doesn't know who he is, doesn't remember he's got a daughter.'

'See, that's what I said. He *could* have lost his memory. Then he'd still sound like himself but he wouldn't remember who he was, or where to find his family. But Mum won't even listen. Not even now, when I *know* he's alive.'

She freezes on the spot. 'You ... *know*?'

I tell her about the voice at King's Cross station.

She stares at me, an odd expression in her eyes. 'St Padraig have mercy! That must have been some shock.'

'So *you* believe me?'

'I ... I'd need to think about it.'

'How d'you mean?'

'Well, let's say, for argument's sake, it *was* your daddy on that platform, there'd have to be some massive great reason for him not coming home now, wouldn't there?'

I'm annoyed to feel tears on my cheeks. 'See, that's what I want to find out. Why? So can you tell me ... Mum and Dad, were they happy? – together, I mean.'

'Much like most couples, I'd say. Sure, they were past the stars-in-their-eyes, lovey-dovey stage, but they jogged along well enough. They weren't *un*happy ... except ...'

'Yes?'

'Except when your daddy went off on his days away with no explanation ... well, none that you'd count. I only knew about those times because your mammy had to ask me to mind you if she had to work late or she had an appointment. It was embarrassing for her, poor lamb. *I* wasn't bothered, sure I wasn't. One more was neither here nor there in this madhouse. And you were good as gold, so you were. But she'd be annoyed with him then for leaving her in the lurch like that. Mind you, I'd have been the same in her shoes. My Dermott, he's always out working so I know I can't rely on him being here; my older kids have to step in. But *your* daddy, that was different. He had regular shifts, working, sleeping – she knew when he should be there. That all changed when he started going off.'

'So why did he?'

She shakes her head. 'Who knows? Not me. But then, I really didn't know him except in passing. God rest his soul, he kept himself much to himself, so he did.'

'Could going off before have anything to do with him vanishing the last time, d'you think?'

'I don't know, sweetie. I simply don't know.'

My hanky's still soggy from last time. It's ineffective now.

She hands me a bundle of fresh tissues and slides another doughnut in front of me. The loose sugar forms a halo around it.

'You tuck into that, my lamb. And don't you forget, there's lots of us who'd do anything for you, so we would. We all reckon you and your mammy, you've had a raw deal. But if I was you, I wouldn't get my hopes up too much about that voice you think you heard. The old mind can play some cruel tricks when it has an idea in its head. I'd say, you concentrate on making your way in this big old world of ours. Make your mammy proud of you.'

'Thank you,' I say shakily. 'And thanks for the doughnuts. They're amazing. I'm totally stuffed, but could I take this one away with me for my mum?' She's reminded me of the need to get home immediately. How fast does the stomach start to absorb sugar?

'Sure you can, honey. Here, take a couple extra for later.'

Please don't let the calories start acting. Please. Please. Please. I'll go without even water tonight if you'll only stop the doughnut from getting into my system.

CHAPTER 24

Tonya

THE INVITATION ARRIVES in a sealed envelope addressed to *The parent/guardian of India Grayson.*

It's to a special parents' evening at India's school. *'Teens, Tolerances and Today.'* The visiting speaker is some psychologist I've never even heard of. *'There will be limited opportunities for one-to-one private conversations after the talk'* it says in small print at the bottom.

I'm intrigued. What brought this on? These reports of young guys who've gone over to Syria to become terrorists, maybe? Or the girls who've run away to become jihadi brides?

Dr Karen Featherstone is middle-aged, in a wheelchair. Would kids confide in her?

She's slick with the technology, I'll grant her that, and her slides are beautifully clear, no doubting what she's talking about. She warms us up with an outline of the physical stages of growth around puberty, freshened up with the accompanying psychological changes. She catalogues the pressures adolescents are under these days – old chestnuts like school attainments, uncertain futures; modern stresses like social media issues, cyberbullying, increasingly sexualised teen culture ... Crumbs, it's a wonder anybody survives to adulthood!

Then she's straight into problems. How to recognise when normal teen behaviours tip towards the pathological – relationships, work/play balance, discipline ... it's a mind-boggling assortment, but she brings it all alive with an example of a youngster she's treated for pretty much everything on her list. Do that many teenagers really go to extremes where they need professional help? She doesn't *sound* as if she's making it up. But ... it's uncomfortable stuff. Even with names changed I don't want to be some kind of voyeur. I wouldn't want her to talk about my India and our family life to all and sundry.

'Ask yourself,' she says, fixing her wide bespectacled gaze on each quarter so every last one of us feels targeted, 'Is my child having black moods that persist for days? Is she exhibiting obsessive behaviours – washing hands, lining things up in rows, ordering vegetables on her dinner plate? Is she becoming secretive, manipulative?'

Now I'm listening.

'Is he always keeping his limbs covered up? Do you *know* how thin he is, if he has self-inflicted injuries? When did you last see him undressed?'

My mind closes down and I rewind through India's habits ...

'... these are all common short-term coping mechanisms for dealing with pressure and managing stress. One in five teenagers in this country report self-harming ...'

She *wouldn't*! ... would she? What good would that do?

'Is your child telling you he/she's having meals with friends? Wearing baggy clothes? Lots of layers? Rushing to the loo immediately after meals? One minute there's food on the plate, next minute you turn round and the plate's cleared ...'

ANOREXIA NERVOSA. Writ large on the screen.

'Anorexia is the deadliest of all psychiatric conditions,' Dr Featherstone says, looking directly at me. 'Between five and twenty percent of patients will die from it.'

I feel physically sick. *Die?*

BULIMIA shrieks at me in bold capital letters.

'Is your teenager suddenly scoffing huge meals, taking food for snacking afterwards? Is she sneaking downstairs at night and raiding the fridge? Or are you finding food going missing, perhaps? Wrappers in odd places? A smell of food in his bedroom? Is he spending a lot of time in the bathroom after meals? Do you smell cleaning agents or bleach after he's been in there?

'Is she doing an excessive amount of exercise? Have you noticed money mysteriously going missing?'

I pull my jacket closer round my shoulders. It's jolly cold in this school hall.

'Contrary to popular opinion, these behaviours are rarely about food. They're much more about control – or the loss of it. Leading to a desperate subconscious attempt to deal with a deep-seated emotional problem.' She launches into another story: 'Hilary'. Father scarpered when the kid was six; older sister ran away aged fifteen; brother abused Hilary. Mother, working all hours to keep money coming in, didn't believe it. A 'toxic childhood', the psychologist calls it. Then the poor kid is bullied at school because she's got victim stamped all over her. Hilary clutches at the only control she feels she has: what she eats. She starves herself and cuts her arms daily.

Would this woman describe India's childhood as 'toxic', I wonder? Her past is littered with loss and cover ups, half truths. Has she secretly been fretting for Victor all these years? Is it all coming to a head in her teens? Should I have taken more notice of her hearing his voice – well, *thinking* she did? She certainly blames me for being low key with the police, them not making him top priority, I know that. But even if he *is* still alive, he's a grown man, he has the right to choose to stay hidden.

I need to spend more time with her. She's away from home far too much with that new friend of hers, and I'm not at all sure Mercedes is a good influence. But when she's at home it's like living with a hedgehog. It's either 'Leave me alone, I'm hibernating.' Or 'I'm scenting the air to see if it's safe to come out, but one false move and I'll be back inside my defences again.' Or prickles fully extended, 'Back off. Keep your distance.' Nothing I do or say is right. She's never ambling along happily beside me these days.

I'm sitting having a coffee when she shuffles into the kitchen next morning.

It's all there. All the layers ... clothes drowning her slight frame. The wrists ... legs ... face. And ... is it my imagination? ... is her hair thinning? It certainly isn't the glorious shining mane it was when I was in charge of the shampoo, but then, loads of teens get skanky greasy heads. And I can't treat her like a baby. That would *absolutely* drive her away. Guaranteed.

Talk, the psychologist said. Stay calm ...

'Indie, stop a minute. I want to tell you what we heard at school yesterday.'

It's a calm, reasonable, dispassionate account ... I think. Unconfrontational.

She picks her nails, doesn't look at me.

'I'm seriously worried about you,' I say evenly. 'You really aren't eating enough, are you?'

'That is so typical! You hear one talk about something and you're an instant expert. You think you see it everywhere. You were the same after that programme about silent cancers, remember? UV rays. Unexplained tummy pains. Moles. All that guff. And when school put out the circular about healthy lunch-boxes. The kids at school made my life hell because you sent me off with all that natural stuff that tasted disgusting and they still had crisps and chocolate bars and everything. You can find statistics to prove *anything* these days. It's just a fad like all the others.'

'No, this isn't just a fad, India. I've been trying to get you to eat more for ages.'

'Don't I know it! You're never off my case.'

'So? It's not only because of the talk yesterday. But I will admit, that's served to reinforce my worry. I am seriously concerned about you. And even you must see, you do seem to be getting terribly thin.'

'I'm fine. It's not healthy to eat too much. Obesity's the real problem nowadays.'

'I know, but you need to have enough fuel on board to maintain your correct weight and function properly. At your age ...'

'I'm fine. There's plenty girls in my year skinnier than me.'

'Please, Indie,' I say, leaning forward to touch her arm. She snatches it away. 'Don't jeopardise your health ... your *life* even. It's never worth risking your *life*, is it?'

'I'm not, but in any case it's *my* life and I absolutely don't want to get fat. Mercedes, she's taller than me, and she weighs less than me, so I don't see why *you're* worrying. *Her* mum doesn't worry about her. She *helps* Mercedes stay slim.'

'Maybe, but I can see with my own eyes, you haven't got enough energy for a girl your age.'

'Okay, I hear you, I hear you.' She gets up and fills a glass with water. 'No need to keep banging on about it. Teenagers sleep – it's what they do. And I can find you plenty of statistics that tell you that!'

I can't resist one last appeal. 'If you don't want to talk to me, will you at least talk to somebody professional? A doctor, a psychologist, a counsellor or whatever? Just to be on the safe side.'

'It'd be a complete waste of time and money. I'm fine. And like I said, you don't see what I pack away at Mercedes' place. And at school. I burn a lot of it off exercising, but exercising's good, builds up muscle strength, keeps the heart and everything in good nick. So, for goodness' sake, change the subject. More to the point, when are you going to do something about finding Dad?'

'I will, I will. I'll ring a few people today, promise.'

She shoots me a disbelieving look and marches off, her skinny frame stiff with the effort.

I'll make an appointment anyway, she needn't know. It'll probably be months yet before anybody can fit us in, if that woman was right yesterday. No need to precipitate a full-scale tantrum at this stage.

My first goodwill gesture is to contact Victor's old nursing pals. It's ages since we spoke.

I'm less tense about it than I would have been yesterday, though. There's a brief report of Maria Davenport in the paper today. Apparently she's been spotted in the London area. '*Definite sighting*,' it says. So that's one murder that *can't* be laid at Victor's door. I didn't realise until today how much that possibility's been haunting me.

I'm suitably apologetic with each nurse: something new's come up; my daughter's upset, blah-de-blah-de-blah. We're simply trying to make sure no stone's been left unturned. Has anything at all occurred to the staff who knew him, since he went missing?

The first three say, no, nothing new, they told the police all they knew at the time. They wish me well. Huh, if they only knew!

The fourth person – name of Kathleen – chats for ages. She sounds really nice. Says lovely things about Victor. 'Brilliant nurse, so caring, kind, went the extra mile for you.' At the end she says, 'Leave it with me. I'll see if anybody remembers anything that might help. Must be agony for you going over all this stuff again and again. I'll get back to you either way.'

It's like a door shutting. I can't go ringing folk now, but I only have her word she'll do anything. Stalemate.

I'm not even thinking about her when the phone rings a couple of days later.

'Hi Tonya. It's me, Kathleen. Kathleen Gregory? Remember? You rang me on Tuesday about Victor?'

'Yes, of course. What's happened?'

'Well ... Listen, Tonya, nothing new's come up, I'm afraid, but ... Look, I'm not sure if this is okay to mention or not, but after you rang, we were having a chat and thinking about Victor and everything, and one of the girls remembered she had a photo of him taken at one of our staff dos. So we wondered ... you know ... if maybe you might like it? It's a lovely happy shot of him and it shows how much he was part of the gang here. He's laughing and looking like he's having a great time and I ... we ... I thought maybe it'd be a nicer kind of picture to hold in your head?'

'When was it taken?' I ask, buying thinking time.

'About a month maybe before he went missing. No pressure though. You don't need to. If it's too painful and everything ...'

'No, I'd love it,' I say, crumpling onto a chair. It's *something* to hang onto. He was apparently happy at work as close to his disappearance as that.

An hour later the email arrives.

I don't recognise him at first. They're five of them in the picture, all wearing ridiculous blonde curly wigs, white feather boas, tiaras, pink dresses, gaudy make-up.

It was a princesses theme, the message reads. *We all went mad. He was a real sport.*

I stare at his face. Yes, totally happy ... in the moment, anyway. Happy with his workmates. So ... what does it all mean?

What horrors were you hiding, Victor? What demons were haunting you? Was it *us* you couldn't live with? Or was it yourself?

India loves the crazy photograph. 'That is so Dad.'

She downloads it onto her mobile.

I've been making a really big effort, cooking all India's favourite foods, complimenting her every time she manages some of her portions. I don't want to do anything to threaten this new truce, but the more time she deigns to spend with me the greater the pressure to talk about Victor. It's a lot harder than I bargained for. Especially talking about the cracks in my marriage. I don't want to tarnish her picture of her beloved father, but neither do I want her thinking I'm always the villain of the piece.

It helps that she vaguely remembers him going off for days together, Kaetlyn O'Leary looking after her.

'For me that felt like desertion,' I say evenly, calmly. 'I was shut out. He had secrets he wouldn't share.'

'Probably wanted some peace. More space to think, be

himself. He was artistic, wasn't he?'

I nod.

'Well, there you are then. He was probably getting away to be creative. *I* like being on my own to write.'

'Well, I must admit that's what I thought too, at first. And I did give him lots of latitude, I really did, I didn't challenge him. But he knew it made me unhappy, insecure.'

Do I sound defensive?

'So? What're you saying?'

'Well, now, I think … Maybe it started off that way. Maybe. But he wouldn't run off *for good* simply because he felt too claustrophobic with us.'

'So why?'

It's a fair question.

Was I right to talk to her openly? Was I right to give her the photo of her father looking happy? I don't know. It's all completely uncharted territory. What I *do* know is she's even more obsessive. Every blessed thing in its place, straight, ordered, checked, double-checked, triple-checked, colour coordinated. And she's even more convinced Victor's still alive.

'That's not the face of a man who's about to kill himself,' she maintains.

She swears she'll find him come hell or high water.

'Even if he *is* alive,' I caution, 'he might be with some other woman, maybe even kids. A new family.'

She doesn't care. He'll still love *her*, she's convinced of that. I wish I could be. I haven't the heart to point out that his behaviour doesn't support that theory.

'I might have brothers and sisters. I always wanted a sister.'

It's like a knife in my heart.

CHAPTER 25

Chris

REA GOT HER FIRST GLIMPSE of a future in the world of theatre today. Wahey! She heard about a team needing an assistant. Well, more like an assistant-assistant to an under-something who's below a deputy-something-or-other-else, lowest of the low in the pecking order, by the look of things. And not even *that*'s certain. She goes for an 'informal chat' a week on Wednesday.

It's not exactly the West End, but The Bush Theatre does sound like a good launching pad. Nourishing. Encouraging. Rea likes that they're passionate about fostering new talent, and that they list as part of their team two resident cats who tweet regularly under their own names, Pirate and Marley!

I have no idea how she'll fare at interview but it has to be worth a shot. Start her off getting some experience of going for jobs at least.

She was cock-a-hoop over Parminder's reference too. Amazingly generous under the circumstances. Parminder may be a saint but she's none too keen on being complicit in harbouring a runaway.

I told her the full story of Rea four days ago. She closed down right in front of my eyes.

'For goodness' sake, Chris! What were you thinking? I have a business to run here. A reputation to maintain. I can't *afford* to get involved in anything underhand or illegal.'

'Ahh. I wasn't ... I'm feeling really bad now,' I say.

'After all you've done for me too.'

'That was different, helping *you*. You're an adult. Your circumstances were completely different.'

'I guess so.'

'What happens if the police get wind of Rea working here? First thing they want to know is: was I aware of who she is? Did I harbour her knowing she was the subject of a police hunt? Why didn't I say something? For crying out loud!'

'I'm really, really sorry. I was only thinking of Rea.'

We aren't fully back to our old easy relationship yet, but at least she hasn't reported Rea. Hopefully this theatre job will lead to something and the girl can move on, we can put it behind us.

Right this minute though, I feel torn in two.

Parminder's been an absolute angel to me. She's given me a job when lots of employers wouldn't. She's given me stacks of opportunities. She's given my career a real hike. And she's been a loyal friend. I owe her big time.

But there's loads more at stake for her this time with Rea. In my case it was a question of being down on my luck, needing to get a job. I wasn't sixteen running away from home, from school, from an academic career, from the police.

On the other hand, from where I'm standing, Rea's a bit like another me. She's the one who needs a leg up now. She needs people to believe in her, give her a chance, and I desperately want to be the one to do that for her. It'd be some miniscule recompense for my past mistakes. Not that one good deed could ever cancel out a betrayal as monumental as mine. Nothing could.

Bless her, Rea tried to defend me, told Parminder what a difference I'd made to her; actually filled in some of what it was like to be homeless and starving when she first went on the run, which is more than she'd shared with me. She laid it on with a trowel how suffocating it felt being in a straitjacket she hated. How being here had given her new hope and opened doors she didn't know existed.

Underneath it all, I think Parminder kind of understands where I was coming from, and she was definitely slightly mollified when I told her about the fortnightly postcards home. There've been no more references to Rea in the papers so hopefully the family have told the police she's safe, no need to continue the hunt for her.

I wasn't prepared for her change of tack.

'Aren't you worried about the risk *you're* taking, Chris?'

I'm not stupid; I know it could easily be misconstrued. Horribly easily.

I shrug. 'It'll be worth it if Rea gets the chance she needs to be happy. Besides what choice did I have? It was take her in, or leave her to fend for herself, homeless, jobless, friendless. In London.'

'You should have told me from the outset.'

'I didn't want to drag you into something that wasn't your choice.'

'But you have anyway.'

'Just as a matter of interest, would you have said yes, if I *had* explained early on?'

'I don't know.'

CHAPTER 26

India

THE STATION'S CROWDED, the noise overwhelming. What a rubbish idea this was. It won't work, even if he's here.

It was Mercedes' suggestion. 'Let's try going to the same platform, at the same time, on the same day of the week, in case it's something he does regularly. I'll come with you. We could go in our holiday week.'

Mum put her foot down, big time, but I harped on and on, and in the end she caved in as long as she came too. She wasn't going to have two vulnerable teenagers alone in London. Full stop.

'You never know who might be there, what might happen. Far too many young girls vanish down there.'

And blow me, Mercedes reckoned she had a point. Huh! It's not *her* mother!

But what could I do? I made Mum promise to stay back, keeping an eye on us but not interfering if we found Dad. The chances of us bumping into him first go were pretty much zero, and I reckon she'll soon get bored.

We get there early – in case he caught an earlier train today. We stay late – in case he was held up. Three hours ... one hundred and eighty minutes ... it feels like forever. Watching, waiting, freezing, running on the spot, and ... all for nothing. No sound, nothing, zilch.

I'm totally scunnered, I can tell you. I *hate* London. I *hate* crowds. Mercedes though, she's so good about the waste of time. 'It was worth a shot. Anything's worth trying.' She's a real trooper. The best. And we do get to see a bit of London

150

on the open-top bus. Like Mum says, we might as well fit in some sightseeing if we're going to pay that much money just to get here.

I do five extra lengths of the pool next evening, take extra laxatives. I have to feel I'm achieving *something*. Failure's so depressing. I'm well into a shed-load more exercises during the night too but then Mum hears me and she reads me the riot act ... yawn, yawn ... tells me to stop it, *immediately*, and get some rest ... yeah, yeah ... she's exhausted even if I'm not, yackety yackety yack yack yack ... yes sir, no sir, three bags full.

Don't bother talking to me about 'exhausted'. There's this hunking great bruise on my backside from the hard chairs at school, and it keeps waking me up when I roll onto it. I'm getting all these little red thread veins in my eyes and sometimes my skin looks kind of grey, which must be cos I'm dead tired. See, once I'm awake everything crowds in on me, screaming and nagging, and my mind just goes crazy. Last night, though, I stuck a pillow underneath my rear end and I slept much better after that, so let's hope that stops me being completely knackered.

Mum was quiet on the way home from London, dozing on the train and everything, and Mercedes and me, we listened to our music and I thought, that wasn't so bad. But then this morning, blow me, she drags up all that old stuff about teenagers who vanish without trace. Not *again*! I lash out. Harder, I guess, because I've been keeping all my resentment and frustration bottled up cos I don't want to distract her from finding Dad.

'You and your everlasting *nagging*! Worry worry worry. Nag nag nag. No wonder Dad couldn't take any more! You drive *me* crazy. I can't *breathe* when you're around. I'm almost *sixteen*, for heaven's sake. *Sixteen*. Old enough to leave school, consent to sex, get married, go on the pill ...'

'How do you know ...?'

'... apply for my own home, change my name, join the army.'

151

Now she's rattled. Serves her right.

'India, it's only because I *care.*'

'Well, don't! I'm old enough to take care of myself.'

'But that's exactly what you're *not* doing,' she flashes back. 'You're destroying your body with this ridiculous dieting.'

'You're never happy, are you? No matter what I do, it's never enough. I promised I'd eat your skanky meals; I've been eating your skanky meals. And this is all the thanks I get.'

'It's not natural to be so obsessed with your weight. You were fine as you were. Now look at you. You're gaunt, Indie, your bones stick out, your legs are like twigs.'

'Well, you're one to talk, I must say. You're such a hypocrite! How about you look in the mirror before you throw stones at me. *You*'re the one who's obsessed. What with your push-up bras, and your control knickers, and your Clairol Nice'n'Easy, and your anti-aging creams and your vitamin supplements. What's that if it's not obsessed with body image, I'd like to know?'

She has the grace to look embarrassed. I quit rapidly while I'm ahead.

Vomiting her chicken casserole up feels like justifiable revenge. I'm so mad at her I do an extra 8 press-ups before even starting my proper cardio workout. My heart rate bombs up to 128 in minutes and I make damn sure it stays there for a whole hour. Afterwards I totally gorge myself on water and green tea (yuck but absolutely *no* cals). My new carbs and cals app is a real godsend.

I wait till I'm at Mercedes' house to send off for energy pills. I read about them on the pro ana site, and she hadn't heard about them. One up to me!

I'll reach my target even if it kills me. I will. *I will. I WILL!* So there.

I wake up to find at least ten pairs of eyes staring down at me.

What? What's happened? Where am I?

Where I am is on a busy pavement in town. I recognise

the Miss Selfridges' sign and the mannequin wearing a pair of leggings and matching jacket I've fancied for ages only they don't have them in my size.

'Oh, thank God.' Mercedes' voice sounds like it's coming through water. 'What a scare you gave me. How're you feeling?'

'I'm fine. What's … what's …'

'You fainted. Just lie still, Indie. The ambulance's on its way.'

'Ambulance? That's ridiculous. I don't need an ambulance.' I scramble to my feet … except … I don't. The world spins and everything closes in on me.

It gets worse.

Strange men in green overalls crouch beside me, their faces fading in and out of focus. They feel my body, listen to my heart, shine a light in my eyes, move my limbs, strap my neck in a collar, tape my head between these ginormous blocks, all the time hammering out questions. I zone out of this nightmare.

Huh! Where are all the queues of folk waiting to be seen in A&E when you need them? We whizz straight in, the ceiling, the glaring lights, hurtling past. I close my eyes against the dizziness. I absolutely *do not want* to vomit in public. Yuck! How gross would that be?

'This is India Grayson, aged fifteen. Collapsed in Hanover Street. Unconscious for about five minutes. Pulse 50, BP 90 on 45, sats normal. Blood glucose 2.9. Shaky, clammy, abrasions on the forehead and on the right hand. Emaciated plus plus. Says she skipped breakfast this morning. And the rest, I'd say.'

'Anyone with her?'

'School friend. In the waiting area. She's contacting the mother.'

At least four different voices are jabbering away, their conversations swirling and overlapping above me. 'Watcha, Roy. How's tricks?' 'Gently does it.' 'Dandy, ta.' 'Went last night. It was ace.' 'Sally, you got the head?' 'Gotcha.' 'Who was in it?' 'Everybody got a piece?' 'Bradley Cooper. He's such a hunk.' 'Right, everybody, let's watch this spine. On my count: one, two, three.'

Between them they slide me effortlessly onto a bed that smells of fresh sheets and disinfectant.

The paramedic pats my leg. 'That's us, then. Bye, India. Good luck.'

'Thank you,' I whisper.

A nurse flicks curtains around me, a second one starts to undress me without even asking my permission. If only I was sixteen, *then* I'd say something. You bet your life I would!

'Let's get you into a gown, sweetheart, and the doctor'll be in to see you in a jiffy.'

They manage to strip me without moving my head, like I was in plaster from head to toe. The replacement gown is exactly like the ones you see on TV medical dramas, shapeless, ties at the back, leaving arms and legs totally exposed. I drag the sheet higher, shivering.

My own clothes are bundled into a plastic bag. I want to leap up and fold them neatly, but I don't dare protest.

'Can I have my sweatshirt? Please. It's cold in here.'

The nurse gives me a 'you're joking' kind of look.

'I'll give you a blanket,' she says, jamming my things into the locker. I visualise everything crushed tightly in that confined space, totally unwearable. A blanket's not the same, but at least I know they aren't rootling through my pockets; they wouldn't understand laxatives, polybags, Listerine, and stuff.

Suddenly I'm alone, those foam blocks limiting what I can see. What are they hiding from me? I lie still listening to the sounds of emergency, desperate to climb up and fasten the curtain hooks that hang open haphazardly around the rail.

CHAPTER 27

India

AFTER WHAT SEEMS like an age a tall man with ginger hair, freckles, and heavy black-rimmed glasses appears, wearing a hideous maroon and purple striped shirt. He looks as if he left university yesterday. Maybe he's only recently started buying his own clothes and nobody told him what suits him. He hooks a chair with his foot and sits down so our eyes are practically on the same level. His hand is poised over a chart. Even his fingers are freckly.

'Hi, India. My name's Angus Cruikshanks. I'm one of the doctors. Can you tell me what happened?'

I try to shrug, but nothing moves except my eyebrows. He waits.

'I dunno.'

'D'you remember anything?'

'One minute I was out shopping with my friend, next minute I'm being dragged in here.'

'Can you tell me where you are?'

'In hospital.'

'And d'you know what day it is?'

'Saturday. I'm fine now. Forgot to have my breakfast, that's all. Can I go now?'

'D'you often skip meals?'

'Nope.'

'Any dizziness?'

'Nope.'

'Feeling sick?'

'Nope,' I lie again.

'Let's have a little feel of your pulse.' His fingers are warm and firm on my wrist, but I hate that he's actually touching my skin, feeling my bones.

He pulls down my eyelids, shines a torch into my pupils.

'Can you raise your right arm for me?'

'And your left.'

'Wiggle your toes.'

'Squeeze my fingers.'

Like some crazy game of *Simon Says*.

'I need to have a little listen to your heart.' It's a statement not a request. He places his stethoscope on my chest. Repositions it. Moves my left breast to get underneath – what's left of it. Thank goodness for small mercies; at least his listening, his touching, are outside the ridiculous gown for this bit.

'Okay, roll her away from me now, please. Go easy, guys.'

Three blue figures appear miraculously. They must have been hovering behind my anchored head all the time without declaring their presence. They roll me like a tree trunk down a slope into a Canadian river. Hands hold me firmly, head, shoulders, legs, my body pressed against a squoogy stomach. Uber gross! And I can't even move away.

Behind me the stethoscope is cold on my bare skin. He seems to 'listen' for ages. I feel his fingers walk down my spine, press lightly on my hip bones, shoulder blades.

'Right, you can roll her back now.'

I clutch the sheet up to my neck, don't look at him.

'When was your last period?'

'Dunno. Can't remember.'

'Any possibility you could be pregnant?'

I shake my head but it doesn't move.

'It's important, India. Look at me, please. Could you be?'

'I *said!* Nope.'

'Right, well, we need to get you X-rayed, young lady, check you didn't do any lasting damage when you banged

156

your head. But before that we'll put a drip up and get some fluids into you, some sugar, stop you fainting on us again, eh?'

Sugar? *Sugar?* Not likely!

'Do I have to? I promise I'll eat something.' I have no control over getting to the bathroom in here.

'Best not to eat anything at the moment, just in case. Don't want you being sick now, do we?'

I don't know about *you*, but ...

'Right, over to you, Jaz, thanks. Get the bloods off. Start IV fluids. Clean up that forehead if you have time before she goes to X-ray. Thanks.'

'Yep. Sure thing.'

It's the squoogy stomach again, but this time she's an arm's length away, carrying a silver tray. She's pretty. Indian, I think.

'I'm just going to pop a wee needle into your arm, pet,' – dragging the curtain half-shut behind her, not climbing up to fix the offending missed hooks at the top. She applies a tourniquet, bends over my right hand, rubs the skin with something pungent that makes me want to retch. 'Wee scratch.' After several minutes she releases the tourniquet. 'Sorry, let's try a different vein.'

'And again, wee scratch,' – bent over the left hand. 'Oh dear. We don't want to give away any of our precious blood today, do we?'

This time she's slapping the crook of my elbow. No pretence at a 'wee scratch' now. I deliberately inhale the alcoholic fumes of her cleaning solution, willing it to knock me out, stop this awful nausea.

'Your veins are hiding.'

The fourth attempt sends blood seeping slowly into her needle. Cannula, she calls it. I want to decline the word: cannula, cannula, cannulam, cannulae, cannulae, cannula.

She sighs. 'We'd better make sure this one well and truly stays in, huh?' Looks like she's got shares in this tape stuff. 'Leave your arm out on top of the covers, India, so we can keep an eye on the site.'

Once I'm back from X-ray Dr Angus reappears. 'Good news, then. We can take that brace off your neck, you'll be pleased to hear. No bones broken. Still feeling dizzy? Sick?'

'Nope.'

'Fair enough. But let us know if you do, right? It's important. We need to keep an eye on you in case you injured your head. Let's get another bottle of Hartmann's up, Jaz, and I'll get Angelina Stockett to come down. Anybody with you, India?'

Mercedes is allowed to come into the cubicle to sit with me while we wait. Thank goodness the neck collar and that hideous foam stuff have gone, although I guess my hair looks a complete shambles after all that rolling and squashing. But first things first.

'Am I glad to see you!' I hiss. 'Get my stuff out of the locker, will you? Fold it properly. They bundled it all up any old how. It'll look like rags.'

It does. But Mercedes soon rectifies that and I'm hoping the weight of everything will iron out some of those creases.

She shuffles closer to the edge of the bed. 'I'm sorry, Indie,' she says, really quietly so no one else can hear.

'What for?' I whisper back.

'I said I'd let you know ... you know, when to stop.' She gestures to my bare arm. I throw the blanket over it, to hang with the nurses, then straighten the edges with my other hand.

Before I can reply, my mother appears. 'What happened?'

She moves in to kiss me. I pull the blanket higher, slide lower down the bed until I'm almost hidden. 'Don't fuss, Mum. I only fainted. It's no big deal. You didn't need to come. You don't need to wait. I'll be fine.' The last thing I need is her going ape.

'Don't be silly. Of course I'll wait, I need to see what the doctors say. How're you feeling?'

'I'm fine. I've got to see some other doctor, then I can go home. I just need to rest for a bit. I'm tired.' I close my eyes and settle as for sleep.

Silence falls between the three of us. I let myself drift. Straight away the nurse is back, peering, calling my name, probing, shining lights, questioning. Seems falling asleep looks too much like unconsciousness in this crazy place.

There's a sound of voices over near the nurses' station. 'I'm here to see ... India ... is it? India Grayson?'

'Cubicle four.'

Next minute a middle-aged woman parts the half-drawn curtain. She's small and plump and has a kind smile. The light blue of her jumper matches the colour of her eyes. Blue's my favourite colour.

'India?'

I nod.

'Hello. I'm Dr Stockett, and I've come to have a wee chat. And you must be Mum – I can see the family likeness.'

Mum nods.

'I'll show you to the waiting area,' the nurse says to Mercedes, escorting her out and closing the curtains. 'There's a drinks machine down the corridor on the right.' I picture my friend swigging back the Diet Coke. Free to leave. Fully clothed. Unquestioned.

It feels secluded inside the curtains but I'm not fooled. I could hear every word the doctors said to the folk beside me, and believe me, you do *not* want to know those kind of details about anybody. I try to whisper my replies to the endless questions.

After ten minutes Dr Stockett speaks directly to my mother. 'I think it might be best if I speak with India alone for a bit, Mrs Grayson, if you don't mind. I'll come and find you when I'm done, and then you and I can have a chat.' Small wonder. Mum contradicted pretty much everything I said. See what I mean? If only I was sixteen, no way would I have her here. No. Way.

Once she's gone it's easier. Dr Stockett lowers her voice too and it's easier to tell the truth.

'Right, India. I'm going to speak to your mum for a

minute, and then we'll come back and talk about where we go from here.'

The panic starts again as soon as I'm alone. What are they talking about? This is *my* body, *my* life. She told me it was all in confidence ... huh, I bet. I straighten up the jug and glass on the locker, turn the edge of the blanket down evenly, put my feet together dead centre in the bed. I try not to look at that damn curtain rail still hanging raggedly.

I never wanted to come to hospital in the first place. Why couldn't they let me be? I'd have been fine after a wee sit down. No need for all this nonsense, all these doctors and everything. And I really *am* feeling okay now. The world's stopped spinning and I'm warm under this blanket. If I didn't have this needle in my arm, I could get into my clothes ... and walk out ... only ... nah, I don't want to *bleed* to death.

I'm testing the water by sitting up, swinging my legs over the side when Dr Stockett reappears. She's alone.

'Ahh, best not get out of bed yet, India. Your blood sugar's low and we don't want you to faint again, do we?'

'Can I go home now?'

'Not today, no. We need to keep you in for a bit and monitor you. You really aren't a well girl, you know. I've had a chat with my colleague who's a specialist in teenagers and he's going to admit you to his ward and we'll take it from there.'

'I only fainted. Heaps of people faint. I forgot to have any breakfast, that's all.'

'It's more than missing one meal, isn't it, India? You haven't been eating enough for your body's needs for a long time. Have you been taking laxatives too?'

Silence.

'Vomiting?'

Silence.

'Exercising excessively?'

I don't see why I should acknowledge any of her questions. She can think what she likes. As long as I get out of here.

'You're dangerously underweight, and I mean

dangerously. It's affecting your whole body. Your faint today, that was nature's way of telling you you have to stop. We're going to admit you and help you get back to a more normal pattern of eating. Build up your strength and stamina. So you can enjoy life again.'

I glare at her. How *dare* she? Honest to God. Of *course* she thinks *I'm* thin. *Look* at her! Thighs bulging over the edge of the seat, spare tyres for all to see, feet puffing over the front of her shoes. Gross! Grosser than gross. Mega mega gross. I'd rather be *dead* than look like that.

That's the last time I tell anyone anything 'in confidence'. I'll go along with their stupid ideas enough to get me out of here, but then I'll do what I jolly well like. I'll soon be sixteen and there isn't a thing they or my mum can do then. Just you wait and see.

CHAPTER 28

India

CHILD AND ADOLESCENT MENTAL HEALTH it says over the door. *Mental?* Heck! Good job the guys at school don't know I've ended up in a loony place.

But at least this ward's full of people my own age. Not like A&E. I couldn't, I absolutely could *NOT* bear to lie there listening to old fogies coughing and spluttering and snoring and shouting into their phones a minute longer. False teeth, hearing aids, lying around on the lockers. I'd go absolutely totally stark staring mad.

As it is, there's far too much time to think, especially during the night. The nurses try. They keep tiptoeing in: 'Can I get you a drink?' 'Want to chat?' 'Need an extra pillow?' It's nice, but it makes me cry cos it struck me, this is what my *dad* did! Did the patients give him a hard time, too? It wasn't *his* fault; he was only trying to help. No point in taking it out on the nurses. No, I blame the doctors ... well no, the ambulance men ... no, *Mercedes*. Yes. It was *her* fault for calling them in the first place. She should have had some patience, let me come to. I'd have been fine. *She* should know that ...

In the daytime there's not much peace, you can't simply loll about listening to your music in peace in here. No, sir! You have to *be somewhere, do something, eat this, eat that, be weighed*. Like a blinking army boot camp with stupid idiotic rules.

Then there's all these kids with 'problems' – it's enough

to *drive* you mad if you aren't already. They're so *miserable*. Depressed. Grumpy. Moody. Obsessed. Sneaky. Mean. Carbon copies of each other. How pathetic is that?

And the nurses *aren't* stupid, not like this girl Amelia says. She's been in before, reckons she knows how to cheat and pretend so she gets out. No intention of changing her ways. Nah, I reckon they'd know if you were pulling a fast one. You can see them watching people. They even stand guard when you're in the toilet! I ask you!

I *hate* being watched; spend a lot of time under the covers. But there in the dark, I can't help thinking about Dad and how I can't search for him while I'm stuck in here, and that makes me cry again, and that makes the nurses pressure me to talk about what's upsetting me, and that makes me cry more and think of Dad and Mum and what it's been like at home since ...

I *hate* them knowing I've been crying.

I *hate* being monitored like a wee kid. Feels like they don't trust you ... hmmm. Why would they?

I *hate* not being able to hide in my own room.

I *hate* having to be polite all the time. I'm screaming on the inside, but so far at any rate, I haven't been rude to the staff ... well, not exactly *outright* rude anyway. Or to the other patients, although I could slap some of them. Stupid immature morons.

I *hate* not being able to throw stuff or hit things or have my music blaring or anything. Everything gets bottled up and I want to *explode*! I guess that's why Mum got it all guns blazing when she visited.

Straight away she starts up again, criticising, moaning on ... telling me what it's going to be like in future ... *she*'ll be in charge this time ...

'It's all your fault anyway,' I snap.

'Me? How is it *my* fault?'

'You were the one who gave me these lousy genes. If you'd been like Mercedes' mum, if you'd understood, if you'd supported me like she supports Mercedes, none of this would have happened.'

'Indie, you're my whole world. Everything I've done, I've done for you. And I've done my absolute utmost to stop this happening. But you wouldn't listen.'

I flounce away from her, pull the covers over my head, refuse to even look at her. When I hear her go it hits me: I didn't say a single nice thing the whole time she was here. That sucks. And I wonder if she'll cry in bed tonight too.

I *have* to listen to the staff though.

First it's this doctor, Dr Ahmed, who reckons he's in charge of my care (as if!). He's lovely actually, like a friendly granddad. I like the way he says my name, *In*dia, all slow and kind of you're-special. But of course I know it's a game. He thinks he can win me over to his side, get me to do what he wants instead of what I want. No way am I going to fall for that pile of pants. Besides this is what he's *paid* to do. I bet he forgets all about me the minute he walks out of this ward. Will he be there to help me when I get home? Will he heck! Nah! None of them will be.

'You want us to treat you like an adult, India, a responsible adult? Then we need you to act like one. Okay?'

I nod.

'You and I, we're going to work together as a team, okay?'

Another nod.

'I'll do everything in my power to help you get well again, but I need you to work with me, okay?'

Well, nobody's going to sit there and say no are they? Stands to reason. Everybody wants out.

His first task, he says, is to start me on a programme of 'refeeding', build me up, make me physically strong and well again. Everything will feel better once I'm more robust. Aye right. Makes me feel ill just thinking about it.

I go inside my head, away from the watching eyes; imagine what it would be like to hoodwink all these people, get myself out as quickly as possible. *Could* I hide stuff in hems and pockets, drink a ton of water, hold pills in my cheeks ... and all the rest? I know how to pretend. I've had tons of practice.

Thank goodness for Mercedes. She was allowed in for ten minutes today; I guess because she told them she was bringing in schoolwork so I wouldn't fall behind.

Only she was grinning so much I could tell straight away it wasn't any old assignments. You'll never guess what she *actually* had in her bag, though.

A letter, that's what!

A letter from a women's magazine. She only went and sent in one of my scribbles to some short story writing competition! And they want to print it! Say they'll pay me £50. *50 quid?* That'll go a fair way towards one of those white ribbed tops from Harvey Nicks that I've been hankering after like for ever. Ever since Mercedes got one anyway.

'I *told* you you were good,' she crows.

'Wow!' I can't stop reading the letter, over and over.

'This is the beginning of a new life, Indie. You've absolutely *got* to crack this stuff' – her sweeping gesture takes in my drip, the vomit bowl, the ward – 'and get out there, blow them away with your stories. And your poems. This is only the start. You've got to believe in yourself. So, the sooner you get out of here the better, yeah?'

'Believe me, nobody wants me out of this lousy dump faster than me! I *hate* it. Hate everything about it. I never wanted to come in in the first place.' I glare at her.

'I know, but you were ill. Everything went too far. And I'm sorry I didn't see that. You've got to take better care of yourself. Value yourself. You're smart, Indie. You can do it. All you have to do is put on some weight and get out, and then we can show everybody how super-talented you are. I'll help you every step of the way. Promise. I could be your agent, huh?' she giggles.

'But you're slimmer than me. How come you can do it and I can't?'

'I eat, right? I lose some of it too, but I'm not starving myself. And my bone structure's different from yours. It's not better. It's different.'

'Well, I just wish I was you.'

'Now you're being ridiculous. Course you don't! You're the one with the brains, the imagination. You're ... *artistic*! I have no imagination whatever. *You* can reach out and touch people.' She lets her voice sink into the depths. '*You* could be *famous*. Me, I'm an airhead. Fashion's my limit. I'll never be anything except some guy's trophy wife, like Ma.'

'Time's up.' The nurse glares at Mercedes. 'Ten minutes, we said.'

She leans close and hisses, 'Write *her* into a poem. Write stuff about this whole crazy madhouse. It'd be a blast!' before scuttling out without even a backward look. I'm left with only the letter to reassure me this wasn't all a dream. And the dent in the bedclothes made by my friend. I smooth it out gently, let my hand rest there.

When the drip comes down they wheel in some *counsellor* woman. Marianna something or other, something unpronounceable. I hate, *hate, HATE* her voice! And all her stupid jargon. And her fat legs. And her unblinking eyes. Wanting to know how I feel about everything ... what I'm thinking ... why I think that way. About my childhood, even! ... my mum ... my dad ... As if I'm going to puke my soul up for some complete *stranger*. I don't even tell *Mercedes* that stuff!

Okay, I've got no choice, I *have* to listen, but that doesn't mean I'll *answer*. No way!

'The first step is to understand yourself,' she says in that voice they use. 'And I'm here to help you do exactly that; look at why you're doing what you're doing. Remember I'm on your side, dear, and we can't start putting things right until we've got to the bottom of what went wrong for you.'

You're joking me! I know perfectly well why I'm doing it, thank you very much. I understand absolutely. I want to be slim and pretty, full stop. What's wrong with that? And you needn't think for one second you're going to get one over on me, missus, with your promises and offers, and that's a fact. I'll do whatever it takes to get out of this madhouse, but if you think I'm going to start putting on fat, you've got another think coming. No chance in hell! Not after all I've done to get to this point.

Even when she spoke to my mum she used the same smarmy tone: 'Eating disorders are a cultural phenomenon, a social problem, and an emotional condition.' What a load of bull! What does it even *mean*, anyway? I can see Mum hasn't a clue what she's on about either. Besides I don't have a 'disorder'. I'm an ordinary teenager who doesn't want to be totally gross. Nothing disordered about that. They're always banging on about obesity being the modern epidemic in young folk, and then the minute somebody takes responsibility for *not* getting obese, they come barrelling in with all this guff! Huh! Give me strength!

HAZEL MCHAFFIE

CHAPTER 29

Tonya

I KEEP EVERYTHING bottled up until I'm sitting in Kaetlyn's kitchen.

Every surface is littered with boxes and pans and dishes and food, dirty washing lies in two heaps on the floor, their new puppy has just peed against the back door, discarded slippers and shoes divorced from their partners lie forlornly in the path of the seeping liquid. Kaetlyn's hair looks as if it hasn't seen a brush since last week, she's still in her dressing gown, stained and missing a button, but she welcomes me in as if she's delighted to see me. I so envy her this unflappable nature.

She has to push used breakfast dishes out of the way to make room for my coffee mug. It's instant, too much milk, too little coffee, but I don't care this morning. As she eases herself down onto the chair alongside me she lets out a contented sigh.

'Any excuse to take the weight off me feet.' She feigns ecstasy.

I half smile.

'Now what brings you here at this hour, lass? Sure, you haven't had any rest at all this night, by the looks of you.'

That's the thing about kindness, it sneaks past your control.

She hands me a full box of tissues, pulls the wastepaper bin closer, and simply waits till I can speak. Sitting there, holding me, when she must have three miles of jobs on her list.

'I miss him so much,' I blubber.

'Who?'

'Victor.'

'Ahh. Course you do, petal. Sure you do.'

'He'd know what to do with India. He'd stay calm.'

'Hey, listen to me, Tonya Grayson. Give yourself a break, will you? It's not easy being a single parent at the best of times, and you've done all right. She's a good kid.'

'She wouldn't have got into this state in the first place if he'd been around. He always knew how to handle her.'

'What state? What's happened?'

I tell her about the faint, the admission to hospital.

'Ach, she'll be home in no time, sure she will.'

'But that's precisely what I'm afraid of!'

I tell her about the anorexia.

She looks perplexed. 'You sure about that? I mean, I don't want to tell tales out of school or anything, but she was here not so long ago, tucking into a doughnut fresh out the fryer, so she was. I watched her with me own eyes.'

I tell her about the vomiting.

She shakes her head, for once lost for words.

'And now the nurses tell me she's threatening to discharge herself. In her state! It'll *kill* her!'

'Saints have mercy!' She crosses herself swiftly.

'I know. It's so *not* the right thing to do. She needs help. But I'm not sure they can stop her, once she's made up her mind. They reckon she's "competent" to decide for herself.'

'She's a *kid*!'

'Exactly. But see, the thing is, she isn't at death's door or at risk of "significant harm or deterioration", now. Apparently, if she was, they could section her under the Mental Health Act. Compulsory detention, they call it.'

'But she's only a *kid*!'

'That's not the point. Doesn't matter what age you are, if you're mentally ill and that's affecting your ability to make good decisions about your health, they have a responsibility – a *duty* even – to treat you, *make* you have the right treatment.

169

But if she isn't as bad as that, they might *have* to let her out and just monitor her.'

'Seems crazy logic to me.'

'I know! But they say she's old enough to understand what she's doing, and take some responsibility for her own actions.'

'Deliberately make herself worse, you mean?'

'Exactly! Perverse, isn't it? She's *"not thin enough"* to be kept in. On some kind of index or other. That's like saying, "Your tumour's not big enough yet. Wait until it's strangling you then we'll treat you." Imagine telling a kid who already looks like a skeleton, "You aren't thin enough yet." They *aren't* saying that, of course, they're telling her she must eat more, but well ...'

A loose curl flops over her eye; she rams a kirby grip in to secure it.

'That's crazy! So *is* she coming home then?'

I nod.

'But, honestly, Kaetlyn, I don't think I *can* handle her any more. She's completely out of control. She won't even *talk* to me, now! And I know she's still absolutely determined to lose more weight. What can I do? I've tried everything I know.'

I sob my way through six more tissues.

'They say it goes way back. Starts with irrational thoughts and beliefs,' I mumble.

'Sorry, you've lost me.'

'These girls who stop eating, they think, if I can only lose x pounds, so-and-so will like me. Or, it's my fault my dad left home; he didn't love me because I'm so fat. Stuff like that.'

'That's sick. But it's not India, sure it's not. She *knew* her daddy loved her. He was besotted with her.'

So Kaetlyn noticed too. Did she ever suspect ...? I push the thoughts aside.

'Sometimes it's a form of bargaining with God. I'll stop having puddings if you let my dad come back home.'

She lets slip a soft expletive. I've never ever heard

Kaetlyn actually swear before, beyond invoking her saints. 'The poor darlin'.'

'Well, we don't know if that *is* what she was thinking. At least, not *consciously* anyway, but you know, that's the sort of example they gave me. At least they're *trying* to get to the bottom of it for India.'

'So, d'they think it's all to do with Victor disappearing?'

'They think that's probably got *something* to do with it. But I don't know, Kaet. It all happened ages ago. She wasn't even eight. I'm wondering ... did she maybe see or hear something that her immature brain didn't really understand? Did she suppress it and now it's coming out in her starving herself?'

Kaetlyn's clearly as mystified as I was when the doctor tried to explain it all to me.

'Only, the thing is, India's pointblank refusing to open up to them. Keeps saying the past's the past, all she wants is to get out of there. I'm starting to wonder ... is someone maybe threatening her? "Tell, and I'll burn your house down. Or kill you. Or kill your mother." But if she *won't* talk, they can't find out the cause of what they call her "unhealthy patterns", and that's not good. We're no further forward. She'll go on slowly killing *herself*.'

Her mouth twists in sympathy.

'And even if they *do* get to the bottom of her anxieties, will she even listen to them? As a first step, the doctor said, she needs to recognise, acknowledge for herself, how these erroneous beliefs are contributing to her problem. And *then* she needs to break away from the old way of doing things, start developing a healthier pattern. Everybody – nurses, doctors, counsellors – they all say it's a long haul, they usually keep relapsing, have to be readmitted. It's really, really tough for the patient and the whole family. And in our case that's only me!'

'Strong brave you.'

'But I'm *not*, Kaetlyn, I'm really not. I'm at my wits end. There're times when I could ... I *do* lose my temper with her. She simply defies me. *Outright*. Or she ignores me completely. I get so *mad* I could ... *throttle* her! She's so *stubborn*. I can *see* she's starving herself and ... I feel so *powerless*. I've tried everything I can think of – bribing her, supporting her, bullying her, punishing her, and she's still hell bent on losing even more weight. You should see her! She's nothing but skin and bone already.'

I blow my nose vigorously.

'What's more, I don't believe a word she says. She only goes through the motions to get me off her back. But underneath she has absolutely no intention of doing the right thing. I know that now. She's *impossible*. I've been too lenient for far too long, given her the benefit of the doubt. I have to accept she's devious, manipulative, secretive. A lying, cheating, scheming little *devil*. And it's *all ... my ... fault*. Victor would have known how to keep her on the straight and narrow. He was always closer to her than I was.'

CHAPTER 30

Tonya

I OPEN THE NEWSPAPER automatically, my mind still with our problems, a leaden weight of responsibility in my chest.

The headline jumps out at me: *MISSING MARIA SEEN IN WEST END*.

Thank you, God. Oh, thank you … and the whole host of Kaetlyn's saints!

The picture's grainy but it certainly *looks* like the same girl. Same curly hair – different colour maybe? Looks lighter but that could be the camera, same oval face, but looking older, dressed up, laughing.

What must her parents be going through? Holding their breath, willing it to be true. They'll be clutching at any germ of hope, surely, whatever happened to drive her away.

I let my own breath out slowly, relief flooding my body. This is one missing girl Victor *can't* be responsible for. She's alive. She's *alive!*

I read the article slowly. Apparently she was recognised by a couple leaving the Queen's Theatre in Shaftesbury Avenue. They'd been to see *Les Misérables*. The guy had the presence of mind to snap Maria on his iPad by way of evidence. She seemed fine, they said, she was with a middle-aged female, also caught on camera in profile. *About five ten or eleven*, it says, *long reddish brown hair, very smart, elegant even, wearing a black chiffon dress and sequined jacket*. Apparently the two women vanished in the crowd afterwards but the police have been informed. Will they follow it up, I wonder? Would they *have* to? Isn't she old

173

enough to make up her own mind where she goes, who she's with? After all she's sixteen. My India's younger and she's considered old enough to defy medical advice; competent enough to decide for herself to leave the security of the hospital, do her best to kill herself.

Looks like Maria and her 'friend' were having a night out with style. A *'red silky dress and a black fluffy bolero-type jacket'* is hardly the clothing you'd expect to find on a runaway in hiding, huh?

I wonder where they went? Will *anybody* follow up this lead? If it was my India ... to hang with rights and being sixteen, I'd be on the next train to London. I'd be on the backs of the police morning, noon and night.

My mind roams over the possibilities: never tracking her down ... finding her ... losing her again. How cruel would that be? The heartbreak ... the terrible revelations ... the recriminations ... the guilt ... the final severance ...

Hopefully this woman is a kindly person who won't harm her. There's no hint of coercion in this shot at least. And tickets for London shows don't come cheap, so presumably Maria's fallen in with a benevolent older soul with an empty nest and too much money.

The sound of footsteps on the stairs makes me slap a tablemat over the article. It covers most of the writing, only half of the picture. It'll do. Last thing I want is India getting ideas. At least if she's here under my roof I know she's still alive, getting *some* food into her. And Dr Ahmed's not far away. She's on their radar now. I only have to make one phone call and ...

She's lost inside a massively oversized forest green fisherman's sweater. Victor's. It still freaks me out when she does that. Even her hands are hidden. *When did you last check your teenager's limbs?* Short of physical restraint there's no way I can get near her arms. She could be slashed on all four limbs for all I know.

My own hands spontaneously clench into fists, my stomach contracts, as I imagine the feeling of a blade slicing through my flesh. How *can* they?

174

I get up and walk to the sink, go through the motions of filling the kettle, although I know she'll refuse all offers of a hot drink. But we're pretending to be a normal family.

'What d'you fancy for lunch? Mushroom stir fry?' Totally bland, no pressure. It used to be a favourite back in the days when we were a fully functioning family.

She shrugs. 'Rather have roasted tomatoes. I'll do it myself. Is there any garlic?'

'In the pot behind the sink.'

'Okay. I'll do my own then.' No sparkle, no energy, no warmth.

I must admit her vegetable dishes smell pretty good but there can't be many calories in any of them. One squirt of olive oil from the spray and that's it. But of course, that's the point.

It's new, this vegan business, just since she got out of hospital. She's got all the arguments off pat too, *and* she's downloaded recipes from the net. But at least I see her making the stuff and eating it, so I know she's getting *some* nourishment at some point in the day. Seems better than forcing her to add protein and finding it in the bin or up her sleeve or in her bedroom. But how long can the body live on veggies alone? We had a kiddie in our nursery once whose mum was a strict vegan, but he got pulses, grains, seeds as well. And after the age of five she said she'd give him nuts too.

I take my time with the kettle, long enough to adopt a calm and indifferent expression. Like they advise.

I hear the legs of the chair grate on the tiled floor as she drags it closer to the table. The harsh sound sends shivers down my spine, sets my teeth on edge. I always wanted to change the flooring in here, but Victor said it was top quality stone, we couldn't afford anything comparable. Me, I'd settle for cheap any day to avoid that particular Chinese torture.

'How about a hot Marmite?'

'No, thanks. Nothing.'

Well, at least I don't get 'I've just stuffed myself at Mercedes' place' now. The Atkinson-Baker house is off limits, although Mercedes is allowed to come here once a week on Fridays, after school, to keep India up to date. It was the hospital that laid down the rules for me: *make sure they stay downstairs where you can see them.* Besides, I'm pretty sure the threat of re-admission to hospital is still enough to ensure compliance at the moment. Mercedes at least is far too scared by all that's happened to be complicit in any of India's shenanigans.

I'm annoyed to find my hand's trembling as I take a mug from the cupboard. I stop, change hands, try again.

'Mum ...!' It's sudden, sharp.

'I'm fine, just cold. I'll be fine.'

'No, Mum ... look!' It's the old India's voice, urgent, energised.

I put down the kettle and walk over to the table.

She hasn't moved the placemat, her skeletal finger is on the photo, obscuring part of the picture.

'Who does that remind you of?'

I move to stand behind her, peer at the picture. 'Let me get my glasses.'

Suddenly the woman with Maria comes into sharper relief ... well, the face, which is all India has left uncovered.

I freeze.

It can't be.

Without the soft drape of hair, the glamorous frock, she could be ...

'It is!' India yells. 'It has to be. It's *Aunty Marjorie*! Like she was in that old photo of Dad's family. You know, in the green album.'

The world seems to fade in and out. If this is my husband's sister, what is she doing associating with a runaway teenager? I lost touch with her after Victor left. We were never close and I felt she blamed me.

All the old horrors come crashing back into my thoughts. What if ... what if Marjorie is in cahoots with Victor? What if Maria Davenport is their next victim?

'Why would *she* be going to the theatre with a missing teenager?' I say slowly.

'Ring her! Ring her!'

'I can't. I have no idea where she's gone. She moved away from Newcastle years ago.'

'If *she's* in London, and *Dad's* in London, maybe she knows where he is.' Under other circumstances I'd welcome this animation.

'But ...' I hesitate. 'What if he has his own reasons for staying hidden?'

'Like what?'

'Something ... bad? Something he's ... done?'

'Meaning?' The single word is loaded with aggression. Her eyes meet mine for the first time in days. They're truly alive now, with anger!

'Because ...' I so don't want to douse the flames of real feeling. 'Maybe ... he's deliberately hiding from the police?'

She stares at me wide-eyed and scornful. 'What *are* you on about? This is *Dad* we're talking about!'

'Why did he run away in the first place, then?'

'*I* don't know. You said *you* didn't know. Was that a lie? *Do* you know?'

I cringe from the blatant accusation in her glare.

'No, I don't know for sure ... but I ... I have my suspicions.'

She's absolutely still, waiting.

Haltingly I tell her about the coincidences, the dates he was absent, the dates the teenagers went missing, the panties I found.

She's frozen in her seat.

I didn't mean to scare her rigid. I was only trying to ...

'I ... can't ... *believe* you'd even *think* like that – for even one *second*,' she hisses. 'He *wouldn't!* He absolutely wouldn't. You've got a totally evil mind. He *wouldn't!*' And suddenly she's sobbing uncontrollably.

I move to take her in my arms but she beats me off.

'Don't *touch* me! Don't come anywhere *near* me. I can't *believe* it would even enter your head. You're sick, you know that? Sick. Sick. *Sick!*'

'India. Dad changed. Something happened. He became

177

distant even when he was with us. And then ... he left and didn't come back. Why, if he had nothing to hide? And now this – you think you hear him down in London at exactly the same time as another teenager disappears. Then out of the blue we see this picture of the missing girl with Dad's sister? It's too much of a coincidence.'

'They must be helping her, looking after her. That's what it'll be, something like that.'

'We absolutely *have* to go to the police this time. We *have* to, before it's too late. We've got no choice. Don't you see? We have to stop him doing anything to harm her.'

'Stop it! *Stop it!* You aren't *listening.* This is *Dad* you're talking about! He wouldn't hurt *anybody.* He absolutely *wouldn't.* There must be some perfectly good explanation. There *must!*'

'I didn't want to believe it either, darling. That's why I didn't tell the police about my suspicions before. That's all they were, suspicions and coincidences. But this man isn't the Dad you remember. Maybe he's sick, mentally ill, not responsible for his actions. Maybe something tipped him over the edge. Maybe he's temporarily insane. I don't know. But *something*'s definitely not right.'

'There must be some perfectly innocent explanation. There *must.*'

'Fair enough. So, if that's the case, it won't do any harm to go to the police now, will it? They can find him and he can explain it all. Imagine if that was *you* with some stranger, and their family were suspicious and did absolutely nothing, and then something bad happened ... It doesn't bear thinking about. I'd never forgive myself. No, we don't have a choice; we *have* to report it. And warn them.'

'About what?'

'To go carefully. Not scare him into doing anything worse.'

'I warn you ... you put that garbage into their heads and I'll *never* forgive you. Never, *ever.*'

'Well, here's a compromise. How about I phone Heather? You know, that nice profiler who interviewed me before. Ask her what I should do. In confidence.'

I dial the number seven times before I summon up the courage to let it ring.

'Tonya, hi. How are you? How can I help you?' Friendly, professional.

I burble something vague about confidences, needing advice.

Her voice is gentle, encouraging.

I choke on disjointed words, buying thinking time.

She uses all her skills, but it's no use. The words won't come. I can't ... I *can't* ...

She must be tearing her hair out. Probably has a million things she ought to be doing.

I try again, my hands shaking so much I need both to hold the phone against my ear.

In the end she interrupts the silence.

'Tonya, can I make a suggestion? How about you ring off now, take your time, think about exactly what you want to tell me, maybe write it down, ring back when you're ready. Or would you rather come here and talk face to face?'

'No! No, I *can't*!'

'Okay, what about telling me why this is so difficult for you.'

I blurt it out.

'Because I can't bear to think ...'

She gives me plenty of time.

'Think what, Tonya? What can't you bear to think?'

'That that girl might be in danger.'

'What girl?'

'Maria Davenport.'

'You know something about Maria Davenport?' Her tone's changed. I can feel her tension.

'No. Maybe. I don't know. She could be ...

A long pause.

'She could be what?'

'Victor might be ... involved.'

'With Maria?'

179

'Maybe.'

'What makes you think that, Tonya?'

She coaxes the story out of me piece by agonising piece.

'And you never mentioned this to the police before?' Her voice is even, expressionless.

'I couldn't! I'm only telling you ... in confidence ... because this other girl has gone missing and ... what if ...? What should I *do*?' It ends in a wail.

I should have known this wasn't a confidence someone in Heather's position could ignore.

I'm summoned back to the station.

This time the police really are listening. And suspicious. And increasingly senior. *Why didn't you ...? What makes you think ...? Can you be sure ...? Why should we believe ...?* But my story doesn't change. It's fact not fiction.

I can't blame them for being short ... and riled ... and sarcastic ... and scornful. Concealing facts? Destroying vital evidence? Keeping quiet? Protecting my daughter's feelings rather than caring about the life of somebody else's daughter? I'd be rattled too in their shoes. How self-centred can you be?

'Well, we can't change that. At least you've come forward now,' is as kind as it gets.

I'm shell-shocked by the time I get home, not in any fit state to see the headline on the lunchtime news. But there it is. They haven't hung around. There's the shadowy picture of the Marjorie-look-alike with the Maria-look-alike. Anyone who knows the whereabouts of either of these people is asked to call a London number or get in touch with their local police. There is reason to believe Maria might be in danger.

Ahhh. Nothing about from whom. Nothing about Victor. Nothing about us. Nothing about those other missing girls.

Small mercies.

CHAPTER 31

Chris

THESE FLORAL ARRANGEMENTS are exquisite. Eryngium's one of my favourites, perfect with green spider chrysanths, Polar Star white roses, eucalyptus, looped bear grass. I've already requisitioned this combination for my own coffin, on one of Parminder's fabulous twisted willow frames.

Somebody's due to collect this order at 10am, so I'm keeping one eye on the clock and the other on the shop floor. Feels good, being trusted, in charge, while Parminder pops out to the market for some extra foliage – apparently a last-minute request for church flowers came in late yesterday.

Her mushrooming reputation means I'm getting more and more experience in the back room, and I love it, love it, love it! All made possible because my godsend Rea's taken on the humdrum tasks. She *seems* content, dreaming of the stage while she sweeps, but I'm personally hoping Parminder will let her dabble a bit in the creative stuff too, give her more incentive to stay. I've given her my floristry books to browse through at home. Anything to keep her here with me. I'm not pushing it, though, we both owe Parminder too much already, and although she doesn't say it, I know she's still worried about having Rea in her employ.

The woman who appears rather breathlessly at 10.05 is not the delivery boy I expected. She's enviably slim, twenties, impeccably groomed in a cream suit, immaculate nails too. Eat your heart out.

'Ahh, you'd better let us carry this lot out for you,' I say with a smile.

Her estate car looks as if it's come straight from a garage valeting.

'Hang on a sec, I'll get some protection for your boot.'

I line it with plastic sheeting, lay old newspaper and bubble wrap on that to hold the boxes securely.

'Sorry, but I'm in a real rush ...' she grimaces, glancing at her watch. 'Can I start carrying ...?'

'No need. I'll get our assistant to help load.' I whip inside and get Rea to carry the boxes of flowers out of the shop while I shoehorn them securely into the limited space. It's a tight fit but the cream suit remains unblemished.

The customer's sufficiently grateful to offer a tip, but we both decline. 'All part of the service.'

Parminder returns with the fresh foliage and I pitch in immediately sorting the ruscus and eucalyptus into different lengths, stripping the lower leaves. It's beautifully fresh. Rea is busy replacing ribbons and cellophane in the dispensers, stacking the compliments cards, humming under her breath. I love to see her so relaxed and happy.

I'm almost finished when Parminder puts her head round the doorway.

'Chris ...', her voice sounds odd, 'the police want a word with ...'

They're inside the backroom before she's finished speaking, too quickly for me to usher Rea out of sight.

'Hello, Maria.' The female voice is gentle, unthreatening. 'How're you?'

'Fine,' she says, back to truculent.

'I think we need to have a chat, don't you?'

'Don't see why.'

'Where are you living now?'

'With her,' she gesticulates in my direction, not looking at me. 'I'm all right.'

'Who's "her"?'

She nods at me this time. 'Ms Taylor.'

'And how did you two meet?'

She glances across at me as if for confirmation. 'She's a

friend of the family.'

Damn.

The police officer crouches so she's lower than Rea, less threatening. Her voice drops to a confidential level, 'Are you really all right, Maria? Has anybody hurt you? Done anything you don't like?'

She shakes her head vigorously.

The police officer stands again, looking directly at me. 'I think we'd better take this down to the station, don't you, ma'am?'

'Is that really necessary?' I ask. 'She's fine. We like having her about the place. She's safe. She's happy.' And it's exactly what I personally dreaded.

'I'm not going back,' Maria hisses.

'Okay, okay, but we do need to talk to you. Check things out. Here's not the right place.'

'I'm sorry to leave you in the lurch, Parminder,' I say. 'I've only just started on the Crawford order.'

'Don't you worry about that,' she mutters. 'You concentrate on your story.'

'I'll do my level best to keep you out of this.'

She looks unconvinced.

As I leave, the sight of her grim face goes with me. I'll never forgive myself if I've harmed her business.

It's the first time I've ever set foot in such a place. I expect to be thrown into a cell, but no, it's remarkably civilised. There's not much more than a table and chairs in the rather fusty interview room but at least it's warm and dry, no evil smells or harrowing groans or blood-curdling screams.

I sit there for twenty-three minutes and fifty-one seconds, nothing to do but watch the clunky hands jerking round the dial on the wall in front of me. The clock looks ridiculously incongruous, about three times the size it needs to be. Maybe they picked it up in the flea market for a pound. Maybe it came out of stolen property.

Presumably they're taking Rea's statement first. Good. Hopefully they'll let her get back to the shop after that.

'Interview commencing at 13.35. Present Sergeant Alan Whitecroft, PC Sadie Frost and ... can you say your name for the tape, please.'

'Chris Taylor.'

'You heard Maria say – back there in the shop – you're a friend of the family. Is that true?'

'No.'

'Why would she say it then?'

'Because I implied I knew her when we met. So it was true as far as she's concerned.'

'Where *did* you meet, truthfully?'

'At a car boot sale in the parking place off South Gloucester Street.'

'So why did you say ... ahh, *imply* you knew her?'

'To gain her trust. There was enough detail in the newspaper to help me convince her.'

'Funny notion that, gaining trust by *lying*.'

'Simple psychology. It worked, didn't it?'

'I don't know. You tell me. Did it?'

'Yes. She came with me.'

'So, why exactly would you want to gain the trust of a teenage girl, a stranger?'

'Not *any* old teenage girl. This *particular* teenage girl. Because I recognised her from the papers, I knew she'd run away from home. You could see she was living rough. I wanted to protect her.'

'Protect her?'

'Yes, protect her.'

'Or groom her for your own purposes?'

That catches me broadside.

'You've lost me. What am I supposed to be grooming her *for*? Other than working in the shop, and that only occurred to me subsequently when I found out what she really wants to do with her life. Oh, and before you get the wrong idea, let me tell you my boss is totally innocent in all this. *I* took Maria in. I told Parminder she was a friend. *I* asked if she could help out in the shop till she got on her feet.'

'So, you weren't grooming her then? Is that what

you're telling me?'

'No, I was not.'

'You didn't have your own agenda for her?'

'No.'

'So. You see a young pretty girl ... no ties ... you pick her up off the street ... you put her in your debt ... and I'm supposed to believe you had no ulterior motive, no designs on her?'

Enlightenment dawns. They think I'm a brothel madame, or a pimp, or some sex-crazed lesbo!

'The thought never entered my head,' I say with a half-smile, 'until you put it there.'

'You sure of that?'

'Absolutely, one hundred percent.'

'So, why take her back to your place?'

'So she could have a bath and a hot meal. Wash her clothes.'

'All very magnanimous. No ulterior motive then?'

'None whatever.'

'But then you offer her a bed for the night. Several nights. Lots of nights, in fact.' The tone has changed now; more suggestive, more aggressive. *A soft answer turneth away wrath.* Why would that suddenly leap into my mind?

'I did indeed. The kid was exhausted, she was kipping on benches. It was too dangerous, a young girl all alone. Any decent civilised human being would have done the same.'

'Oh, I hardly think so. London isn't full of benevolent people housing the homeless, and all the waifs and strays that find their way here, now, is it? So come on, what else have you offered her?'

'Shelter. Companionship. Honest work. Well, that's Parminder. It's her shop. But like I said, I was the one who asked if she'd let Rea ... Maria, come to the shop with me. I didn't want her running off again, getting into who knows what trouble.'

'I bet you didn't. You'd got her exactly where you wanted her. You'd become her guardian angel. She'd do anything for you, huh?'

'You've got it all wrong.'

'Tell me this then, Ms Taylor, you knew Maria had run away, you knew her parents must be frantic, and yet you didn't tell us? Didn't report finding her even.'

'She begged me not to. She's sixteen, legally allowed to make her own decisions.'

'You must have known her family'd be beside themselves with worry.'

'Course I did. That's why I got her to contact them to say she was alive and well. But she didn't want them to know *where* she was. She's been sending a card every two weeks. You can check. I don't even know the address. But she didn't want them to call you. If I'd gone behind her back, she'd only have run away again, and heaven knows where she'd have ended up. At least I knew she was safe with me.'

'Was she, though?'

'Yes, of course she was.'

'Why would you want to be stuck with a kid young enough to be your daughter?'

'It wasn't for *me*; it was for *her*. To protect her till she could get back on her feet again.'

'And you really had no other motive than that?'

'None.'

'Why should we believe you?'

'Because it's the truth.'

'What did you say your name was again?'

'Chris Taylor.'

'And is *that* the truth?'

'Yes.'

'So you deliberately conspired to waste police time by not reporting her whereabouts. You knew we were looking for her.'

'I had no choice. It was a question of her safety. Keeping quiet was the price she demanded.'

It's after 5 before they let us go, but I know Parminder will still be in the shop. I might yet be of some use to her. Whether she'll even speak to me is a moot point. Rea insists she'll come too although she's welcome to take the key, let herself into my flat.

'You okay?' I ask her as soon as we're outside the police station.

'Yeah. You?'

'Sure. Did they say what put them onto your whereabouts?'

'Yeah. Seems somebody saw my photo in the paper and then saw me coming to work here and told the police. And that woman that came in this morning to collect the flowers, 'member? – she was a plain clothes person. She came to check out if it really was me.'

'So it's my fault. Damn. I shouldn't have got you to help me load up. You should have been safely in the back room out of sight. I'm so, so sorry, Rea. I didn't think. We've got so used to having you around, I'd kind of forgotten you were in hiding.'

'No sweat, it's not your fault. I told them: don't tell my folks. I'm staying here. I like it here. I'm sixteen, I can stay if I want.'

'So, did they agree not to tell your parents?'

'Nah. They have to tell them I'm safe, why they've stopped looking, but they don't have to tell them where I am.'

'You okay with that?'

'Yeah. S'long as they *don't* tell Mum and Dad.'

'So they didn't know about the cards you sent?'

'Yep, they did. But seems Mum thought I might've been forced to write them.'

'Ahh. But fair enough. I guess I'd have been suspicious too. She'll be relieved then, knowing you're not being forced into anything.'

'Maybe.'

I glance sideways at her. 'The police suspect I'm up to no good, that I have evil intentions. That I might be hurting you.'

'Yeah, I know. They asked me about that, but I told them.'

'What? What exactly did you tell them?'

'To go see a shrink! You *wouldn't* do anything mean or nasty. I feel safe with you.'

'Thanks for that.'

'Even if you did tell a load of cobblers to get me here.'

'What cobblers?'

'That you knew my parents.'

I grin back at her. 'It was for your own good.'

'Yes, Grandma!'

Parminder is outwardly her usual unflappable self but the shop's been busy, she's behind with her order for first thing tomorrow. She's terse with me. I fill her in briefly, tell her I did everything possible to protect her. That Rea did too. And the fact that she wasn't personally dragged down to the station looks promising.

'I've been thinking,' I say hesitantly. 'There's a load to do. Could Rea maybe secure the oasis, start the foliage, to speed things along?'

She thinks for a moment before turning to the girl. 'You up for that, Rea?'

'You betcha!' She's positively beaming.

'Fair enough. Let me show you.'

She watches Parminder's expert fingers deftly setting the scene for the first of eight baskets. She soon gets the hang of it.

We've all moved up a notch and the vote of confidence comes at exactly the right time for Rea. And for me.

CHAPTER 32

Chris

IT'S A DIFFERENT SERGEANT who saunters into the shop with WPC Sadie Frost three days later.

'Can I help you?' I keep it neutral, willing Rea to stay in the back with Parminder. The police aren't exactly discreet if this is their idea of surveillance.

'We'd like you to accompany us down to the station.'

'Who? Me? Why? I haven't done anything.'

'We need to ask you some more questions.'

'Again? But you questioned me for hours already. I haven't done anything wrong. And I have work to do.'

'Some new information has since come to light.'

'What information?'

'D'you really want me to spell it out here, in public?'

Parminder's voice is at my elbow. 'I hope this isn't harassment, Officer. Ms Taylor is a valued employee and I can assure you, has my complete trust.'

Wow!

'No. It's not harassment, ma'am. Routine enquiries, that's all.'

It's a different room; no monstrosities on the wall, a convoluted Picasso scored into the table as if someone got bored waiting and decided to leave something original for posterity.

And this time I appear to be higher up the pecking order. In less than ten minutes Sergeant Mace takes his seat opposite me, lips curled in what looks remarkably like scorn.

He lets his eyes wander slowly over me in a way that makes me shiver inside. Bad memories stir. I'm suddenly acutely aware of my own body language.

'This time we want the real truth, none of your make believe. Tell us your real name.'

I sit in silence.

He leans forward. 'You see, we *know* who you are. We traced you all the way back to Edinburgh.'

'So why ask me?'

'Because you have a bit of explaining to do, *Victor*.' He leans back with a smug smile on his face. 'Victor Grayson.'

'That's not my name. I'm Chris Taylor, and I know my rights.'

'Do you now?'

'Yes, I do.'

'And what exactly *are* your rights, Chris Taylor, *sir*?' He packs a vile sneer into that title. I see the WPC flinch; she knows he's out of line.

'As you well know, it's my right to be treated fairly under the Equality Act. To have my lived gender respected.'

'Is that right? Your *lived gender*, huh? Got all the patter, haven't we?'

'It's not patter. It's my legal right.'

His eyes narrow and he leans forward aggressively, the questions firing at me like enemy bullets. I no sooner dodge one and another one whistles past my ear.

Why did you change your name?
Why did you run away?
Where have you been living?
How did you support yourself?
Was that job legal?
How did you pay your way?
Why did you pick up Maria Davenport?
Do you like young girls, Chris, <u>sir</u>?
Where were you on 17th July 2006?
Or 11th August 2007?
Can anyone vouch for you on those dates?
What? Nearly a decade ago? You have to be kidding!

Not only have I absolutely no idea what I was doing back then – who would? – but I no longer have my diaries from that time. And I certainly have no intention of dragging my family into this to give me an alibi. I long ago forfeited the right to their loyalty.

Does the name Eva Demarco mean anything to you?

What about Rebekah Quindlan?

Vague bells ring, but no, I can't place them.

What if we told you they were teenage girls who went missing in Scotland when you lived up there?

'Ah, of course. I do remember teenagers going missing, now you say.'

And what if we told you that on the nights in question you were reported to be missing yourself – not at work, not at home?

Eva, Rebekah, Maria ... you see where this is taking us?

Ahh ...

Eva's dead, Rebekah's still missing, we've found you with Maria ...

'I can explain.'

'I'm listening.'

By the time I'm released from the relentless questioning, I feel bruised and stripped naked. I'm a mess. Not helped by the sergeant reappearing on his own to hiss, 'You can go for now, you pervert, but you can bet your life I'll get you for this.' This time there's no witness, no more enlightened WPC to restrain him.

I ring Parminder. I'm in no fit state to come back into the shop after this mauling. I'm scarcely coherent.

'Look, Chris, never mind about work. Get yourself a taxi home. Rea and I will finish up here and then we'll come out to you and we'll get this sorted. Oh, and I'll bring a takeaway. Have a long soak in the bath or whatever. Hang in there. See you soon.'

It's all I can do to hail a cab. Mercifully the driver isn't looking for conversation. My brain recycles the past hour, my horror mounting with each retelling.

Parminder takes one look at me and sticks the takeaway in the oven on a low heat.

'Ahhh, you poor thing. You need a proper drink. We'll eat later.'

CHAPTER 33

Chris

NOT TILL WE'VE ALL GOT a glass in our hands does she say any more.

'Listen, Chris, leaving aside Rea's case, as far as I'm concerned your business is your business. If any of this stuff with the police affects your work then you can tell me, and I'm sure we'll work something out. But otherwise … it's your life.' She dismisses it with a quick flick of her hand.

'Thanks, Parminder. That means a lot. You've been a real friend. And I truly am sorry you've got dragged into all this.'

They both wait while I compose myself. A great big bit of me wants to protect Rea from my problems – she's only a kid – but she's in this up to her neck already now the police are involved.

'I haven't done anything criminal, nothing that affects my work in the shop, I can assure you of that. But … I think it'd be best to get it out into the open. I owe you both that.'

'Is this about you being a guy before?' Rea says.

I stare at her.

'We did about that stuff at school: LGBT, equality, rights, discrimination. Happens. Like Parminder says, it's your business.'

'My name was Victor Grayson.' I stop to take gulps of air. 'I've known since I was about six that I was a girl, but I couldn't share it with anyone. My parents were very old school, my brothers were … *are* very macho, so all through my adolescent years I had to keep my feelings under wraps.

193

'Then in my twenties I got married. We had a baby ... things were better for a bit. I adored that girl. She and I – well, we had a really special bond.

'I was a nurse back then too, and I loved my job. So work and family kept me busy. I thought maybe the other thing would be less important if I concentrated on helping other people. But no, gradually, everything built up and built up until I felt I would *suffocate* if I didn't express my real self somehow. So eventually I started occasionally going out publicly as a woman, in places where no one knew me.'

'What did that feel like?'

'Mixed. On one level it felt totally liberating to look in the mirror and see the outward trappings of a woman; an outward image that matched the me inside. But in practical terms it was also really tough – early on especially. I had no idea how to carry it off and I got loads of abuse. Looking back I guess I was a bit like an adolescent trying out make-up, clothes, new experiences, experimenting, like teenagers do. Getting it wrong. I guess I must have looked like ... well, a tart, I suppose! I used cheap wigs and loads of mascara and some pretty brassy jewellery back then.' I shudder remembering. 'And I hadn't a clue how to manage boobs. Then there was all the business of going to female loos, dressing rooms, things like that ... well, let's just say I learned the hard way.'

I look at Rea for a moment and give her a half grin.

'I could tell you some hair-raising stories – but I won't! I got chased out more than once, accused of ... I won't sully your ears, but "pervert" was probably the least foul name they threw at me. I got ridiculed, taunted, abused in the street. Harangued by little old ladies who promised me I'd burn in hell if I didn't mend my ways. I howled myself to sleep many a night.

'I wanted to confide in my wife and I tried several times to introduce the subject but ... well, she was pretty squeamish about stuff like this. She hated hearing about cases I looked after, anything like that. I coped by going away to hotels for a few days, and being my real self. But in the end it simply

194

wasn't enough.

'I looked up stuff on the net and back then they recommended making a complete break with your past. Go right away and start afresh.'

I feel Rea tense.

'I know! Seems brutal now, but that was the official advice back then, eight years ago. It wouldn't be today, but nowadays there's much more tolerance and understanding for this kind of thing.'

Parminder nods her head.

'It's all relative, of course. There's still a lot of resistance and ignorance. And I know all about the statistics on transgender people who're killed because of who they are. Anyway, I took the advice. And that's why I came to London.' I stop abruptly.

'Leaving your little girl behind,' Parminder says softly.

I nod, feeling the tears gathering, gritting my teeth.

She reaches across and covers my hand with hers till I can speak again.

'It killed me to do that. Absolutely *killed* me. Not a day goes by that I don't grieve for her. And as for what it did to her ... I try not to think about it. I did what I did *for* her, but now I think she must have paid a terrible price for being protected like that.'

She waits before speaking again, steering the conversation into safer waters.

'So when did you change your name to Chris?'

'Not till I met up with other trans people. Till then I was just "Vicky" if I ever needed to give a name. I was pretty lonely down here initially. Knew nobody. Then one day I met this lovely lady, Christine, and we got talking. She was so kind and supportive. She put me in touch with somebody else who in turn introduced me to the transgender community. And at my second meeting they asked outright, "What's your name?" I was actually thinking about Christine so her name popped into my head, and it just came out: Chris ... Chris Taylor – my mother's maiden name. And it stuck.'

'Cool,' Rea says.

'Parminder, I can't tell you how grateful I am to you, taking me on with only the bare bones of my past. You've been terrific. You get it, I know. But you turned my life around. '

'My cousin came out about five years ago,' she says to Rea by way of explanation. '*I* was pretty clueless too before that. I admit it.'

'So?' Typical teenager!

'So, she wasn't scared about taking on a trans woman,' I chip in. 'It's a big deal in my book.'

'Why *would* you be scared?' Rea asks. 'Chris's great. Kind and ... everything.'

'You and I know that, but the world can be a pretty cruel place when people don't understand something,' Parminder says.

'As I know to my cost,' I say. 'And loads of people in the retail trade are reluctant to take on people like me in case we frighten off the customers. I kind of get where they're coming from too – especially in the early stages, before we pass, it's pretty obvious what we are. Anyway, ages before I met Parminder, when I first came to London, I had to get some kind of a job. So I started off working in a hotel kitchen. Well out of sight! They were desperate for staff though, so they took me on, no questions asked. At least it got me started down here.'

'So what *was* it like?' Rea chips in. 'Changing, I mean.'

'Rea!' Parminder says sharply.

'No, it's a fair question,' I interrupt. 'Pretty horrendous, if I'm honest. And there aren't any shortcuts. I had to go through all the stages exactly like everyone else – well, unless you're loaded – like Caitlin Jenner. You know, Jenner? Related to the Kardashians? Famous American athlete, known back then as Bruce Jenner? No? Well, anyway, she could afford to pay privately for the best of everything. That's why she looks like a supermodel.

'But for the rest of us it's a slow painful process. You have to try going out as a woman at first before they'll even consider you for treatment. So skirt, wig, make-up, heels, but with a man's voice, facial hair, masculine walk, all that stuff. And then, even when you're accepted for treatment, it takes years to fully transition. People see the discrepancies and contradictions and they don't know how to react, what to say. And because they're unsure, scared, they can be pretty insensitive, lash out even.'

'Well, more fool them,' Rea says. 'I think you're terrific. I've had the best time thanks to you – the theatre and working in the shop and planning my life and ... everything. *You* see where I'm coming from, and you don't try to force me into what *you* want me to be. I like that. *And* you let me pay you something for staying. Makes me feel grown up, like, not a silly kid that needs everything done for her. I want to make my own way. I can't do it yet, but you've helped me get started. And I don't care if you're a man or a woman or something in between – no offence!'

'None taken.' I can't help but laugh at her comical expression.

'I told those idiots at the station that'n all.'

'I'm very much afraid they don't share your enlightened view of the world, sadly for me, Rea. Well, not the sergeant anyway. A complete dinosaur, I'd say.'

'Was it ghastly?' Parminder chips in.

I shrug. 'I've had worse. And I guess they're used to dealing with criminals. It's not their fault they're suspicious and expect the worst. The sergeant couldn't quite bring himself to believe I had no ulterior motive for helping Rea. Not even when I told them about my own daughter and how I'd have wanted somebody to do the same for her if she'd ever been in a similar position.'

'You said just now about leaving her, so how did she die? Or ... well, no need to talk about it if you don't want to.' Rea peters out. 'Sorry.'

'No, I owe you both an explanation. She isn't dead, and to be fair, I never said she was. I only said I'd lost a daughter. I did lose her ... when I left her and her mother.'

Rea is staring at me open mouthed. 'You ran away? From *her*? From your own *daughter*? And she's still *alive*?

And you haven't told her where you are?"

'I did. And I'm not proud of it.'

'See, that I don't understand,' Rea interrupts, eyes narrowed, body taut. 'If you loved them, how *could* you?'

'Because I knew what kind of flak they'd get if I stayed and came out as a woman. The rejection, the humiliation, the ridicule. I could at least protect them from all that.'

'You know something? You're a hypocrite,' she hisses fiercely. 'You *made* me tell *my* family, to stop them worrying. But see you? You didn't have the balls to do it for yourself.'

'It was different.'

'Nah, you're just making excuses. If they loved you like you said, they'd understand. They'd want you around. You hurt them big time, pretending you were dead. You don't ever get over something like that. I bet your girl still hurts really bad.'

'Rea ...' Parminder cautions, but I hold up my hand to stop her.

'No, let her have her say. She has a point.'

Rea has her say all right! And there's more than a grain of truth in her accusations, my tears are testament to that. How *could* I have done it? Fair enough, that was the advice the experts gave you back then, but what did it do to my daughter? And to Tonya? *Was* I being selfish? *Was* I really thinking of them? I don't know. How can you unravel their best interests from mine?

When Rea finally dries up I feel shattered and deflated.

'Well, Rea, we can only do what we think is right at that point in time with the information we have available to us.' It sounds feeble even to me. 'I've had years to think about all this: what I did, the effect it must have had on my wife and my daughter. Back then I did what I did for all the right reasons. I loved my little girl more than life. Still do. I'd have died to spare her pain. I thought that's what I was doing, but now, looking back? I'm not so sure it *was* the right thing. Maybe I should have given them the choice.'

'The thing that's worrying me,' Parminder says quietly when Rea dries up finally, 'is, what's to stop the police telling your family they've found you now? Presumably they've been doing checks, tracking your past history and everything. And your family would know about that.'

'Yeah,' Rea chimes in. 'And there's that picture of us in the paper, when we went to see *Les Mis*. They'd *have* to say they'd tracked you down, wouldn't they? Maybe not the address or anything. "He's alive but he doesn't want you to know where he is," maybe, something vague like that. Imagine! Well, what would *you* think if somebody breezed up and told you your husband, your dad, who you thought died yonks ago, is still alive and well and living in Hounslow?'

'I don't ...'

'Oh *pu...lease*! You know what I mean! Hounslow, Chelsea, Acton, Wimbledon – it's all the same. And don't try to dodge the question.' She grins suddenly. 'Grandma!'

I have nothing to say. I don't even correct her pronouns.

'It sucks. Big time. You *owe* them, and you know it. You said a minute ago you owed Parminder and me, but that's *nothing* compared with what you owe your wife and daughter. I'm right, aren't I, Parminder?'

'She has a point, Chris. It'd be cruel for them to find out from somebody else, wouldn't it? The police or whatever.'

CHAPTER 34

Chris

I'M NOT PREPARED for the sound of India's voice answering the phone. Last time I heard it she was a little girl all giggles and exuberance, now she sounds like ... I'm not sure ... jaded? world-weary? depressed?

'Hello.' No name. No warmth.

I deliberately disguise my voice. 'Hi. Could I please speak to Tonya Grayson?'

'Who's speaking?'

'An old friend from way back.'

'What name shall I say?'

'Just tell her it's a surprise. Someone she used to hang out with years ago.'

Tonya is understandably cautious.

'Who is this?'

'Tonya, hi. Is India still in earshot?'

'No ...'

I can almost hear her holding her breath.

'Is that ...?' her voice cracks. '*Victor*? Is it really ... *you?*'

'It is me, but not the me you remember. Listen, is this a good time to talk or should I ring later? Once India's in bed maybe? '

'Don't you dare ring off,' she hisses. 'Don't you *dare*! Not before you've told me what the hell's going on.'

'Well, let me know if she comes in, then. I need to explain everything to you first before I speak to her.'

'Wait a minute while I close the door ... Right, I'm listening.'

'First of all, how are you? How's India?'

'Apart from having been to hell and back, you mean?'

'Tonya, there's nothing I can say to undo the last seven years. But for all sorts of reasons now I need to let you know I'm still alive and I'm living in London. I couldn't let you hear it from ... somebody else.'

'Well, that's big of you.'

I let it go. But she rushes on anyway.

'So, all this time you make us think you've gone for good, you're probably *dead*, and then suddenly you ring up out of the blue ... in case *somebody else gets there first*? I don't believe I'm hearing this.'

'I don't blame you for being cross ...'

'Cross? *Cross*? Cross doesn't *begin* to cover it!'

'The thing is ... the police have found out where I am and they've been asking questions and I don't want them calling at the house ...'

'The police? Why are the police involved? Victor, what's going on? What ... have ... you ... done?'

'Nothing to worry about. Nothing criminal. Honestly. I just helped somebody else who the police were looking for. They were hunting for her and that brought them to me.'

'What kind of a "her" are we talking about here?'

'A teenage girl who ran away from home.'

'You're ... involved ... with *a teenage girl*?'

'No, not like *that*! I've just been helping her get back on her feet.'

'I think you need to go right back and start at the beginning.'

'I will, but there's something you need to know first.'

She doesn't speak.

'I'm not Victor any more, Tonya, I'm Chris. And I'm a woman.'

Nothing.

'Tonya?'

'I heard you.' It sounds all ragged and raw. 'But ...'

'I've always known I'm a woman. But now I've transitioned properly.'

Silence.

'That's why I did what I did.'

Nothing.

'Look, I'm desperately sorry I left you like that. You have to believe me. At the time I did what I thought was best for you, for India. I didn't want you to suffer because of me. Better that I sacrifice everything than that you were hurt. Now, though, thinking has changed. People are more accepting, less ignorant. I'm not so sure it *was* the best thing. Maybe we could have worked something out. I don't know. But we can't change what's happened.'

'No. We *can't change* ... you simply vanishing, no explanation. You leaving me to bring up India on my own. You not even contacting us all these years. You ringing up out of the blue *now* when it suits *you*. You pretending nothing's changed.'

'Oh, I'm not pretending that. I *know* things have changed, Tonya. Lots of things have changed. I've been to hell and back too, just a different kind of hell.'

'And I'm supposed to feel sorry for you, am I? Believe your hell was worse than the hell you put us through?'

'No, I'm not looking for sympathy. I did what I did because I believed it was the only way we could all survive. Living a lie was killing me; living the truth would expose you to all kinds of humiliation and abuse. I thought you'd be better off without me. I thought people would rally round and support you if they thought you'd been widowed or your husband was simply missing, you were a single mum. A clean break was best for everyone, they said.'

'*You* thought. *You* thought. What about what *I* thought? How *I* felt?'

'I'm sorry. Like I said, maybe I was naive, but I honestly did it with the best of intentions. Whatever else, you need to believe that.'

'Hang on a minute ... so ... when you said ... you aren't Victor any more ...'

'I'm not. I'm Chris. I'm a transgender woman, Tonya. I always was a girl inside. I did everything I could to deny it. I tried, I really, really did. But as the years went by, it became more and more impossible. I was so much in the wrong body. I tried to keep it secret. Those times when I went away? That was so I could be my real self for a while. I did my level best to protect you. But the deception was suffocating me. I couldn't keep living like that. I need to be a woman all the time, outside as well as inside. This is who I really am, and now, as Chris, I've finally found peace with myself.'

'It's all you, you, *you*, isn't it?'

'I'm only trying to explain.'

'I know. But try telling that to your daughter. Your *daughter*! You've wrecked her life, d'you know that? She's been grieving for you all these years. How could you *do* that to her? How *could* you?'

'It was the price I thought I had to pay to protect her – both of you. I need to talk to her too, but I think it would be better face-to-face. What d'you think?'

'You know what? I have no idea whatever at this precise moment. Damn it, you ring up out of the blue after all these years and ask me something like that? I have absolutely no notion how she'll react, or what to tell her even. Whether I should tell her at all. What right have you got to come back into our lives now and stir things up all over again? And if I tell her you're alive, what then? Does she get to see you? Will you become part of her life again? Will you bunk off when it suits you and leave her grieving all over again?'

I take a big breath, force myself to speak quietly.

'You know what, Tonya, I think we should leave this for now. I appreciate it's been a shock. Give yourself time to think things through and decide what's best – for you and for India. Whether I should come up to see you – either, both of you. You mull over what's right for you and we'll talk again. When's best for me to ring?'

I pour myself a stiff drink, swallow it in one gulp. It's done. No, of course it's not. Who am I kidding? That's only the first tiny step. We have so far to go before it's done and I have no picture at all of how this story will end.

Tonya will need time to take all this on board. She'll probably Google everything about transition. And talk to people about the best thing for India. I have no choice but to await her decision.

Imagine ... she says, no, I want nothing more to do with you. No, you can't speak to India. No, I'm not even going to tell her you're alive. No, you can't contact us ever again ...

Imagine ... she says, yes. I get to meet my darling daughter again ...

CHAPTER 35

Chris

FOR OUR FIRST MEETING I go up to Edinburgh, choose a hotel five miles from my old home, so they don't have to travel far. It's the least I can do; after all, I was the one who left.

I have absolutely no idea how I should greet my fifteen-year-old daughter after so long an absence. She'll be so grown up now. Who does she take after, I wonder? How broad or narrow-minded is she? Kids can be very black and white, hurtful in their arrogance. I'm still smarting from Rea's onslaught. And Tonya's anger. How will *India* react to her dad sitting in front of her as a woman?

Our first conversation was harrowing. She begged me again and again, through her weeping, to come home, but that was only my disembodied voice on the phone. Should I read anything into her insistence that she be the first to see me, and on her own? Her mum was objecting apparently – something about not trusting me. But India was adamant.

'*I* never gave up, Dad. I *knew* you'd come back one day.'

They've reached a compromise. Tonya insists she will be just outside, waiting, 'in case'. And she's given us half an hour before she'll have her own turn to question me.

For a pretty modest fee the hotel agree to my using a small ground floor room they reserve for private meetings. It's decorated in deep reds, complementing the rich dark wood of the table and chairs. Shaded lights cast a soft glow in the darkness of a room with no natural light. In other circumstances I'd relish the colours, the feeling of peace.

Not today. Today I'm in turmoil.

I pace up and down rehearsing again and again the first words I'll say. How I'll react if ... Or if ... Or if ...

Nothing prepares me for the sight of a tall, skeletal girl with sparse hair, parchment skin and the gait of a woman twice my age. Her smile is wide, but seems too cavernous in her gaunt face. In spite of her frailty she almost runs into my arms and her bones close like a vice around my waist. I want to return the embrace with interest, but I daren't. I fear she might break. Hot tears fall unchecked. Mine.

Eventually she lowers herself cautiously onto one of the leather chairs, still clutching my hand as I take my seat inches away from her ... after all this time ...

Her eyes never leave me.

She declines all refreshment, but I've already ordered biscuits and juice and a pot of tea to be brought in as soon as she arrives.

'I can't tell you how good it is to see you again. I've missed you so, so much. How are you, sweetheart?'

'I'm fine. You won't leave me again, will you, Dad? Please. *Please.*'

'Sssh. We'll talk about the future in a bit ...'

The refreshments are delivered quietly and we're alone again. I give her space. I re-order the cups and plates and biscuits into straight lines.

'You do that as well,' she says almost under her breath.

'Sorry. It's annoying, I know.'

'Not to me it's not. I do it too.'

'A chip off the old block, huh?' I keep it light.

She leans forward for a moment, her bones prominent through the tightened clothing.

'You *won't* leave me now, Dad, will you?'

'Not if I can help it. And not if you want me back. You're the most precious person in the world to me, India. But we have lots of talking to do, and Mum has to be part of that conversation. So for now, let's just agree that I want more than anything to be part of your life. Exactly how that will happen is something we need to discuss.'

'You mean it? You really mean you want to be my dad again.'

'I've always been your dad. Always will be. Are you asking about the staying? ... or the what-dad-means part?'

'Everything, I guess.'

'I certainly want to be an active dad to you for the rest of our lives, but ... India, I can't go back to being the dad you remember. I can't. Not now.'

'Oh, I know *that*! That doesn't matter. As long as you're here.'

'So what do you want us to talk about now?'

'I want you to tell me *everything*. And I want it to be true. I'm grown up now and I'm fed up with all the lies and deception. I want to know what *really* happened. Why you left. Why you came back. *Everything*.'

'Absolutely. I know I owe you that,' I say softly, but my heart is breaking. She looks unutterably fragile and vulnerable. Other-worldly. How can I bear to shatter her picture of her father so completely.

'Go on, then,' she urges, irritation sharpening her tone.

'India, this won't be easy for you to listen to, so stop me if you want a break, or you want me to explain anything. Right?'

She nods, eyes wide, shaking fingers plucking at an uneven nail.

I take a big breath and send up a wordless prayer.

'I don't know how much you know about transgender people so stop me if this is all old hat to you, okay?'

She nods.

'We did about it at school but I want to know what it was like for *you*.'

'Well, gender's pretty important right from the word go, as you know. It's the first thing the parents ask when a baby's born, "What is it?" Then off goes the dad to ring all the aunties and uncles and grandparents and friends: "It's a boy," or "It's a girl." And only after that does he fill in the details: weight, name, time, and all that stuff.' I smile at her.

'I remember doing that after you arrived. "It's a girl!" I was bursting with pride. "She weighs seven pounds and half an ounce. It was one minute after midnight. Her name is India Gwendoline. And she looks exactly like her mother." Granny was funny: "*What* did you say her name is?" "India Gwendoline." "*India?* But that's a *country!*" I'm not sure she ever really got used to it.'

India manages a wry grimace. She remembers her paternal grandmother.

'And it's the same once the baby goes home. People peer into the pram, they smile and coo, and want to know the gender. But actually, you know, the boundaries between what makes us male or female aren't quite as clear as people think. Sometimes babies are born and you can't tell from the *outside* which they are. "Intersex", it's called. It may be that the genitalia are neither one thing nor the other; it may be the inside organs don't match the outside ones; it may be the chromosomes have different X and Y combinations. There's a range of things under that umbrella term. You know about all that, yes?'

'Not all of it, but in any case that's not you, is it?'

'No. Sometimes it's clear on the *outside* which they are, but as the person grows, the way *they feel* on the *inside* doesn't match what they appear to be to everyone else. *That* was me. Although nobody else knew I was in the wrong body, *I* knew. At first, of course, I couldn't understand why I felt like something wasn't right. People didn't talk about that sort of thing when I was little. There were no TV programmes about it or anything. Not like today. So I did what was expected. I wore boys' clothes, I played boys' games, I used the boys' cloakrooms, exactly like everyone else. It wasn't until I was about eleven, twelve, that I began to really question what was going on, why I was more in tune with girly things.

'So basically when I was little I felt horribly confused. But then, when I hit puberty, when my body started changing to a man's ... Fair enough, I know most teenagers feel churned up about things at that stage, but for me there was an extra layer of bewilderment and ... horror, I guess. I *hated* my body. It felt like I was unravelling at the seams. I raged against the changes that were trapping me in this cage, blocking my escape from maleness. I can tell you I was ... despairing, depressed ... and I mean, seriously depressed. There was nobody to talk to about it. My parents would simply have told me not to be so stupid. I was a boy. Full stop.'

'Our teacher told us nobody talked about this stuff twenty, thirty years ago.'

'That's exactly right. So I had to figure it out for myself. And I came to the conclusion I had no choice, I needed to fight these "unnatural" feelings. I must *force* myself to suppress my softer side, *make* myself one of the lads.

'But of course, it wasn't that simple. The emotions, the convictions, didn't go away. I *couldn't* simply crush them at will. That's not how it works. I was still a girl inside. So then I tried to rationalise things. I thought, it's a bit like being in tune with my feminine side – only more so than the rest of my male peers. So, how about I use that to my advantage, be more sensitive, more considerate, more thoughtful than other guys. And lo and behold, I found girls quite liked that! I had a whole new crowd to run with. Girls! Great. But I still went along with the fact that I was a bloke outwardly. I would occasionally give in to my inner feelings in private, but I honestly don't think anyone else suspected how I felt.'

'How d'you mean, "give in"?'

'I'd dress up in girls' clothes, wear make-up, wigs, stuff socks up my jumper. All in the privacy of my locked room, I hasten to add. My mother would have had a heart attack if she'd known. And my father would probably have belted me to knock some sense into me!'

'I can't imagine you doing that. Hiding. Stuffing socks up your jumper.' She half grins.

'Sounds bizarre now, I agree. But it was the only release I could find back then. And then along came your mum. She was kind and gentle and altogether lovely. We instantly clicked. And pretty quickly we fell in love. That at least was real. And for the first time in my life I started to be glad I was outwardly a man. Feeling like I did with her gave me hope. She would be my ticket out of this nightmare.'

'But ...' She stumbles. I wait. 'Did *she* know ... about the other things?'

I shake my head. 'No.'

'How could you *marry* her, knowing ... you know?'

'That's a good question. I've asked myself the same thing hundreds of times. Honestly, India? I *did* hesitate at first but she let me know she wanted us to marry, and we got on so well together and back then, I honestly thought that our love would be enough. The other stuff would be almost ... incidental. I could keep it locked away, out of sight, and it wouldn't hurt anybody. It would be like a secret fantasy life.

There's a tap at the door. It opens a crack.

'Are you all right, India?' Tonya whispers.

'Course I am. Go away. Leave us alone.'

I'm shocked by the insolence in her tone.

CHAPTER 36

Chris

SHE'S PICKING AT THE EDGE of her sleeve, her skinny fingers restless now. I reach across and place my hand over hers. She doesn't respond, but she doesn't pull away either.

'You okay to continue, sweetheart? Need a break?'

She shakes her head vigorously. I see the dizziness overtake her; watch her closed eyes flickering while she stabilises.

'Where were we? Ah yes, why did I marry Mum. I know this is hard to understand, sweetie, but back then, I was desperately trying … to be a proper man. I wanted more than anything to have proper male feelings, behave in proper acceptable male ways. And the last person I ever intended to hurt was your mum. She was the best thing that had ever happened to me – back then. Before you.

'And I genuinely believed that she and I would work. We *did* work! We were happy together. And then we had you, and you were the icing on the cake. And I kept telling myself, you were only possible because I was a man – biologically anyway. I fell in love with you the minute I saw you. Actually no, *before* you were ever born. I would feel you moving inside Mum and think, this little person is partly mine. I helped create you. And I can't tell you what that did to me. I loved you – unconditionally, overwhelmingly, so, so much.

'When you were tiny Mum had a bit of a hard time, so I had plenty to do looking after you. With that, plus work, there wasn't much time for anything else. But then when the other feelings didn't go away, I felt so guilty. Why wasn't what we had enough? I had to find some way to deal with all my other baggage. So I sectioned off that part of my life – to make sure it didn't contaminate the life I had with Mum and you. I went away occasionally and let myself be the woman I knew I was inside. I would buy pretty things – soft silks and fine wool, things that felt lovely on my skin. I told the assistants they were for my girlfriend. And I'd dress up in them. But I should probably clarify, India, it's not the clothes *per se* that are important to me – they're simply the outward expression of what I feel on the inside. When I'm wearing dresses, heels, tights, earrings, make-up, perfume, my outside matches my inside.'

'They told us that, too.'

How much more worldly-wise she is than my generation.

'I kept the clothes locked away so there was no danger anybody else would find them, and for ages I confined these real-me times to some hotel room or other. But then I needed more, so I went further away from the people who knew me and I started to venture outside and pass myself off as a woman. Oh, it was bliss to have people call me "madam" in a shop, or refer to me as "she" or "her".' I close my eyes recalling the exhilaration. 'For those brief periods of time I could relax in my own skin. No conflict. A wonderful feeling of peace with myself.

'But then I'd go back to being perceived as Victor, male colleague, husband, father, son. He. Him.' I shudder. 'And the depression really set in then. Now I knew what I *could* feel like, the situation was far, far worse. I knew this wasn't something that would ever go away. I *was* a woman trapped in a man's body and I'd never be truly happy until I lived like one.'

India looks so lost I want to reach out and hug her but I daren't, not when she's looking at me like that, trying to reconcile the stranger in front of her with the father she thought she'd found.

'So, why did you go away?' she says. 'That's what I

don't get. Why leave us?'

'For your sake. Because I wanted to protect you ... from me. I couldn't – I simply *couldn't* – continue living a lie. It was destroying me, killing me. I *had* to finally accept myself. But I couldn't drag *you* into all that confusion. I loved you too much to hurt you like that.'

'But you *did* hurt us, Mum *and* me, going away. Making us think you were dead.'

'I know. But I genuinely thought that would be a healthy, acceptable kind of hurt. It felt like the lesser evil ... for *you*, not for me. You could look people in the eye and say, "My dad died." Or "They think he drowned at sea but they didn't ever find his body." People would be sorry, sympathetic, kind to you.'

She doesn't look convinced.

'Believe me, India, it would have been altogether different if I'd stayed around and become a woman. I know! I've gone through this, remember. I've lived with the rejection, the scorn, the discrimination, that look in their eyes, the whispers, the sneering, the snide comments. I *know* what it's like to live in constant fear of humiliation, abuse even. I couldn't do that to you, my precious girl. I couldn't bear to think what I did would cause you that kind of grief. I simply couldn't do it. It was better for you this way.'

'So, *were* you happy?' Her voice is a crackling whisper.

'Happy? Seriously?' I shake my head slowly, swallowing hard several times. 'No. I still knew you were out there, growing up, sad at first but making a new life without me, but I couldn't make contact with you – or so I thought. I missed you every second of every day. It was like ripping out my heart. And Mum. I felt guilty all the time about what I'd done to both of you.'

'But ... all this? Did *it* make you happy?' Her gesture takes in my clothes, my figure, my face.

'Oh, you mean about being a woman? Ahh, India, it was like coming home. The transition wasn't easy, of course, plenty of hiccups along the way, but it was worth all the problems to finally really be myself.'

'So, did you go to London straight away?'

'Yes. Where else? I couldn't go abroad – no passport, no identity.' I grimace. 'But in London I could be whatever I wanted to be. I started to relax into my new self.'

'And you changed your name.'

'Yes.'

'Can you do that? I mean, is it ... you know ... legal?'

'Oh yes, for all practical purposes you can change it any time you want, simply by usage.'

She takes time, absorbing this. 'Weren't you lonely?'

'At first? Desperately. I missed you more than I can ever tell you.' I have to stop, my voice fraying.

She stares at me as if X-raying my reaction to her question.

'I'm sorry ... Sorry ... Give me a minute ...'

When I can, I continue.

'Once I'd decided to transition, I started to meet other people ... like me. That helped. I was part of a community – one that accepted me for who I was. And understood. I could be myself with them. And a couple of them recommended a therapist who was tremendously supportive. Rosemary, her name was. I think I must have driven her mad with my calls outside of our sessions, but she was always calm, always reassuring, always helpful. She got me through many a crisis. And she helped me understand what was happening to me.'

'*I* don't understand – *any* of this,' India says. 'I think you should have stayed. You wouldn't have been lonely with us.'

'Bless you, darling, you can say this now, but you're a lot more enlightened than anyone was even seven years ago. I honestly don't think people would have understood back then. You'd probably have been bullied, and I'd have been ostracised. We'd have been the targets for hate mail, smashed windows, verbal and physical abuse.'

She looks sceptical but lets it go.

'How did you live? Did you have a job? What were you *doing* all day?'

'I found a flat, a cheap place where I could hide until I

decided what to do. Then I took the first job I could get – washing up in a hotel, actually. Employers are pretty suspicious of transgender people; think we'll put customers off, that kind of stuff. Or we'll get bullied in the workplace and they'll have a court case on their hands. Anyway, this hotel took me on as long as I stayed hidden in the kitchen. Which actually suited me while I was transitioning. And once I'd properly become Chris, and accumulated enough money to pay for a course, I enrolled at college. Flower arranging. Turns out I'm a natural. Remember? I always loved doing that sort of thing at home?'

She shakes her head. No, of course she was too young to remember. Another wave of sadness washes over me. My own daughter has so many blanks in her growing up.

'Then I went to work in a florists with a lovely, lovely woman called Parminder, who's an absolute genius with flowers. And she's taught me so much. Plus she's a real pal. Turns out her cousin went through something similar to me. So then I wasn't so lonely, although I still missed you, so, so much.'

All the while I'm speaking she's surveying me with a questioning look.

'You're different. It's not only the clothes, the hair, the make-up, and everything ... Something else.' She stares at me. 'I don't know ...'

I smile. 'It's the treatment. I had help to change my skin, my shape, my hair, my voice, my smell, the way I speak, my non-verbal communication – it's made me softer, more feminine. Although nothing could be done to make my feet smaller. I still have size ten clompers!'

She glances down, gives a small giggle.

There's a tap on the door.

She frowns. 'Wasn't my idea to make it this short.'

'I know. But Mum's only trying to protect you.'

'There's no need. I'm not a kid.'

'I know.'

'Next time I want to know why you decided to get in touch now. Promise?'

'Promise. I've taken two weeks off work and I'm staying up here. Between us we'll all three agree something more definite before I go back, I promise. Once we all know what we want.'

'I know what *I* want. What I've always wanted.'

'And that's what I want too, sweetheart, but I have to listen to Mum too. I owe her that.'

CHAPTER 37

Chris

IT'S NOT JUST THAT Tonya can't trust me with India; she can't trust me full stop. Fair comment. Why *should* she? The old me let her down about as badly as anybody could. She hardly knows the me I am now.

As she passes India in the doorway, she gives her a long look. But India gives nothing away. She vanishes to the foyer before they can exchange even a word.

Tonya looks a lot older than I remember. All my fault. I hesitate as she approaches, but she takes my outstretched hands in hers. I lean in to kiss her cheek, feel her tense. I draw back.

'I'm so sorry, Tonya. Truly I am.'

She nods. 'I guess so.'

I pour her a cup of tea, black, no sugar. She accepts a biscuit but lays it in the saucer, doesn't attempt to drink or eat either.

'Why didn't you warn me about India?' I begin. 'I was so shocked to see …'

Her eyes widen. 'Well, that's rich, I must say, *you* accusing *me*! Why should I tell you *anything*?' She's clearly finding it hard to manage more than an occasional glance at me. '*I'm* the one who's had to deal with her.'

'Fair enough. Sorry. I wasn't accusing … well, I didn't *mean* to, at least. But am I allowed to know? Is she getting help?'

She fills me in sketchily, making it abundantly plain that I have no right to a parental stake.

She returns fire. 'Why didn't *you* tell *me*? That's much more relevant in my book.'

'I couldn't bear to see you recoil from me.'

'I wouldn't have ...'

'Yes,' I say, struggling to keep my voice even. 'You would have. I told you once about a transgender patient I looked after and you ... well, you made it clear you were revolted by the whole thing.'

'Did I? I don't remember.'

'Maybe not, but I do. And we had a long discussion another time about people who hate one part of their bodies. Remember?'

'Vaguely.'

'There was a programme on TV about it. People who laid down on railway lines so a train ran over their hated leg. And surgeons who agreed to lop off perfectly healthy limbs.'

She shudders.

I nod. 'Yeah, you had real problems with all that stuff. Gender dysphoria came into the same category for you.'

'So, my fault again.'

'No, that's not what I'm saying.'

She looks so defeated, hunched in the chair, hugging herself. But the barriers are palpable.

'So, why does it feel like that where I'm sitting?'

'Because now it's personal. Now you know I went away because I knew you couldn't handle it.'

'You could have *said*.'

'My problem. I had to deal with it. And trust me, I didn't talk to *anybody* about it. Not just you, *anybody*.'

'You *should* have told *me*. I was your *wife*.'

'I couldn't expose you to the ridicule and all the "scandal". You'd have absolutely hated it.'

'Don't turn this all back onto me,' she flares.

'I'm not. I'm only trying to answer your question.'

'Yeah, by blaming me.'

'I was trying to explain, not blaming you. Fair enough, I didn't talk about it, but I did try to find a way through it. Typical man, huh? What was your gripe? "Why do you

always feel you have to come up with a solution?" Huh?'
Time was she'd have responded to that. Not any more.

'And your way through it was running away!'

'I was in hell, Tonya. Sheer bloody unadulterated hell. I even thought about ending it all.'

She stares at me for the first time, eyes wide.

'You?'

'Yeah, me. Me who always maintained life was sacred. That's how bad I felt.'

'So ... when you left your clothes on the beach ...?'

'No, that was deliberate. So the police wouldn't start searching. I wanted everyone to think I'd drowned. Draw a line under Victor. Start again.'

'Me included.'

'I thought it'd be easier for you, thinking I was dead. No scandal. You knew I was a strong swimmer. I thought you'd put two and two together and think I'd got into trouble out there and drowned.'

'You have no idea what it did to us.'

'Tell me then.'

'I will, but first I need to know what happened ... after that. How did you change ... you know? I've never understood how ...'

'I *can* tell you, but, are you sure you want to know?' I lean forward and look directly into her eyes.

'I don't *want* to; I *need* to. I need to know where I stand.'

'Fair enough, but I want to make one thing absolutely clear at the outset, Tonya. We can't go back. You have to accept that. I can't go back to being the man you married. It's about me; who I truly am.'

'Well, at least that's telling me straight.'

I grit my teeth. No point in antagonising her further.

'So, you want to know about my transitioning? First of all I needed to convince the medics that I was totally sure it was what I wanted. *I* knew I was psychologically ready, of course. I'd been through years and years of confusion and unhappiness. I'd tried fighting it, and it hadn't gone away. I'd also tried pseudo-transitioning, so I knew without a shadow of a doubt I was only truly happy as a woman. But I had to satisfy *them* too. Is this the kind of thing you're after?'

She nods.

'Once they accepted that I was ready, I took hormones – combination of oestrogen and anti-androgens – to start the feminisation process. And gradually that made my skin softer, my body shape changed, redistributing fat to hips, breasts, thighs. And gradually I started to feel so much better mentally. I began to relax in my skin, be fully me at last. Although I must admit, the anxiety never quite leaves you.

'To start with I thought that'd be enough. But I knew there were other things that gave me away – the way I communicated. Men and women are so different in lots of little ways. So I went to a specialist who helped my speech – pitch, intonation, patterns – and my posture, facial expressions, things like that. Body language. And that all helped me ease into my new self. I was *Chris*.'

'So, no ... surgery?' She flushes in that telltale way I remember. Ah, does she still think there's a chance ...?

'Well, I didn't have surgery to change my voice, or liposuction or anything like that, but I did have top surgery. Implants. I looked too ridiculous with my flat chest, being my size. Falsies were too ... false.'

Her flinch is involuntary.

'The next step would be genital surgery, but I haven't felt the need to go down that route at the moment. I might not ever. Lots of trans women are happy to stay at this stage.'

'And are you? Happy, I mean?' Her voice sinks to a whisper.

'About my lived gender, my own body? Yes, I am. Finally.'

She closes her eyes and sits breathing in and out slowly, deeply, like someone warding off a panic attack.

'So ... are you ... do you ... fancy *men*, now?'

'No. Trans people can be straight, gay, bisexual, asexual – anything on the spectrum. In fact I haven't had a sexual relationship with *anybody*, male or female, since I left you. But to be perfectly truthful, Tonya, I'm not that interested. I guess the hormones don't help. In any case, that's not what this is about. It never was.'

She looks bewildered.

'It was never about sex. It was all about gender.'

'Oh.'

'And for the record, it's not actually that uncommon. There are something like three to five hundred thousand trans people in the UK. It's only in the last few years it's been openly talked about, but even now it still attracts a lot of negative reaction. Largely because people don't understand it.'

'So, did *you* get all that ... negative stuff?'

'Rejection, ridicule, discrimination, violence, you mean? Been there, done that. Got the t-shirt. And the mug.'

She closes her eyes.

'Ignorant people can be very cruel,' I say quietly. 'They don't understand so they lash out.'

'I feel bad about ...'

'I didn't mean you, Tonya ...'

'Yes, you did. You said it yourself. That's why you went away.'

'No, you didn't reject me, or ridicule me. I voluntarily went away so you and India weren't involved in all that unpleasantness, not because you caused it. I couldn't bear to have you suffering on my account. That's why I changed my name, didn't make contact, let you think I was dead. I reckoned a clean break would be the best thing all round. That was the official advice back then. But in any case, the Victor you knew *was* dead. Gone for ever.'

She lets the tears fall unchecked. I guess it's the end of hope. She has to begin mourning all over again.

After a long time she mops her eyes and looks at me directly. 'So, where does this leave ... *us*?'

'I don't know. It's something we'll all need to work out together. But first you need time to adjust to this new situation. Chris is alive and well and here; Victor is no more. What do you want from me? What does India want?'

'What do *you* want?'

'That depends. I can see you're still mad at me – for leaving, and for changing, I guess. And I can understand that. But we're *both* different people now. So we need to take this one step at a time. How do you feel about being with *Chris*? What's best for *India*? What does *she* feel?'

'I know what *she'll* say!'

I wait.

'She'd want you back at any price! They learn about this kind of gender stuff at school nowadays. It's not such a big deal for her. And ... right now, I know she needs you more than she's ever done.'

'She looks to be in a bad place at the moment.'

'You don't know the half of it.'

'Tell me.'

I listen in absolute silence to the horrors of my daughter's obsessions.

'I'm desperately, desperately sorry you've had all that to deal with on your own, Tonya. I truly am.'

'I'm at my wits end with her.'

'I'm not surprised. Could I ...? It must be so tough doing it on your own. Will you at least let me help you now? Could you accept that?'

To my surprise she suddenly shrinks into herself visibly.

'What *now*?' I say more sharply than I intended.

'Did she tell you?'

'Tell me what?'

'About my ...'

'What?'

'My ... suspicions.'

'No.'

She buries her face in her hands and rocks back and forth in the chair.

When she shows no sign of stopping I get up, crouch beside her chair and put a hand tentatively on her arm.

'Tell me what's wrong, Tonya.'

'I can't. I *can't*,' she wails.

'You must. I've been honest with you. If we're to stand

any kind of a chance at all, I have to understand where you're coming from too. Come on, tell me. I can take it.'

She pulls away and covers her face. I move back a pace.

'After you went away, I needed answers. Why did you go away? Why had you become moody and withdrawn? Why did you start going away for days together? Why were there ladies' panties in your drawer? And I started to put two and two together.'

'And?' I prompt.

'Those girls – teenagers – who went missing ... You were away both nights ... the knickers ... I thought ... maybe ...'

Ice cold fingers reach into my soul, freezing me into immobility.

'You thought ... *I* ... was responsible ... for *that*? ... Hell's bells, Tonya. Don't you know me *at all*?

'I ...'

'Was it *you* ... that told the police ... *that*?'

'Not at first. Honestly, I didn't. I *didn't*! Not for ages. I even got rid of the panties! I didn't *want* to believe it. But where *were* you on those nights? What *were* you doing? I didn't know. I couldn't give you an alibi. But then, when you were seen with Maria ... it was in the paper ... Well, we thought it was your sister, Marjorie. You look exactly like her. So then I thought she must be in on it too. I *had* to tell them. I kept thinking, what if that missing girl was India? What if *she* was the one in danger? I couldn't live with myself if I didn't stop someone hurting her. That's why I told them. So they'd do something. Find you. Put her in a place of safety.'

I back away, reaching blindly for the chair.

'So, was there anything *else* you suspected me of?' It sounds harsh, sarcastic.

'I'm sorry. I'm desperately sorry. I truly am. I know better now ...'

'Go on. I can't get much lower in your estimation surely. *Tell me.*'

'I was afraid ... maybe ... you'd had ... you might

have ... *feelings* for India ...'

I'm too appalled to speak.

She looks up, her face blotched, her eyes wild.

'All the time you spent with her in her room, going off together, having secrets and ... her behaviour ...'

'You thought ... I was capable ... of ... *abusing India*?'

'I didn't know what to think,' she gabbles. 'You'd always been terribly close. She was only eight. So when she started with her obsessions ... her eating fads ... compulsions ... lining things up ... I tried to find a reason. Was it just because you'd gone away ... or was she reacting to what had happened when you were here? Had you gone after other teenagers because you couldn't handle how you felt about India?'

I push my chair as far from her as it will go, feeling the colour draining out of my face. I can't trust myself to stand, I think I'd crumple.

'Bloody hell, woman. Bloody, bloody hell. How could you even *think* ...?'

'I don't know. I didn't know *what* to think. None of it made any sense. You should have *told* me about the dressing up thing.'

Somehow I manage to restrain myself enough to grind out, 'You know what? You can forget talking about any kind of future – for us, I mean. If it wasn't for India I'd walk out this minute and never speak to you again. The only thing that happened when I was here was that I loved that girl to bits – like a precious *daughter*.'

'I know,' she whispers. 'I know that now. But ... you were so close, unusually close. I was ... jealous. I felt left out.'

'You're something else ... you know that? If you felt left out, well, tough. I *did* spend loads of time with her. All her life, from the very beginning. You were a mess, Tonya, a total mess. She *needed* me! And you were so paranoid about everything, *somebody* had to let her be a normal kid. We *were* close, of course we were. I adored her. I still adore her. But there was never *ever* anything unseemly in our relationship. *Never. Ever.*'

224

'I know that now. And I'm sorry. But I was only trying to make sense of things, find some plausible explanation. It never *occurred* to me it could be ... *this*.' She sweeps a hand down the length of me.

A terrible thought strikes me. 'So, does India know ... what you suspected?'

She shakes her head vehemently.

'Well, thank God for small mercies!'

'And for what it's worth *she* didn't ever think you were involved with those missing girls. She was furious with me for doubting you.'

'So you did discuss *that* with her.'

'Only when we knew about you maybe being with Maria Davenport. I needed to give her a reason why we *had* to go to the police, get them to find you ...'

'... in case I was about to do away with yet another teenager,' I finish for her. 'Did you by any chance fill her in on where I really was at those times? What I was actually doing for Maria?'

'Yes. Yes! I *did*. I was glad to.'

I shake my head, the horror threatening to overwhelm me.

'Damn it, Tonya. You really are a piece of work. You talk about *me* ruining India's life; what about *you*? Imagine if she'd *believed* you!'

'I had no choice. You *have* to see that. What if Maria had been India ... with some stranger ... a middle-aged man masquerading as a woman?'

I nod slowly seeing the logic in spite of my revulsion. And in some small corner of my mind acknowledging that at least she didn't associate gender transition with paedophilia. She had no idea I was transitioning when she harboured those suspicions. One day I might live to be grateful for that. Right now I'm appalled, revolted, angry enough to lash out. Instead I retreat into silence, wave her away.

Trust can be demolished in seconds; it could take a lifetime to rebuild. If then.

CHAPTER 38

India

I'M BURSTING TO TELL somebody. *My Dad's not dead*! He's alive! *And* I know where he is. *And* I've met him. I've actually seen him in the flesh, *hugged* him even, so I know he's real. Only ...

I mustn't say 'him' or 'he' any more. Feels weird.

Mum and Dad are both so ridiculously cautious, though. *Both* of them. Go carefully, don't shout it from the rooftops. Give it time.

Time? I've given it *seven years*! Now I want the whole world to know.

But it's like they think everybody's out to make fun of us, or shout stuff, or stick dead rats through our letterbox, or something. Me, I think it's the best thing that's happened in my entire life. And when I wake up I have to look at the photo of Dad and me I took on my phone that first day in the hotel, just to be sure it isn't another of those dreams that splinters into tears as soon as you wake up.

Mum was all for telling Mrs O'Leary, but I reckon it didn't go quite like she expected, cos she looked sort of stunned and it was obvious she'd been crying when she came back from the O'Leary's place. I tried to quiz her, but all she said was, 'The Irish have a different way of seeing things.' I guess that means Mrs O'Leary wasn't over the moon about Dad being a woman. But then, Mum isn't either, so *she* can't talk. Only see, she's never been very good at seeing what she's like herself. Drives me insane. I mean, she's quick enough to criticise *other* people – Dad, me, Mrs O'Leary, school, the hospital – everybody. Accuse them even. I mean, look what she thought Dad might have done! You can't get much worse than that. But she can't see that *she*'s prejudiced and judgemental and gets the wrong end of the stick and doesn't give me any room to be grown up, make my own decisions. I reckon it'll be a whole different ball game living with Dad. I can't wait!

Only that's tricky too now. Apart from the 'her' and 'she' thing, we haven't worked out what I'm going to call her instead of Dad. Chris, maybe? Or CT. Or DD. Something will feel right eventually, she says.

I know! Yeah! 'Mad' about sums it up. '*Hello. This is my Mad.*' '*Mad, can we have salad tonight?*' I reckon I could get used to that. Thing is though, I can't imagine anybody'd be too chuffed being called Mad to their face! 'Mud', maybe?

In the end it's Mercedes I tell. You should have seen her. Eyes on stalks doesn't come near it. Totally gobsmacked, more like.

'You'll absolutely *have* to write about this,' she says when I finish telling her – an edited version.

'I absolutely will not!' I flash back. 'This is my *Dad* we're talking about.'

'Well, nobody needs to know it's for real. You can change names and details. But it's a *brilliant* story, you must admit. Who'd believe it? Two teenagers go missing. Middle-aged man – let's call him MM (middle-aged man) – vanishes, feared drowned, leaving a wife and daughter grieving behind him. Wife suspects him of child abduction, murder even. Years later he's photographed by a stranger hundreds of miles away, dressed as a woman, with a third teenager. Wife sees the photo in the paper, tells the police cos she thinks he might be going to kill off this next girl. MM's arrested. Turns out he's now a woman – MW. He hasn't done away with anybody except his old self. The family are reunited and they all live happily ever after. I mean! What's not to *love*?'

'Sounds to me, you ought to write it yourself,' I say sniffily. This is all too raw. 'And stop saying "he". It's "she".'

She stares at me. 'Now that *wouldn't* work in a story.'

'What wouldn't?'

'Talking about "Dad" and saying "she" or "her". Far too confusing. People wouldn't stick with it.'

'Okay, Mrs Expert. Write the damn story yourself since you're such a know-it-all all of a sudden.'

'Don't be daft,' she snorts. 'Since when did *I* ever get an A for an essay?'

'Well, shut up, for goodness' sake. You don't know the first thing about it.'

She's instantly contrite. 'Sorry, Indie. Didn't mean to upset you. I'm totally chuffed for you. But, you must admit, it's like some kind of psychological drama.'

'To you, maybe,' I say. I know I sound grumpy. She doesn't get it. 'It's *real* for me, though. It's my life. My *family*. So back off or I'll never tell you anything ever again.'

Instead she launches into the whole business of LGBT and discrimination and the definition of family and parent, stuff we had in lessons at school. But you know what? I haven't got much appetite for it this time round. I would absolutely *hate* for my classmates to talk about *us* like we talked about other families in class and in the playground. Shows you, doesn't it? It's altogether different when it's you.

'Hey,' Mercedes says suddenly, 'What d'you call him now? Is he ...?'

'She,' I interrupt instantly.

She rolls her eyes. 'Is *she* still Dad? Or is she another Mum?'

'We haven't decided,' I say. 'And it's nobody else's business except ours, so butt out, Mercedes. I mean it. Or I shall wish I'd never told you. Well, I already do.'

'Hey, lighten up, Indie. I'm only pointing out that there's a load of stuff you could use in your writing, specially if you want to be a serious writer. You do still want that, don't you?'

'Yep. And Dad says she'll help me every step of the way. And she's exactly the right person to have on my side. She's so totally into books and writing and everything.'

'Brilliant. I'm so made up for you, Indie. You deserve a break.'

'I'm not sure about deserving, but it feels like a fresh start, knowing Dad's alive, back with us, picking up where we left off. It's like a huge great shadow has gone away.'

'So will he ... sorry, *she* ... move back up here now?'

I shake my head. 'Nope. She says she's better off staying where nobody knew her as Victor. Folk down there've only ever known her as a woman, and mostly she gets left alone.'

'So can you *tell*? You know, that she's a man underneath?'

'She *isn't*! She's totally a woman. Looks like it, behaves like it, everything.'

'So where does that leave your mum?'

'She needs time to get used to things.'

'I guess it would be odd – for her, I mean. One minute she's married to a man. Next she's married to a woman. She thought she was a widow; now she's not. Only *she's* not changed. Y'know what I mean?'

'Yeah. Only I don't want to talk about it.'

'So, will you go down there to see her?'

'Better than that. The idea is, I'm going to *stay* with Dad!'

'What's your Mum think about that?'

'She was the one that suggested it. She reckons a new start's exactly what I need too, and I'd be better off away from her. Dad won't freak out over every little thing, like she does.'

'Is that right? I mean, d'*you* think so too?'

'I think it'll be totally cool. I can't wait.'

'Fantastic,' she says. 'Mind you, I'll miss you like crazy.'

'Nah, you won't. You'll soon be thick as thieves with some other loser.'

'Speaking of losers, what's happened to that girl your dad picked up in London?'

'She didn't pick her up!' I give her a push. 'She took

care of her. She kept imagining Maria was me and thinking what would she want somebody to do for me. That's the kind of person Dad is.'

'Wow!'

'And the girl – Maria – she wants to go on the stage. So Dad's helped her get a foot on the bottom rung of the ladder. And her parents know and they're cool with that cos they reckon she's settling down now she's earning and studying and everything. And Dad did that for her.'

'Wow. She sounds like something else.'

'She is. She's the best.'

'So will Maria be there too?'

'Not sure. To be honest, I'm not too keen. I mean, I've waited seven years to get Dad back. I'm not sure about sharing her with this stranger now. But Dad's looking into finding somewhere big enough where Maria can maybe be a kind of lodger meantime, but there's plenty room for *us* to be a real family.'

'You cool with that?'

'I don't know. Time will tell. I haven't even met the girl yet.'

'Wow, an actress, a writer, and a hero. I reckon you'll have tons of ideas for your stories down there in the big city. But don't you forget, India Grayson, when you get to be a bestseller, *I* was the one who discovered your talent first.'

'In your dreams!'

Acknowledgements

One of the joys of exploring different subjects is that it brings me into contact with a whole new raft of people. For a writer who spends vast tracts of time alone and unseen, these forays into the real world are truly refreshing. But there's also something reassuring about the endorsement of established friends, and during the writing of this book, *Inside of Me*, I appreciated both more than I usually do.

In thinking about body image, I travelled further outside my comfort zone than ever before in my writing life. I have long-standing issues of my own; I was also very ill for six months of the book's gestation, unable to write or work, which posed a serious threat to my sense of identity. So in the creation of this book, I've been hugely grateful for the support of many people who helped to boost my mental wellbeing and keep me from drowning in negativity and failure, supporting me during the long road back to work. Family, friends, I salute you all.

When it comes to the various contributions made to the material in the book, there are several reasons why I can't itemise the specific backgrounds of the experts; their personal stories as well as the integrity of this book could well be compromised. Suffice it to say that they included medical specialists, spokespeople and members of organisations, as well as those with a wealth of personal experience, who between them encouraged, critiqued, reassured, advised and challenged me. I'm grateful to them all.

Charlotte Lindsay guided me in the right direction to find appropriate experts in areas outside my normal ken.

Becky Kent and Jo Clifford steered me through the sensitivities around the character of Chris. Becky went far beyond the original brief and taught me so much.

Jane Morris and Shaun Maher were excellent critics on matters medical.

Becky Fletcher checked my knowledge of floral art with great charm.

Anne Wilson shared her experience of the financial ramifications when someone goes missing.

Abbi McHaffie refined my ear for teen-speak in return for quality time together and lots of favourite foods. Special hours, Abbi.

Jonathan McHaffie held a helpful mirror up to my faults frankly as only a son who aspires to be a novelist himself can.

Rosalyn Crich was as usual my first and most loyal port of call.

Patricia McClure, Tony Miller, Barbara Miller, Christine Windmill, Helen Balsillie, Anne Vann, and Roslyn Edwards read early drafts with immense care and provided invaluable feedback. And in the later stages David McHaffie's eagle eye homed in on all the remaining anomalies and typos.

Tom Bee gave me choice and wise guidance in equal measure when it came to the cover design.

Without their input the book would never have reached publication level and I would have sunk without trace. Thank you all.

I'm also grateful to the authors of about forty books – fact and fiction – which I read as part of my research. They introduced me to the worlds and minds which the Grayson family inhabit and gave me the insights necessary to spin my own tale.

Discussion Points for Book Clubs

• The story is told through the voices of three characters: Tonya, India and Chris. Why do you think the author chose this format?

• Five teenagers form the focus of this novel. Two play relatively minor roles and yet are essential to the plot. What is the significance of their relative ages and family backgrounds?

• Tonya is portrayed as a neurotic mother and suspicious wife. Is this fair to her? Did you share her anxieties? Why do you think she didn't go to the police earlier? Why does she destroy evidence?

• Food plays an important role in this story: a response to bullying; a means of control; a maternal obsession; teenage rivalry; a measure of achievement. How significant is food in your life?

• India, Mercedes and Maria are all parented differently. How effective would you say each family dynamic is? Is Tonya's jealousy of Victor's relationship with India justified? Mercedes' mother treats her as a responsible adult in order to generate a responsible attitude in Mercedes: is she right?

• At what point did you realise who Chris was? What clues betrayed her? Why does she play a game in the London Underground?

• The author avoids giving specific figures for India's weight and measurements. Why do you think that is? How healthy is the relationship between Mercedes and India?

• Penelope Atkinson-Baker says: '*Nobody wants to see real life people in magazines and photo-shoots. We can all see them in the mirror, on the bus, in our streets – for free.*

Fashion magazines are about <u>fantasy</u>. Dreams. Ideals.' Do you agree?

• How do you feel about Kaetlyn's role in this story?

• Parminder asks Chris: *'Aren't you worried about the risks you're taking?'* (by having Maria staying in the flat). What risks? How would you balance the pros and cons? If you were Maria's parents how comfortable would you be with this situation?

• India challenges her mother: *'You're the one who's obsessed. What with your push-up bras, and your control knickers, and your Clairol Nice'n'Easy, and your anti-aging creams and your vitamin supplements. What's that if it's not obsessed with body image, I'd like to know?'* Is this obsession? How does it differ from controlling food intake, laxatives and exercise?

• What did you think about the doctors' and nurses' treatment of India in A&E? Is India competent to make her own decisions in relation to her health, as the nurses say she is? Tonya feels the medical team are telling her that India isn't thin enough to warrant being kept in hospital. She would need to be *'at death's door or at risk of significant harm or deterioration'*. What do you feel about that?

• Should the police tell Tonya that they've found her husband?

• Chris says: *'Trust can be demolished in seconds: it could take a lifetime to rebuild. If then.'* Do you think the Graysons could ever rebuild theirs? Who do you most sympathise with in the meeting in Chapter 37?

Questions Exploring Ethical Issues Raised in this Novel

• Should open-access pro ana sites be permissible?

• To what extent should a) parents and b) doctors be allowed to overrule minors' decisions which threaten health and life? What factors would persuade you of a teenager's competence to decide for herself? Given what you know about the parents of the girls in this story, how competent would you say they are to make ethical decisions on behalf of their daughters?

• Modern communication has raised the profile of the sensitive issues covered in this book. What are the pros and cons of increased awareness? Has this story challenged any of your opinions?

• In Chapters 26 and 27 India is subjected to treatment in A&E. To what extent were her rights and dignity and autonomy respected? Should the information she provides be kept confidential?

• The nurses tell Tonya that India is 'competent' to make her own decisions. Would you agree if you were a) her mother and b) her nurse/doctor?

• In this story patients in the Child and Adolescent Mental Health Unit are manipulative, deceitful and suspicious. To what extent should their behaviour be acknowledged or go unchallenged? What are the pros and cons of nursing them together?

• In Chapter 29 Tonya and Kaetlyn have the following conversation:
Tonya: 'Exactly. But see, the thing is, she isn't at death's door or at risk of "significant harm or deterioration", now. Apparently, if she was, they could section her under the

Mental Health Act – compulsory detention, they call it.'
Kaetlyn: 'But she's just a <u>kid</u>!'
Tonya: 'That's not the point. Doesn't matter what age you are, if you're mentally ill and that's affecting your ability to make good decisions about your health, they have a responsibility – a duty – to treat you, make you have the right treatment. But if she isn't as bad as that, they might have to let her out and just monitor her.'
Kaetlyn: 'Seems crazy logic to me.'
Tonya: 'I know! But they say she's old enough to understand what she's doing, and take some responsibility for her own actions.'
Kaetlyn: 'Deliberately make herself worse, you mean?'
Tonya: 'Exactly! Perverse, isn't it? She's '<u>not thin enough</u>' to be kept in. On some kind of index or other. That's like saying, "Your tumour's not big enough yet. Wait until it's strangling you then we'll treat you." Imagine telling a kid who already looks like a skeleton, "You aren't thin enough, yet." They aren't saying that, of course; they're telling her she must eat more, but well ...'
What do you think about such an index?

• In Chapter 37 Chris mentions patients who want healthy limbs amputated because they feel strongly the body part doesn't belong to them. Is such mutilation ever justified? Should surgeons perform such operations?

• By the very nature of their condition, people with mental disorders could be said to have an imbalance in their minds. Does this render them incompetent to decide what is in their own best interests?

237

If you are interested in further information about medical ethics or the issues raised in Hazel McHaffie's books, visit her website and weekly blog.

www.hazelmchaffie.com

By the same author

Over my Dead Body
ISBN   978 0 9926231 0 4   PBK and eBook

When her daughter, Elvira, and three year old granddaughter are fatally injured in a car crash, Carole Beacham, is passionately opposed to their organs being donated. She has been haunted for thirty years by a dark secret and will do anything in her power to keep it from shattering their lives. But unknown to her parents, Elvira has been in a close relationship with a man they have never met, and he insists her wishes were clear: their organs should be used.

Eventually, reassured by the safeguards in place to protect the identities of donor and recipients, Carole is reluctantly persuaded to give qualified consent. But no one has factored in the aspirations of a budding journalist and a young poet. As the family struggle to deal with their crippling loss, barriers crumble with potentially devastating consequences.

Saving Sebastian
ISBN   978 1 906817 87 9   PBK and eBook

Sebastian Zair is four years old, but a rare blood disorder means that he won't live much longer unless he gets a stem cell transplant.

His mother is determined to save him. With no one in the family a match, she appeals to the Pemberton Fertility Centre for help to create an embryo the same tissue type as Sebastian.

But will her resolve falter as her fortieth birthday approaches? When hormones play havoc with her confidence and control? When the Pemberton becomes the focus of a major inquiry following the birth of a white baby to black parents? When an unscrupulous journalist starts to invade the family's privacy? When militant pro-life campaigners protest against the wanton destruction of life?

It's a race against time, and time is not on Sebastian's side.

Remember Remember
ISBN   978 1906817 78 7   PBK and eBook

Doris Mannering's secret has been safely kept for 60 years, but now it's threatened with exposure.

In her early twenties during World War II she made a choice that changed the course of her family's life. The evidence was safely buried, but now, with the onset of Alzheimer's, her mind is wandering. She is haunted by the feeling that she must find the papers before it's too late, but she just can't remember ...

Jessica is driven to despair by her mother's behaviour, but it's not until lives are in jeopardy that she consents to Doris going into a residential home. As she begins clearing the family home ready for sale, bittersweet memories and unexpected discoveries await her. But these pale into insignificance against the bombshell her lawyer lover, Aaron, hands her.

Right to Die
ISBN   1 906307 21 0   PBK and eBook

Naomi is haunted by a troubling secret. Struggling to come to terms with her husband's death, her biggest dread is finding out that Adam knew of her betrayal. He left behind an intimate diary – but dare she read it? Will it set her mind at ease – or will it destroy the fragile hold she has over her grief?

Gripped by his unfolding story, Naomi discovers more than she bargained for. Adam writes of his feelings for her, his career, his burning ambition. How his dreams evaporate when he is diagnosed with Motor Neurone Disease, as one by one he loses the ability to walk, to speak, to swallow. How he resolves to mastermind his own exit at a time of his choosing ... but time is one luxury he can't afford. Can he, will he, ask a friend, or even a relative, to help him die?

Vacant Possession
ISBN 1 85775 651 7   PBK and eBook

Following a serious accident, Vivienne Faraday has been in a persistent vegetative state, looked after in a residential home, for years. How can she suddenly be pregnant?

She can't speak for herself so who should decide what happens to the unborn child? Who knows what's in her best interests? Her father, her brothers, her estranged mother who is now a nun, the medical director, the police, all have different opinions as to the best way forward. They also have their personal interests and values.

As events gather momentum, and the baby grows, someone must make medical and moral choices on Vivienne's behalf, choices beset with uncertainty, which profoundly affect their own relationships and futures. And all the time suspicion mounts: who exactly is the rapist?

Paternity
ISBN 1 85775 652 5   PBK and eBook

When Judy agrees to marry Declan Robertson his happiness knows no bounds. But from the very first night of their marriage cracks appear in their relationship, which only widen until Judy finally reveals the demons that haunt her.

Then tragedy strikes, threatening their new security: a child dies. Questions follow, questions that rock their foundations to the core. A history of deception and half-truths masquerading as love begins to unravel, challenging their very identities. Who are they? What have they inherited? What are they passing on to future generations? Do they have a future together?

Declan has always lived by a strict moral code; now he must ask himself just how far he will go to protect his wife from the consequences of her parents' actions.

Double Trouble
ISBN 1 85775 669 X   PBK and eBook

 The Halleys are a close-knit, successful, loving family. Relationships become strained when identical twins. Michael and Nicholas, fall in love with the same girl, Donella, herself a twin. On the rebound from Nick, Donella eventually marries Mike, but their lives become entangled again when Nick returns from work overseas. His new wife, Heidi, is Swiss, reserved, and haunted by her past; she finds it difficult to find her niche within the demonstrative Halley family.

But Donella's three daughters gradually break down the barriers and a new order is established. Later, when Heidi finds she can't have children of her own, new tensions emerge. Fresh alliances are forged; old feelings return; jealousies develop; mental illness and a surrogate pregnancy threaten the delicate peace the couples have established. Will the family survive intact?

16000168R00144

Printed in Poland
by Amazon Fulfillment
Poland Sp. z o.o., Wrocław